USERNAME:
BLADEN

USERNAME: BLADEN

J.V. CARR

WestBow
PRESS
A DIVISION OF THOMAS NELSON

WestBow Press books may be ordered through booksellers or by contacting:

WestBow Press
A Division of Thomas Nelson
1663 Liberty Drive
Bloomington, IN 47403
www.westbowpress.com
1-(866) 928-1240

Because of the dynamic nature of the Internet, any web addresses or links contained in this book may have changed since publication and may no longer be valid. The views expressed in this work are solely those of the author and do not necessarily reflect the views of the publisher, and the publisher hereby disclaims any responsibility for them.

Any people depicted in stock imagery provided by Thinkstock are models, and such images are being used for illustrative purposes only.

Certain stock imagery © Thinkstock.

ISBN: 978-1-4497-8282-5 (sc)
ISBN: 978-1-4497-8283-2 (hc)
ISBN: 978-1-4497-8281-8 (e)

Library of Congress Control Number: 2013901582

Printed in the United States of America

WestBow Press rev. date: 3/28/2013

For Him and for all of those He has put into my path

"Life is like a game, one that is not always easy to solve."

TABLE OF CONTENTS

SWEET FREEDOM

Sometimes life is like jumping out of an airplane and hoping the freaking parachute deploys. You know, the adrenaline kicks in like mad; the heart pumps so fast it feels like there's no pause between the beats; you pray you don't have to use the reserve chute, and all because nobody wants to be mutilated on the ground and kiss life goodbye.

That's what happened to me. I made a choice like jumping out of an airplane ... with the chute. It all started the day I took off for my freshman year in college. I was in my bedroom saying goodbye to the sentimental and packing the purely functional when my iPhone rang in an unusual tone. I picked it up off of my tall oak dresser and answered it.

"Hello?" There was nothing but silence. "Helloooo?" I sang out. Humph! No one's there, I thought. For a brief moment, it illuminated in front of me with the caller ID displaying a blinking "Bladen." My name? I wondered. Why is it showing *my* name? Then a cold chill ran through me as I realized that the phone felt as rough as my grandma's face and as boney as a skeleton's hand. I stared at the phone in disbelief and felt more than a little on edge.

To get my mind off of it, I stretched out on my full-size bed, tapped my iPhone's screen, and began to play my brand-new video game Arcis. I soon forgot about my phone's bizarre behavior and named my avatar Thorn. I had just discovered how to make his body teleport. Wow, that was awesome. He landed inside an ominous courtyard. The massive domes and columns had eerie shadows cast on them that restricted Thorn's view of the vile demons stooped in the corners. One lone demon with Medusa hair leaped in front of Thorn. It appeared with slimy snakes oozing out from under the hood of its blackened cloak. Thorn wrestled desperately with all the strength I could give him to gain every ounce of power over it, until the demon's long, fingernail-like claws drew blood, when they dug deep into Thorns arms. Crap, I thought, I'm gonna lose.

I tapped the screen hard and made Thorn drive his sword into the beast. I hoped I'd beaten it and won the level, but its face altered into a pretty blonde girl. Even Thorn gasped and stumbled back. I had no control over that part of the game. The beast hurled Thorn to the ground. I continued to tap the screen. Finally, I got Thorn to reach for a dagger that hung from the right side of his armored belt. He plunged it into the jerk—blood and guts everywhere. Level I over. I won. At least I thought I won. I wasn't sure when I saw two black eyes glaring at me from inside the basilica. The man's penetrating stare made me feel like he actually saw me Bladen not me Thorn. He looked my way, curled his finger, and motioned for me to enter into the game. I swear his lips mouthed my name. Nice…and…slow. Whoa, I thought, sketchy. I threw my phone on my bed, jumped up, and began to pace.

It didn't occur to me at first, but the courtyard in my game looked familiar, like the one outside of St. Peter's Basilica in Rome, Italy. Trust me I know. Gram has pictures all over her house of it. She said it was the best vacation of her life. Anyway, I reread the game objective on my app. Win the first ten levels in the faraway land of Arcis, on your quest to the final level at the basilica, where demons are stealing the pearl of peace. Destroy the demons, capture and restore the pearl back to its home in the golden box inside the basilica, and win the game before time runs out and Earth is destroyed.

There's something wrong with the game, I thought. Why did I play my first level at the basilica, if my quest is supposed to lead me there in the end?

I racked my brain—until my heart and body felt moved to take care of my phone as though it was a real person. Yeah. It freaked me out. That's when it started. I *had* to take care of the phone. I knew it had something to do with my new game, but I didn't know what. I had to find out. If I didn't, I knew something bad would happen. I began to sweat. My heart pounded—hard. I wondered if falling in love felt the same insane way—total obsession. Other than video games, I had girls tattooed on my brain.

My phone rang again. It lit up like unbelievable fireworks. After what happened before I didn't expect to hear anyone on the other end. When I clicked it on, I couldn't talk.

"Hello...hello?" A female voice rang.

"Uh...uh—" I stammered.

"Bladen?" The voice asked, with uncertainty. "This is Julia."

Get your head together, Bladen, I thought. "Julia? It's me...I mean... you're talking to Bladen." I felt like an idiot.

"Did your mom tell you I was going to call?" she asked.

"Yeah...yeah she did. She said you'd give me a tour of Freefall and that even though you're a freshman too, you are familiar with the campus because you don't live too far from there."

Julia and I made small talk as a couple of people who haven't spoken in years would. She sounded amazing with a voice like chimes. I was sure she'd changed from the freaky, awkward girl I had known from long ago.

After I hung up, I placed my phone on my dresser and finished packing. Towheaded Christiana, my six-year-old little sister, ran in the room, giggling wearing a pink, polka-dot dress. She grabbed my phone and started to push buttons.

"Hey, don't mess with my stuff Christiana." I snapped at her. The sick obsession to protect my phone came back.

My older brother Nicholas strolled in, as I was taking my phone away from Christiana. I gave her a big hug and swung her in the air to make sure I hadn't upset her.

Nicholas shook his head and grabbed the phone. "My precious," he squeaked while imitating Smeágol from the Lord of the Rings trilogy, and pretended to stroke it. "Bladen, you are *way* too into the video games on this phone. Now if you were wigged out because a girl called, I'd understand."

"Yeah, well Julia just called," I said, as I grabbed Nicholas and threw him in a headlock. I tried to hide the returning obsession I felt for my phone. I *didn't* want him touching it either.

"Truce," Nicholas screamed, laughing. "You win."

I let him go.

"So Julia, huh? That quirky girl Mom used to *force* us to hang out with. How is she?" he asked.

"She sounds cool," I answered.

Christiana stuck her tongue out at both of us and skipped out of the room.

Later that morning, when I backed out of my driveway in my old, red Saab 900, the balmy, August breeze blew on my face through my car window. I couldn't wait to go. I was heading to Freefall College in Burlington, Vermont. Sweet freedom. Nicholas was riding along with me. He's twenty and an engineering major at the University of Costa Rica in San Jose. He didn't have to leave until the following week. My parents followed behind us while my other four, younger siblings stayed behind.

"How was your date last night?" I asked my brother.

"Not so great."

"Why not?

"I knocked Christie's soda on her lap."

"Well that was stupid," I joked.

Nicholas dropped his head low and continued, "When I took her home to change clothes, she told me to wait in the car. She sent her mom out to tell me the date was over. Talk about humiliation."

"Oh I'm sorry, man," Was all that I could say. It's not like I could offer any relationship advice. I have never had a serious girlfriend.

Nicholas grabbed my arm. I looked at him like he was crazy.

"Dude, let go of my arm. I'm driving!" I yelled.

He looked at me with a big smile on his cleanly shaved face and a twinkle in his eye. "Like that would ever happen. The date was awesome. We're going out again tonight."

Yep, he had pulled one over on me again! I should have known better. Nicholas was pretty much perfect. He was a few inches shorter than my six-foot three-inch, burly frame. His looks mirrored his demeanor. He had thick, sandy-brown hair and dark-green, piercing eyes. His glasses and pressed clothes gave him an intellectual look. He was a straight A student, valedictorian of his senior high class, and everything in life seemed smooth for him.

I, on the other hand, was *anything* but smooth. I had good looks on my side, though. At least that's what Nicholas had always told me. I was unusually muscular with night-black, medium-length hair. My sea-blue eyes contrasted against my pale skin. Nicholas used to tell people an artist chiseled my face. My life wasn't filled with ease like my older brother, though. I had a loose temper, struggled in school, and was a klutz around girls. I hoped college would be a fresh start for me.

"You must be psyched for Freefall, huh?" Nicholas asked.

"Can't wait,"

"Don't let the workload from those engineering classes get in the way of your social life," he joked.

"Thanks, I'll keep that in mind."

"You didn't forget any video games, did you?"

"Funny!"

My iPhone began to ring. Nicholas went to answer it. I grabbed it off the dashboard. "I got it," I said, feeling my insane need to protect the phone return.

Nicholas pulled it out of my hands. "Dude, you're driving. I'll get it. Hello? Who is this? Get a life." Nicholas slammed it off and put it back on the dashboard.

"Who called?" I felt my face grow hot when Nicholas touched it.

Some prank call, heavy breather. They said have a nice swim in the abyss," Nicholas laughed.

The abyss? I thought. My game? There was an abyss in my game, whatever the heck that is. I didn't mention anything about it to Nicholas. He'd joke and tell me I was high on something. I nonchalantly picked up my phone from the dash and put it in my pocket, out of Nicholas's reach.

It was no time before we pulled into one of the campus parking lots. The drive from Manchester, VT took two and a half hours. I had my phone still safe in my pocket.

Mom knocked on my car window. "C'mon, let's go!"

"Okay okay, Mom, I didn't know you'd be so happy to ditch me."

"You're silly," she said, as she gently rubbed my cheek. I'm going to miss you so much, but I know how much you've been looking forward to this day."

"Thanks, Mom," I said, and pushed her hand away from my face, as she got the digital camcorder ready. I checked around to see if any hot girls noticed. Luckily, I didn't see any nearby. My phone rang once more, then stopped. I gripped it, still feeling a little tense.

Mom aimed the camcorder toward me. "I just want to record the beautiful campus. Look here and smile."

As I reluctantly smiled, she filmed the handsome, older buildings that were made of rusty-colored brick. It was a small school, only two thousand students, and the land surrounding the central campus was close to Lake Champlain—a lake over one hundred miles long, twelve miles wide at its widest point, and astoundingly vast and beautiful.

My mom's camcorder was new, and she did *not* want to stop filming. She was pretty crazy whenever she bought a new toy. Eventually, my dad gently ripped it out of her hands. Everyone but Mom agreed; it was time to find my room.

We found the freshman welcoming committee in the auditorium, picked up my key, and walked to the second floor—room number 222. The first two floors were for the guys, and the top two floors were for the girls—a coed dorm. Cool, I thought.

When we arrived at my room, the door was open. I stuck my head in and was welcomed by a super loud voice.

"Roomieee," Robby bellowed, "you're finally here." He gave me a firm handshake and was genuinely happy to see me. This was our first time meeting face to face. We had exchanged a few get-to-know-each-other phone calls and emails over the summer once we found out we were roommates.

My new roomie was bony and lanky. He wasn't as tall as me, maybe a couple of inches shorter and quite good looking. His hair was jet-black and spiked in a wild fashion, which suited his personality. His grin spread so wide it seemed to stretch from ear to ear, and it revealed sparkling, white teeth that glowed against his black skin. His chocolate eyes sparkled full of mischief. He wore a burgundy T-shirt that said, 'Girls you gotta love 'em' and a pair of ripped blue jeans. Numerous gold chains dangled from his neck. I thought, this is gonna be fun.

I took a quick glance at my room, the place where I was going to crash for the next year. It was a medium size space with a metal bunk bed in one corner, a long unadorned desk with two, russet plastic chairs on another side, and a measly double closet that didn't even take up half the wall. I felt claustrophobic in this room. A brief visual image of me trapped in a prison cell came to mind. It felt eerie and made me shudder. My parents chose this dormitory because it was affordable and practical. That was just like them. I suppose they were being a good example. Who was I kidding? The room sucked.

And seriously, I couldn't shake the creepy feeling I had about the room. My stomach felt a little sick. I didn't know why. I was sure it wasn't from the well-done scrambled eggs I had cooked earlier that morning.

My phone rang, again. I picked it up and checked caller I.D. It read PRIVATE CALLER. I hesitated, "Hello?" The person on the other end sounded like Darth Vader from Star Wars. I heard a laugh in the room. It was Nicholas pulling a prank. He had called me from his phone. "Funny Nicholas. Did you make up the whole thing in the car too?" I felt on edge.

Nicholas laughed. "No, but you should've seen the look on your face."

Mom sent us both a warning glare.

Robby made all the necessary introductions with my parents. He explained his family had headed back home earlier to Concord, NH, except for his sister Alyssa. She was a junior at Champlain College nearby.

Robby had impeccable manners. When I looked at my parents' faces, they shone with approval. Yeah, he knew how to suck up real good.

While my parents continued to talk with Robby, Nicholas and I unloaded my Saab and brought in my stuff. Nicholas threw his arm over my shoulder. "You know you can always call me. I'm sure *you'll* need advice," he said.

I put him in another headlock. "Yeah, right. You still fight like a girl."

I forgot about my phone for a while. Nicholas and I laughed about our childhood. He gave me a few tips about my studies and told me to make sure I studied enough. He definitely had more strength in that area. What could I say? he had the A's and I had the—ahem—occasional D's. I was talented at making up excuses for why I had them, but hey I figured at least I wasn't failing.

Later I heard a loud knock on the door. It was more like a *Bang! Bang! Bang!* I looked and that was the first time I saw him—this short, little dude barely five and a half feet tall. He had spiky, black hair and black soulless eyes. His eerily angelic smile made him look like a kid who could kill someone and then sweet talk anyone into believing he was innocent. He wore tan slacks and a psychedelic-orange, button-down shirt that was buttoned all the way to the top. It was gripping his neck so much I thought it must have been choking him. I guess he didn't feel the need to breathe.

"Hello," he said, in an unusually deep voice that didn't seem to match his body at all. "I'm Berard. I'm staying across the hall." His voice scratched like that of some old guy, yet his face looked like a teenager's. My sisters would have called him a creeper.

My mom Jasmine, who was nice to everybody, went over to Berard and gushed at how charmed she was to meet him. If you ask me, my mother's naive sometimes. When someone seemed as odd as Berard, how could she be so friendly—let alone charmed?

My dad cut to the chase. "Okay," he said, and slowly walked toward the door. "It's time for us to go." I bet my dad was creeped out by Berard, too.

Everyone said goodbye, except my mom. She took the last of a series of too many photos—wow, I thought she'd never quit.

I walked my family out to their shiny, new Honda Pilot. I told my parents I'd visit in September, one of my favorite months, when the leaves on the trees burst into a multicolored array of scarlet, golden, and rust—super beautiful.

"Make sure you call Julia," my mom reminded me.

"I will. I already talked to her, remember?"

"Oh right. Say hi to Lisa for me too."

"I will Mom. No worries."

Lisa Simms is Julia's mom and one of my mom's best friends from high school. She's from Essex Junction, which is a few miles northeast of Burlington. When I was around eight years old I met her for the first time. We spent some vacation time with them for a few summers. Now I haven't seen her for at least five years or more. Julia's parents were divorced; she's an only child. I couldn't remember much about her, except that she had heaps of freckles, wore zany glasses, and always had her pale hair toppled in high, messy pigtails. She was a rather quirky girl, though she seemed different when I talked to her on the phone before I left home. I was excited that she was also a freshman at Freefall.

When my family was set, they stepped into the Pilot, fastened their seat belts, and just like that, they split.

My now annoying phone rang again, showing PRIVATE CALLER. I figured it was Nicholas pulling another prank, so I answered it and began to breathe heavily.

"It was nice to see you in the game," a creepy, unrecognizable voice interrupted me. It sounded like an older man, definitely not Nicholas.

"Who are you?" I asked, and then heard a click on the other end. They had hung up. Just out of curiosity, I clicked on my apps to pull up my game Arcis. When I turned it on, it went directly to the basilica again. The infuriated man was still there pacing. I wondered who he was. He wore a dark shirt and pants, though he didn't look like a religious man. He turned to look at me, a smirk on his face. There's no way, I thought. "Hey, weirdo, did you call?" I whispered to him. He continued to smirk. I shut off the game.

I decided to go to room 223, Berard's room, to see if he was around. He made me curious and not in a good way. I pounded on his door.

"Wrong room, dude," Robby said, with his friendly grin.

"I'm looking for Berard," I said.

"I haven't seen him, but how 'bout cruising around Burlington together?"

"Do you have a car?" I knew he didn't. He had told me that last summer.

"No, but you do," he laughed. "Besides I don't feel like taking the bus." I liked Robby and knew he'd have a calming effect on my temper.

"Let's go," I said, and shook my keys.

As we drove along the street entering downtown, Robby quickly rolled his window down. I understood his eagerness when he whistled at two, cute girls on the sidewalk. The girls briefly glanced in our direction, as Robby hollered a silly, "Helloooo!"

I shook my head. Robby was insane, in a good way. I knew being his roommate would be entertaining to say the least.

We found a parking spot near Church Street and stepped out of the car. Cars weren't allowed on Church Street, which was cool. It was filled with a lot of people walking around, though.

The street was lined on both sides with a multitude of restaurants, quaint cafés, and retail stores. One set of large doors opened up to a sizable mall inside. Robby and I enjoyed ourselves as we people-watched. It was a college town and a melting pot of students.

Robby and I were starved, so we paused at a concession stand and bought falafels—a first for both of us. Falafels are a popular fast food in the Middle East made of deep-fried, chickpea balls. We also got some colas to wash them down.

"Tell me more about yourself Robby," I said. "You know, what's your family like?"

"Not much to tell. My life's pretty boring. My sister Alyssa has some hot friends, though. You'll have to meet 'em."

I laughed. I had hoped he had some crazy family story, but at least I understood why he wore his girl-crazy T-shirt.

We finished our falafels and sodas and tossed them in the trash. Robby continued to check out girls, while I daydreamed about Lake Champlain and its countless beaches. I knew there was an extended bike trail that followed along the seemingly endless shore.

Robby pulled me out of my thoughts. "Hey Ladieees," he drooled. He reminded me of a cheesy car salesman, as he began to talk with a small group of college girls. I *was* envious of his ease with females. I would've felt stupid talking to girls like that, but from what I could see, the girls didn't mind.

I wandered around and pretended to look busy, as I glimpsed at items for sale through various windows. I came to an out-of-the-way store that sold fencing equipment, swords, and other extraordinary weaponry. In one of the windows, an illuminated sword caught my eye. It had unusual polygon shaped engravings traversing down the sides of the shiny, silver metal. I couldn't take my eyes off it. I felt hypnotically pulled into the store, where a young man about my age was literally polishing the heck out of the swords. Geez, my mom would love you to come clean our house, I thought.

"Hello, I'm Anthony. May I help you?" he asked rather flatly and without looking up.

I found myself drawn to him, as though I should have known him. "I was admiring the swords you have for sale here." I picked one up in awe.

"They're quite expensive." He studied me up and down.

I'm sure he was thinking, No way you can afford it, dude. "Thanks anyway. Are you a student nearby?" I asked, as I placed the sword back into its sheath.

"Yes, I attend Freefall College." He sounded like a snob. "I'm very busy now and need to get back to work. Let me know if there's anything else I can help you with." He rudely walked away.

I left the store and could've sworn I saw Berard out of the corner of my eye, but when I turned, nobody was there.

I found Robby writing down his phone number for the group of girls he'd been speaking with. When they walked away, one of them, a tall, redhead with shining, green eyes tossed the phone number into a nearby trashcan. She glanced up at me and winked. I hadn't spoken to any of them, though I began to blush ridiculously. What was wrong with me? I was a college man now. I ran my fingers through my thick hair and walked real cool, until I almost bumped into an annoyed lady who wore the expression, *college kids kill me*. When I glanced at the redhead again, she smiled and shook her head from side to side. Told you I'm a klutz.

"Hey, man, that babe's gonna give me a call." Robby announced to me with a smug expression.

"Are you kidding?" I asked. "Didn't you notice? She threw away your number."

"No way bro. In case you haven't noticed, I'm a pro wit' the ladies."

"I'm not arguing with you. I just think you might be a little too forward," I said.

"Nah...nah...that can't be it." Robby shook his head. "I know I just met you dude, but I bet I know more about babes than you, but that's okay, 'cause I'll help you out." He patted me on the shoulder and nodded his head like I really needed the help, like he meant it with all sincerity.

I punched him lightly in the ribs. "Maybe I'll help *you* out."

Robby squinted his eyes. "Maybe. 'Cause you aren't ugly."

"Gee, thanks."

We decided to cruise down to Lake Champlain, but before we got to my car, there was an old, blind man playing acoustic guitar and singing. We stopped to listen.

"Fight the bloody battle!" he belted out. "Live the unknown dream! Don't waste time! Don't lose steam!"

"He's pretty good." Robby looked impressed.

The man heard him, took off his hat, and set it on the ground. "Money for an old, blind man?" The man continued to strum the guitar and sing, "The tears I hide, I offer to the sky in retribution for unlawful pride...yeah... fight the battle hard. Don't let your courage wane. Try to stay on guard..."

I pulled some change and a couple of dollars out of my pocket and flung it into the blind man's hat.

"Thanks lad. Don't forget what I sang. I sang it for you."

Robby was already heading for my car and didn't hear the old man.

"What are you saying?" I stammered. "W...what do you mean?" It was too late. A group of people clustered around the man, and he didn't respond to my question. Who is he, I thought? How could he know me? I glanced back at him as I strode to my car. His head never turned back my way.

❖ ❧ ❖

Robby and I drove down to Lake Champlain. The lake gleamed as intensely as I had imagined. It almost blinded me as I stared out at the shimmering waves. A variety of birds chirped and flapped their wings high above the water. The excitement of the lake made me forget the blind man's ominous song.

I loved sailing. It was one of my favorite things to do, and we happened to come across a shop that rented all types of sailboats. The Hobie Cat was my favorite catamaran because of its speed and ease to maneuver. I knew I wouldn't flip it over. I was imagining myself flying on the water with the wind whipping, when, oddly, I gazed out at the water and thought I saw Berard, again—in a motorboat. I clutched my fists in irritation, but when I looked for him a second time he was gone.

I felt paranoid, with my animated phone and all the weird stuff that kept happening. I knew I wasn't crazy, but I could no longer contain my anxiety. I needed to find Berard—find out who he was and why he was such an annoyance. He was like a buzzing fly I wanted to swat with one of those super big fly swatters, and that's putting it nicely, the way my mom would want me to say it.

The activity of the day finally wore on me. I was ready to go back to campus. Robby wanted to return to our dorm as well. He wanted to finish unpacking and wander around to meet new girls. No surprise.

"P.A.R.T.Y.—par-tay," he sang, and begged me to come with him, but I had other things on my mind.

When we arrived on our floor, the unforeseen was waiting for me— Berard. Strangely enough, he was expecting my return.

"Hello Bladen," he said, in his aged voice. "I know you wish to see me. Why don't you come in now?"

I turned to see what Robby was doing to see if he had any reaction to Berard, but he waltzed into our room as though he hadn't noticed Berard at all.

I hesitated, before I went into room 223. My heart pounded—not knowing what to expect. I stepped in and was amazed to see a myriad of posters plastered against the walls. Most of them were of historical places like the Coliseum in Italy or Myndos, Turkey. A breathtaking poster of the Grand Canyon in Arizona hung from the wall as well.

Then my eyes rested on another fascinating poster. At first, I knew I recognized it, although I couldn't immediately place where I'd seen it before. When it illuminated on its own like a frigging spotlight, the color drained from my face. The poster was an illustration from my video game, Arcis. I knew something was messed up with my phone, I thought. I slowly edged closer to the poster and placed both my hands on it. My fingertips found their way across the scene and explored it—in the same manner that a blind person reads Braille.

The poster looked busy with legendary creatures like Minotaurs, prehistoric flying birds, and unnaturally large stallions with wings. In the backdrop, there were immense, snow-capped mountains and threatening storm-like clouds. In the foreground, marching armies emerged ready for battle, while freakish demon-like monsters with horns charged at them. The creatures looked so vile, I trembled with dread.

I reminded myself that I *had* already played this game. It was only a video game. No big deal. I took a deep breath, swung around to face Berard, and demanded with distrust, "Who are you? What do you want with me?"

"Calm down," he said, walking toward me with his hands up. "I'm your patriarch. You've been chosen to become a life player. My mission is to help you."

OPTING IN

"**H**elp me? I spat. "Help me how?"

"Bladen, take a seat, and I'll try to explain what I can to you."

I saw a semi-comfortable looking, purple lounge chair—another eccentric color that clashed with Berard's vibrant, orange shirt. I sprawled out on it and tried to put my feet up. Feeling uptight, I placed my feet on the hard floor and leaned toward Berard, waiting for him to speak.

"So go on," I pressed.

Berard paused before he began his explanation, "Okay...first, I know Arcis is your new video game."

"How could you possibly know that?" I interrupted. This guy's whacked, I thought.

Berard spoke with authority and ignored my question. "You've been chosen among thousands of players to be pulled into the game to play it...for real. You have a choice. Even though you've been selected, you don't have to play the real-life game. But if you say yes, whenever the maker of Arcis needs you, he'll pull you into your iPhone to play. Like I said, you have a choice."

Not only did this guy sound old, but he also sounded like a freaking robot.

"That's ridiculous," I argued. My head spun in confusion. "What are you talking about? Look, dude, you're nuts. I'm out of here." I stood up to leave.

Berard sighed and went on. "We'll work on your disposition later. Look do you want to play the real game or not?"

"If you're not lying to me, yeah, of course...but why me?"

Berard continued, "I know it might take you a while to trust me, but eventually you will." I sat back down. "We want you because we *have* to win, and you're a genius at playing video games. You already know how the game works, but now you'll be a real life player. When you're in the game, you'll be the one to fight against the beasts and demons. It's pretty simple. If you win against the beasts in the land of Arcis, Earth wins too. But if you lose the game, major catastrophes occur on Earth like plane crashes, hurricanes, and the like. "

"That already happens in the game," I said, in awe.

"You're right, but this time, it's for real. If you lose in the game, real catastrophes occur on real Earth, not just in the game. If you win, real Earth wins too, meaning fewer catastrophes. Get it? Can you really sit back and put your future into the hands of another life player? You *know* you can win, but do you really know for sure that whoever your replacement is can too? " Berard challenged.

I wasn't one to back down from a challenge. I really wasn't worried about losing the game at this point; it seemed pretty easy. "What's the objective of the game when it's played this way?" I asked. Berard seemed to relax at my apparent interest.

"It's similar. If all ten levels are won by just over half of all life players around the world, Earth will live in perpetual peace, the game Arcis will be destroyed, and so will everything and everyone in it, including anyone good who isn't fortunate enough to get out before it happens—if it happens."

"And what if life players don't win the game?" I joked. "Will Earth self-destruct?"

"This isn't a joke, Bladen, and, yes, Earth will be destroyed...forever... and that includes you. If we lose, the consequences are grave."

I still wasn't worried. Seriously, I hadn't lost a game yet, although I hadn't played that much, either. I mean the game *was* new.

"There is a catch you should know about," Berard said.

"What catch?"

"When it's time for you to enter the game, your body will split into two. One of you will battle the levels, while your other body stays on Earth. In that way, nobody on Earth will ever guess you're a life player."

"Far out," I breathed in amazement. "What else can you tell me?"

"You'll learn beyond the passing and fading away of time and more frequently than every new moon." Berard, like a lunatic, pointed both index fingers dramatically up to the sky.

"What? Can you speak in English?" I asked, my eyebrows raised. I wondered if Berard had a clue. Maybe he *was* crazy and made all this up. His voice still sounded old and freaky. I found him irritating.

"You won't travel on this quest alone," he emphasized. "You'll experience a multitude of beings that will assist you on your journey, and you'll always be learning." Berard walked over to me and waved his hand behind my left ear. "There's one more thing I need to do for you." I felt a warm sensation. He picked up a gold mirror and handed it to me. "Go ahead and look."

I gazed in the mirror behind my left ear, which was pretty darn hard to do, and saw an emblem that depicted Spero, the benevolent king from my game Arcis. He was the king the life players fought for. "How did you do this? What does this mean?"

"It marks you as a life player."

I continued to stare in the mirror. The mark blew me away. "Is that it, or is there more to this?"

"There's more, but if you try to learn too much too quickly, it *will* weaken you. If you learn to be forbearing, you're instincts will become stronger."

I thought about the obsession I had felt toward my iPhone. It began to make sense, now that I knew about the real game of Arcis.

For a few moments after Berard spoke, the room was silent. I absorbed his comments like a sponge and couldn't wait to play the game. "Tell me Berard," I challenged, "did I see you earlier today when I went downtown?"

Berard nodded.

"I saw you. Then you disappeared. How? It was like, poof, you magically went into thin air."

After a pause, he broke into a fit of laughter. I couldn't understand what was so funny.

"I'm irritating you, am I not?" he choked out, talking oddly again. He seemed to enjoy making fun of me.

I was ripped. How dare he test my anger on purpose. I wanted to show *him*. I jumped toward him to take hold of his scrawny arms, and believe me they were…well…petite. Anyway, I almost had him in my fists when he disappeared. I leaned forward and lost my balance. Before I could regain it, I dropped to the floor.

He laughed so hard; he cried. Jerk, I thought. "H…how did you do that?" I stammered, in anger and disbelief.

His chuckling eventually subsided, and he took on a more considerate tone. "I'm sorry; this shouldn't be so entertaining for me. Believe it or not, I'm training you to control your temper. You need to get a handle on that one. It's truly your biggest weakness. You shouldn't have tried to attack me. As for my vanishing act…I can disappear and reappear wherever I need to go. I don't need transportation. Pretty neat trick, huh?" He crossed his arms and raised his chin, in conceit.

I was speechless—blown away. Maybe he wasn't as geeky as I had originally thought, maddening yes, but maybe…he was sort of cool. After all, he could do cool stuff. I turned and stepped out of his room without saying another word.

Robby never noticed me enter our room; he had his iPod on. I tapped him on the shoulder.

"What's up?" he asked.

"What are you doing back so early? I thought you wanted to meet some hot, new girls."

"Tomorrow," he answered, "it's kinda late, and I promised my grandma I'd call her."

Normally I would've joked with him about his grandma, but instead I sat down across from him. "So...what do you think of Berard?"

"I don't know him yet," he said, as he pulled off his headphones. "Why?"

"Well," I started, "what do you think of his voice? Do you think he sounds peculiar...sort of old?"

"Nope, not old at all; he's our age, man; why would he?"

"You mean you haven't noticed *anything* different about him." I stood up.

"Not at all."

"Did you see him earlier, when we were downtown? I asked. "I saw him a couple of times."

"No I didn't. Why all the questions, man?" Robby stared at me like he was thinking, Dude, what's your problem?

"I just think he's...weird that's all."

"Look man, you just met the guy," Robby said. "Lighten up on him."

With that remark, our conversation ended. Robby's phone rang; it was his parents. While he went on and on about how awesome Burlington had been, I left our room and crossed the hall. Once again, I pounded on Berard's door.

"Do I have to open?" he asked.

"Yeah that'd be great," I answered, in the kindest voice I could muster.

Berard opened the door. He glanced around to make sure nobody could hear him, and he didn't wait to explain. "No...no one else can perceive the prehistoric hum of my voice apart from you," he whispered. "To everyone else I sound and behave like any ordinary eighteen-year-old. I've been alive in various forms for over one thousand years." He glanced down at his body. "This human form was given to me, so I can help you."

I shook my head in disbelief. "How'd you know I wanted to ask about your voice?"

Berard smiled. "Normally I'll only be near you when you need me—like if you're in danger. This time…I *was* eavesdropping. I wanted to know your reaction to me. I can be around you without you seeing me. Apparently, I'm fonder of you than you are of me. I don't think you're weird."

"You were spying on me? Dude, that's…that's…just creepy; don't do it again," I warned, "and so you know; you talk crazy too."

"Am I bothering you, again?" Berard mused.

I smirked and thought, Dude, I am so gonna get you back.

"Something funny, perhaps?" Berard asked.

"Not at all," I said, and began to walk away.

Berard's somber voice stopped me. "I feel you should know your path won't be a simple one. You're going to think that you're this super hero…I just hope the struggles you're going to experience won't kill you."

"Um…thanks…I think," I said, and walked away unsure again of what he meant, though, it sounded like an insult. Not surprising.

Robby and I stayed up late that night. We talked about girls and shared gory stories of our past. His crazy stories far outshone mine.

Before I fell asleep, I made up my mind to call Julia the next day. She had said she would give me a tour of the campus, so I could find my classes on Monday. Later, my sleep was filled with a turbulent dream…

I was alone, drifting down the current of a narrow river in a boat that looked the tiniest bit like a canoe, but it was only large enough to hold me. Intriguing Roman architecture rose up within the waterway that encircled me. Other ancient-styled structures were standing nearby, including a stone bridge built with four huge arches. The air was saturated with misty steam like a sauna.

The eerie river below looked shallow and trifling enough. With great ease, I plunged my paddle to the floor. A loud crunch reverberated on the rocks below. I shivered from the chill in the air. I couldn't tell if it was dusk or dawn. The surrounding light showed no apparent sun, moon, or stars as the source of it. I heard a whisper in my ear; someone called my name. "Blaaaden." Every hair on my body stood on end. I searched around.

The water splashed up, angry at the world. A toothless, disproportionate giant with wild, brown hair past his shoulders stormed out of the river high above my boat. Irate, he screamed, "I am ailing; heal me!"

Caught off guard and gripped with fear, my heartbeat quickened. I stood up, stumbled, and fell out of the craft, only to be wholly submerged by the river. I never took a breath of air before I dropped and inhaled the cool water deep into my lungs. They burned like fire.

I woke up startled and gasped for air. I was relieved to find myself in my bed, although my throat and chest still blazed. My head spun—a dream or a vision? It had all seemed so real. Even the blue T-shirt and shorts I wore to bed felt chilly and damp when I touched them. Was it sweat or the remnants of my unwanted swim in the river?

I wanted to get up right then and ask Berard about it, but when I looked at my red digital clock, I saw it was only 3:00 a.m.

I glanced around in the dark, and, once again, my dorm room sent chills down my spine like it had the previous afternoon. I couldn't understand why my room set me ill at ease.

I tossed and turned for the rest of the night.

I woke up around 6:00 a.m. with the sound of Robby's voice as he sang "Here Comes the Sun" not badly, but not as well as the Beatles.

"Ugh," I groaned. "Are you always so annoying in the morning?"

"Hey, I sing so awesome you should thank me. Besides, *you* need to get out of bed; it's late."

"This is *not* late," I articulated. "No one living should be up this early. We need to set some rules, or you're gonna be a serious morning enemy."

Robby threw a pillow at me. "Aren't *you* a grumpy bro in the morning. Maybe tomorrow I'll throw a cup of ice-cold water on you to wake you up instead."

"Funny," I remarked.

Robby was already dressed. He grabbed his toothbrush and paste and headed for the door, apparently, to go to the bathroom down the hall. I rolled over peacefully to go back into oblivion, until Robby came back and shook me hard. I sprang out of bed, seized Robby, and wrestled him to the floor in a headlock.

"Okay okay," he cried. "Truce. I'll leave you alone. Come on bro, if you get your hands off me, I'll share my breakfast with you."

"No you'll cook it for me. Breakfast today, and if you wake me up tomorrow, You're a goner."

"Deal," he relented, "but you'll need to help me cook. I'm a lousy chef."

"What do you have to eat?" I asked.

"Eggs," he replied.

"No problem—eggs, I can do."

We cooked a hearty breakfast in the dorm kitchen: scrambled eggs, toast with melted butter, and sweet, tangy orange juice. I ate plenty, since I wasn't sure when or what I would be eating next. Robby offered to clean up. Actually...I *made* him. Well, not really. I helped him–a little.

Back at our room, I picked up the phone book and looked up Julia's number. I realized I had forgotten to pack it. My hands grew clammy with sweat. Girls—they always had this maddening effect on me. I reminded myself that she was just an unconventional girl I had ridden bikes with as a kid. I had loved to pull her pigtails and make her scream. She was kind of a nerd.

But the way she had sounded on the phone back home made my hands sweat. My heart jumped. I flipped through the white pages, found her number, and dialed—fast. The phone rang once, twice, then at least five more times. I was about to hang up when a female answered, "Hello," in a groggy voice.

"Um...hi...Julia? It's Bladen."

"It's awfully early you know," she said—not exactly the greeting I had hoped for.

I glimpsed at the clock—8:12 a.m. on a Saturday. "I'm sorry. My roommate woke me up at the insane hour of 6:00 a.m. It feels late now. I called to schedule my tour of the campus."

When do you want to meet?" Julia asked. I took a deep breath and glanced in the mirror, noticing that I needed a shave. Robby strolled into the room. "Bladen, are you still there?"

"Uh yeah, Julia. How 'bout today? Do you have time?"

"Yes, I do."

"Cool, what's your street address?"

Julia laughed, "You won't need that. The directions are *really* simple."

"Maybe, but my sense of direction is *really* horrible. I'm a complete GPS guy."

Julia laughed some more. Man, I love her laugh.

"Well, if you insist. It's 8454 Walt Way, zip 05452.

"Got it! Is noon okay?"

"Noon it is!" she sang with a little lilt in her voice then hung up.

It was then that Robby stuck his face in mine.

"So…you're holding out on me, aren't you?"

"What…I don't know what you're talking about," I countered.

"You were on the phone with a girl. Don't act like you weren't. I know. I have girl radar."

"It's not a big deal. She's just a peculiar girl I knew when I was younger. She and my mom have been friends since high school, and she goes to school here too. I asked her if she could show me around." I shrugged, hoping he'd drop it.

"All right, you're off the hook, but I want you to bring her back here. I wanna meet her."

"No way!" I said adamantly. "I've never met anyone as crazy about girls as you. You'll probably humiliate me."

Robby put his right hand across his heart and threw his head back, pretending to be in pain. "I'm hurt."

"Yeah whatever," I answered, "somehow I think you'll live. Now if you'll excuse me, I need to take a shower."

As I headed down the hall toward the showers, I decided to see if Berard was in his room. This time I knocked lightly, but nobody answered. I knocked a few more times—still no answer. I wondered where he could've taken off to so early. I wanted to ask him what he thought of my dream.

Since Berard wasn't around, I went to the men's bathroom and took my shower, letting the hot, steamy water pound against my back. Endless hot water poured from the showerhead. At home, I shared and fought with my siblings over whose turn came next in the bathroom. If you were last in line, frosty, cold water met you at the other end.

When I finished, I picked out what to wear—a faded pair of jeans and my favorite olive T-shirt. I wanted to look decent for Julia. I thought twice about why I even cared. I even styled my hair, carefully making sure strands of it didn't stick out. Robby took off for a moment, and was no longer around to give me a hard time about Julia.

By 10:00 a.m., I was ready to go. I had an hour and a half of time left to kill, before I had to meet her. I decided to take out my guitar and play for a while. The temptation to crank the volume on my amp. and wake a few people up struck me, but I didn't do it. I put on my headphones and strummed out "Dreams." It was one of my favorite songs to jam to. I closed my eyes, rocking with the beat, until Robby came in and pulled the plug on me. I yanked my fingers away from the strings. Man was it loud. Before long, someone pounded on our door.

This gangly kid with red, curly hair and glasses walked in. He was a scary-looking dude.

Robby spoke up a bit too honestly. "Bro you're a mess. Your eyes are so red and swollen, they're practically shut."

"Look dude, turn down the racket or else," the kid spat, and moved forward toward Robby. Robby walked in his direction, with his hands balled into fists at his side.

Yeah. I tried to keep the situation calm.

"Hey don't worry about it," I said, glancing at the guy. "We won't turn the music back on. What's your name, anyway; I'm Bladen."

"Jared," he answered.

I put my right hand out to shake his. Respectfully, he shook my hand too. "I'd appreciate you keeping the noise down," he said. "I wanna catch more sleep."

"Sure, why don't you stop by another time."

Jared walked to the door. "Thanks. See ya later." He glared at Robby before he walked out.

After the door closed, I spun around. "What were you thinking? That kid looked like he wanted to pulverize you."

"You mean Jared? He looked messed up on drugs, bro, and I could've taken him down. No problem."

"How do you know it was drugs?"

"Gut feeling," he said.

Later, I headed to my car to drive to Julia's. I was a nervous wreck, and at times, this slice of my life frustrated me. My dad had always encouraged me in the girl department. I should've called him before I left.

I started the ignition in my car and typed Julia's address into my GPS, recalling that Julia was definitely *not* a girl I needed to be anxious about. I drew in a deep breath and drove off.

I pulled into Julia's driveway and was glad I had arrived at her house on time. I glanced at my appearance in the rearview mirror—to make sure my teeth were clean, no breakfast foods stuck anywhere, and to make sure my hair didn't look like a mop. Then I proceeded up to her front door. I knocked twice before she opened, and with one glimpse at her, my jaw fell *wide* open. It didn't really; that would've looked stupid. But I'm almost positive my eyes bulged out.

SKIN DEEP

Julia threw her arms around my neck and almost knocked me over with a hug. "Bladen I'm so delighted to see you. It's been too long."

At that moment, I heard a voice in my head whisper, *She's* the one. I looked around but didn't see anyone.

Yeah. This time my mouth did drop open, and I felt like an idiot. I couldn't stop saying, "Uh...uh...uh." I knew where I had seen Julia before. She looked exactly like the blonde girl from my game Arcis. I couldn't believe it. How could that be? My blood pumped hard. I tried to pull it together.

A look of alarm crossed over Julia's face. "Are you okay?"

"Low blood sugar," I muttered.

"Do you want a glass of milk or something to eat?" Julia's voice rang, sweetly.

"Milk."

I followed Julia into the kitchen. While she poured me a glass of milk, she glanced up at me, still concerned.

I stared back at her, breathless by how much she had changed. She no longer wore glasses, and somehow her collection of freckles had minimized, revealing milky, smooth skin. Her light, blue eyes radiated against it. Her lengthy, pale hair had deepened to a darker shade of blonde and fell straight to the middle of her back. Her smile sparkled and lit up her entire face. She wore a dark blue T-shirt that fit just right and faded blue jeans that showed the contours of her slim hips. She was so beautiful; I immediately felt intimidated, again.

She handed me the milk. I drew in my breath, "Th...thanks," I managed to stammer. Then it occurred to me, maybe she was a life player too, and played in the game like I was going to. "Do you like video games, by chance?"

"No, I hate them, always have. If you feel better, I'll show you around."

I nodded, disappointed. The uncanny resemblance between Julia and the blonde from the game was a strange coincidence. Bummer.

I gazed around the house. It was impressive. The wide, open space had high cathedral ceilings. I entered the living room first and saw a puffy, white couch, white chair, and matching ottoman. Off the living room, there was a guest bedroom with an adjoining bathroom. Just outside the bathroom door, an indoor Jacuzzi tub sat, invitingly. Sweet, I thought. The kitchen bordered the living room and had granite, marble-speckled counter tops, and shiny, spotless stainless steel appliances.

The walls were almost entirely made of glass. Julia showed me the switch on the wall that controlled the blinds inside the glass walls. If you pushed the switch, the blinds closed and gave the indoor space complete privacy from the outside. In the middle of the living room, a remarkable stone hearth rose all the way to the ceiling. A striking wood stove made out of green and black checkered soapstone sat at the base of it. A black-metal, spiral staircase in the middle of the room rose up to a loft upstairs. Julia told me she and her mom's bedrooms were up there, each with their own adjoining bathroom.

I glanced around. "You and your mom have a nice place."

Julia pulled her long hair up to the top of her head, giving me a better look at her flawless face. "Yeah," she answered, "it's a lot better than the last house we lived in. You and your family visited us there, remember?"

"Yeah, I think so," I answered, in a dazed voice, mesmerized by her good looks. "It was so long ago, and we were much younger. I don't remember it that well."

"Are you okay?" Julia looked puzzled. "You kind of look out of it."

I have this child-like habit of being outrageously honest with my feelings sometimes, and, unfortunately, this was one of those times. "I'm sorry. It's just that...well...do you know what a knock-out you turned out to be?"

"Excuse me?" she said, startled. "Um...thanks. Your girlfriend probably wouldn't appreciate you telling me that."

"No...no," I answered, flustered. I've never had a serious girlfriend... not that I don't like girls...because I do...never mind."

She glanced away and appeared to be staring out the window. I thought I saw a glimmer of a smile on her face. She circled around toward me. "You mean you've *never* had a girlfriend?"

"N...no...are you going to make fun of me because of that?" I asked, sure my face was turning crimson, as I felt freaked by the stupidity of my end of the conversation.

"Of course not...you turned out pretty good yourself, you know. I'm sure girls must tell you how cute you are."

"Oh, he's sooo cute," I teased in the highest girlie voice I could muster. Cute? I thought. How insulting.

"You're funny," she laughed, and ran her index finger leisurely across my chin. My heart pumped at her touch.

She made me feel so jumbled inside, I foolishly revealed my thoughts—again. "There's a character in my video game that looks like you, by the way."

Julia let out a slight giggle, "Interesting."

"So, if you don't like video games, have you ever modeled for one?"

"That's flattering, but no; I don't play them or model for them." Julia's smile grew wider as she let her finger slide down my right arm.

Gently, I moved it away and changed the subject. "Are you ready to go back to campus to show me around?" I tried to appear unscathed from the prior moment, even though my insides felt like Jell-o.

"Sure," she replied, and walked away from me. I thought she looked disappointed.

While girls made me generally nervous, I didn't always care what they thought of me, but I cared what Julia thought, and I knew exactly why... she was hot...and nice, too.

Julia and I arrived at my car and got in, when I realized I hadn't seen her mom, Lisa. I couldn't believe I hadn't thought to mention her. "Where's your mom, anyway?"

"You finally noticed my mom's respectable missing presence?" Julia asked, her voice laced with sarcasm. "She works...a lot. She's a V.P. at one of the local banks in town, and she's frequently away on business trips. 'That's the reason why we have such a comfortable home, and I can help you pay for your college', blah, blah, blah." Julia imitated her mother's words.

"You sound bitter," I said. "I gather you'd rather have your mom around more often."

She peered at me with scowling eyes. "Who wouldn't?"

I tried to lighten up the moment with a lame joke. "I guess one whose mother's a convict."

She rolled her eyes.

Clearly, my joke sucked.

After we both sat in my car, I asked, "Isn't your mom alone...I mean without your dad?"

"Yeah, she is. They're divorced. You can say the word—DIVORCED. They've been divorced for so long, I hardly remember what my dad looked like, and I know Mom has to work to support us. It...just hurts because she's hardly ever around. She's always off somewhere."

Julia sat silently for the rest of the car ride. When we arrived at Freefall, I parked the car near my dorm.

"Where do you want to start?" I turned, and looked at Julia.

"Let me see your schedule, and we'll go from there." She didn't seem to be having as much fun, as when I had first arrived at her house.

I stared at her for a moment. "Julia," I said softly. "I don't know the whole story about your parents, but I'm sorry it upsets you so much."

She gazed back at me with her face brightened, and flashed a spectacular smile at me. "It's okay, forget it. It's cool seeing you again. I'm glad we're both going to Freefall. Now let me see your schedule. I don't want to sit in your car all day. Oh, and by the way, my mom *is* an ex-convict," she giggled. "I *do* have a sense of humor, just in case you thought otherwise."

I laughed and handed her my schedule.

I watched her scan my list of classes. Her eyes widened. "What are you trying to do, commit academic suicide? You're taking biology and chemistry with labs, pre-calc, and intro to psych. What's with all the science and math?" She stared at me with quizzical eyes.

I defended myself. "It's only fourteen credits."

"But the science and math are hours of work, and why are you taking psychology? It doesn't exactly go along with the others."

"I'm taking psychology, so I can figure out people like you," I said. "Never mind me, what classes are you taking?"

"I'm taking a couple of introductory education classes, an English writing course, Vermont history, and Spanish."

"What kind of job do you want when you graduate?" I asked.

"I'd like to be an elementary school teacher someday. Little kids are sweet and fun." Julia stared wistfully out the window. Her thoughts looked miles away.

I gave her a poke in the stomach. "Hey!" she exclaimed, and pulled back in surprise.

"Come on. Let's get out of here," I said, as I opened my door.

When we both got out of my car, Julia took my schedule and directed me around various buildings. She was amazingly easy to spend time with. We both talked nonstop as we wandered around.

After two hours or so, we had explored the entire campus and approached my car. "Thanks for showing me around. I owe you one." I opened my car door, ready to hop in.

"Wait. Hold up. You mean that's it. Don't I get to see your room?" she asked, one hand on her hip.

When she said that, my first thought was, No way Robby.

"Well... what do you think?" she wouldn't let up.

"I think...I'm hungry, that's what I think." I felt uneasy. "How about lunch? I'd rather take you out. Are you hungry?"

The thought of her meeting Robby made my palms sweat. I mean I liked the guy, but I didn't want him to blow it for me.

Julia still held one hand on her hip and stared me down. She flipped her hair out of her face and didn't budge.

"What?" I asked, widening my eyes.

"Are you hiding something?"

"It's my roommate, Robby," I started to explain.

"You're hiding your roommate?"

"No...no...my roommate's kind of wild over girls, and after he takes in one look at you, I'm not sure what dumb thing might come out of his mouth."

"What dumb thing do you think he might say?"

I leaned toward Julia and whispered, "He might mention something about your good looks."

Julia smiled and changed the subject. "I'm a little envious. I wish I could've stayed in a dorm with a roommate, but my mom said 'no' because we live so close."

"I think you're lucky to live in your house," I said. It's awesome. Come on, let's go to lunch. It's on me, on one condition...tell me more about yourself. Your life is a mystery to me. Even my mom doesn't know much about you or your mom."

"Hmm," she hesitated. "My life *is* a bit cryptic. How do I know I can trust you won't tell anyone?"

I gave her the Boy Scout salute and answered, "I promise, cross my heart, hope to die, stick a needle in my eye."

"You're *so* juvenile," she smirked, and hit my arm.

"Seriously, I can't wait to hear your story. If you're worried about trusting me with it, it must be good. And then after I'll take you to my room."

"Deal," she said.

Julia and I drove down to Church Street. She knew of a little bistro, where they made tasty calzones. We each ordered one, along with a soda. We sat at a table just outside the restaurant on the street. I waited for Julia to talk first, excited to hear her story, but she remained quiet for what seemed to be—forever.

Just when I couldn't stand the silence any longer, I heard a familiar voice sing in the distance. I snapped my head up to see where it came from and saw the blind man.

"Hold on," Julia said, "I'll be right back." She sprang out of her seat and went over to the blind man. I watched him whisper something in her ear. Then she dropped money into his hat. Just as quickly, she sprinted back into her seat and faced me.

"What was that all about?" I asked.

"I—helped out a person." Julia answered, not offering an explanation.

"I saw him. He whispered something in your ear. What was it?"

Julia took a long, slow sip from her straw. "Nothing, it doesn't matter."

"What did you say to him? It matters to me." Oddly, the obsessed feeling I had with my iPhone came back. I had to know.

Julia stared at me. "Why does it matter to you?"

I told her about the song he sang the previous day and how he seemed to know me. Her eyes grew.

Julia leaned forward, putting her face close to mine and spoke in a low tone. She glanced around to make sure nobody could hear her. "His nickname on the street is the Psycho Psychic, which I don't think is too kind, but I've heard other stories like yours. This is the first time he's ever talked to me. He told me I should trust you."

"How can he know who we are or that I'm here, if he can't see us?" I whispered.

"I don't know," Julia answered. It's weird. He appears and disappears out of nowhere."

"Don't the police pick him up off the street?"

"The police are never here when he is," she answered. He's a bit of a myth. There's been a lot of talk about him recently, because he's been hanging around more than usual."

At that moment, a flock of white doves like a puff of smoke descended on Julia and me. We tried to hit them away, but they continued to flock around us. As quickly as they appeared, they were gone—except one. It landed on Julia's shoulder and chirped sweetly. It nudged at her cheek. She hit it away, but it continued to sing to her. Its musical chirp sounded surreal, until it put its head down in a sign of defeat and flew away.

"That was strange," I said.

"I sees doves often," Julia answered, and shrugged.

"Don't you ever wonder why?"

"I guess."

I put my elbow on the table and rested my chin on the palm of my hand. "How about telling me your family story now."

Julia sighed. "Okay, you win. I can't believe I'm telling you this so soon, and...I need to give you the compact version. The entire story's too long."

I reached out and placed my hand around Julia's and stared into her eyes. "The blind man told you, you can trust me, and you can."

Julia nodded her head in understanding. "I might as well start with the worst of it. My father's...a criminal. He's murdered...countless people, but he was never caught. He always had an alibi."

Julia stopped to see my reaction.

"Go on," I said, reassuringly.

She swallowed hard then continued. "That made my mom believe in the beginning that he was a good man wrongly accused. When they first met, my father wined and dined my mom. She fell deeply in love with him and believed all his lies. They lived in Chicago at the time. My mother became suspicious when she found blood on his clothes. After that, my father disappeared for weeks at a time. The police kept showing up at our door, yet my mom never knew where he was. So they harassed her, believing that she was covering up for him. Eventually, she was afraid and became convinced that he had committed the crimes he was accused of, but she didn't leave right away. She stayed in Chicago, because she was pregnant with my twin sister and me. Then, when we were six, my father pushed his way back into our lives. He favored my sister Jessica, while he treated me with intense cruelty. Jessica grew heartless when he was around, even though she was only a little girl. My mom never called the police. She was afraid my father would kill us. But when I cried all the time, my mother couldn't stand it anymore. She took me in the night when I was seven and fled to Alaska. We lived there in hiding for one year with my mother's friend Adonis. Then we moved to California. Adonis followed us to protect us. Finally, we moved to Vermont. That's when my mom looked up your family. She wanted to regain ties with old friends she trusted.

But someone ransacked our home. They ripped it to shreds. My mother thought it was my father again, but the police couldn't find his fingerprints anywhere. That's why my mom had the house we own now, built. The reason for the beautiful windows and enclosed blinds: so that at night, we don't have to worry about anyone peeking into the house. The glass is bullet proof.

My mom was concerned for everyone she cared about, so she chose to not keep in touch with your mom. She was afraid your family would get hurt because of her." Julia laughed with scorn; her eyes watered. "It's ironic you're here with me now. Isn't it?"

I didn't know what to say; her story stunned me. I had believed she was an only child from a divorced family. I had no idea she was in so much danger.

"Wow," I began, "I didn't know your life was so complicated." I squeezed Julia's hand and made another one of my pitiable jokes. "You should tell Inquire Magazine. If your dad knew that you had talked publicly about him, maybe he'd show up, and the police could lock him away. Then you could make lots of money on talk shows, or maybe write a book."

The corners of Julia's mouth turned up, and she laughed. A small laugh tumbled out at first, but then she breathed her soda in the wrong way and started to cough. The waitress came over and asked if she was all right.

"She's fine," I teased again. "I just asked her to marry me, but she turned me down. So, if you don't mind, I'd like the check." The waitress stared at us like we were crazy.

That sent Julia into a greater fit of laughter. I waited a few minutes before she caught her breath, surprised that she thought I was so funny.

"I can't believe you're making a joke out of this, but even more...it feels good to laugh. I can't remember the last time I did."

"I'm happy to be here for some comic relief—even if my jokes are pathetic."

"They're not pathetic. If my mom and I made money at his expense, it would make up for the years of pain he's caused us. Because the police never found him, we don't know if he'll show up on our doorstep again. My mom always lives in fear. Her friend Adonis won't leave us, because he feels responsible. Every time we've moved, he's bought a house next to ours, and I've had to live a sheltered life." Julia squeezed my hand. "So you know, I've never had a serious boyfriend." The only reason I'm out with you now is: My mom knows and trusts your family."

"I'm flattered," I confessed. Actually, I was pumped; she had never had a serious boyfriend.

The waitress came back and gave me the check. I slipped her some cash. "Keep the change."

"Have a great afternoon," she said, as she checked out my generous tip.

"C'mon." I took Julia by the elbow. "It's time for my end of the bargain. Let's go see my room, and if all goes well my roommate Robby won't be there."

Julia wrinkled her forehead. "You're so mean."

When we arrived back on campus, I reached for the door to get out of the car. "Wait," Julia held onto my arm. "I've never told anyone that story about my dad before—not even my best friend Gloria. Promise you'll keep it to yourself?"

"Your story's safe with me, and I know I tried to make you laugh... but I can't imagine what you've been through. If I could change it for you I would."

"Thanks, that's sweet...now I want to meet your 'wild about girls' roommate," Julia grinned.

"Let's go," I said.

We were both quiet as we walked to my room. It gave me a few moments to think about the dream I had the night before – the eerie river, the irate giant, the whispery voice. I wondered if it meant anything, or if it was related to Arcis. The scenery did look a lot like the game. Maybe it was some sort of strange preparation. Unfortunately, I spaced out and Julia noticed.

Julia waved her hand in front of my face. "Hello?"

"Oh sorry, we're here." I took out my key to unlock the door, but Robby beat me to it.

He flew the door open wide and greeted us with his usual grin. "Hi, come on in. You must be Julia; so nice to meet you. You're much prettier than Bladen described you. He didn't do you any justice."

Julia laughed.

I whispered in her ear. "Told you so."

Julia's phone rang. "Hi Mom…yeah, I'm with him right now. I don't know…sure. I'll ask…okay…love you too…bye." Julia hung up her phone. "That was my mom. She would love to see you. She invited you to lunch tomorrow, if you'd like to come."

"Obviously he'd like to come," Robby answered for me.

I glared at Robby and punched his arm. "I'll answer for myself, loser."

"Hey bro," he yelped, clutching onto his arm, "stop showing off for the lady."

We all talked for a while. I was grateful that Robby acted surprisingly normal.

I noticed Julia yawn and figured she was either bored or tired. I turned toward her, "Are you ready to go?"

"Yeah, hey Robby it was nice meeting you. You're not as eccentric as Bladen described you."

"Thank you." Robby took a bow. "I know Bladen's a little hard on me, but I'm really a gentleman."

Julia giggled.

When Julia and I drove to her house, we remained silent, until we reached her driveway. I thanked her for showing me around. She told me to be back at her house the next day at 12:30 p.m. for lunch. My heart pounded inside my chest at the thought of seeing her again.

Back at my dorm, I gave my parents a call and described my first two days at school. I wished I could tell my father about Berard and my "real" game, but I couldn't. After I hung up, I decided to try to find Berard again. I trooped across the hall and knocked on his door. I pounded, but no one answered. Was he in there and just not answering?

I walked down the hall to ask the resident assistant if he could open the door for me. I told him I was worried because I hadn't seen Berard all day. He went back with me to Berard's room and pulled out his master key. He took his sweet time. I thought, dude let's go.

At last, he put in the key, turned it, and twisted the knob. It made a delayed clicking noise as he rotated it. The door creaked as it leisurely opened. The room was out-and-out black. I heard the R.A. fumble for the light switch. When he found it, after what seemed like forever, the light lit up the room. I was shocked. The room was entirely barren, like a desert. I couldn't move. Berard was gone, and everything he owned was gone with him.

ALMOST THERE

"Hello?"

"Hi, Dad?" My voice rang, semi-panicked.

"Bladen?" my dad asked, startled, "are you all right?"

"Yeah, I'm fine; I'm calling again because a minute ago I went into Berard's room, and he's gone. I mean *he's* gone. All his stuff is missing too. What do you think happened to him?" I didn't give my dad time to respond. "You know I spent the day with Julia today. She's amazing."

"Slow down, Bladen," my dad interrupted me. "Who's Berard?"

"That weird kid Mom was so nice to. You know...the one from across the hall."

"Why does it matter if he's gone? Bladen, are you all right?" my dad asked, concerned.

"Yeah, yeah, forget it."

"Um...okay. You said you saw Julia. How are Julia and Lisa?" he asked.

"Okay I guess. I didn't see Ms. Simms today, just Julia, but her mom invited me to lunch tomorrow."

"Make sure you tell them your mom and I said hello."

"Yeah sure."

"Say hello to Adonis for us also, okay?"

"You and Mom know Adonis?" I asked, surprised.

"Of course, he's been part of Lisa and Julia's lives for many years. You never met him when you were little, because he didn't go to our family gatherings. Oh, and let me know what happens with Julia; since…you said she was amazing."

My dad threw in that last part casually. I knew what he was getting at. "She's incredibly beautiful, Dad. I think she and I will become good friends."

I talked with my dad on the phone for a while longer and then hung up. Okay, so the idea of becoming a life player already made me paranoid, a little on edge. I needed to chill, but Berard, where the heck did he go?

Robby came back; we went out for a quick bite to eat and then hung out in our room for the night. We stayed up for hours, talked, and played video games. When I played Arcis, I wondered which players were real humans. I knew my character Thorn wasn't, but as I passed others I wondered…in amazement. It was so cool watching my screen, like reality TV.

Later as I was falling asleep, Robby whispered, "Bladen? You awake?"

"Yeah."

"You never told me about your day with Julia. She's real pretty and seems nice too."

"Yeah she's cool," I agreed.

"So ya gonna ask her out?" Robby asked.

I thought, if there were any girl I'd want to ask out, it would be her no doubt, though I answered, "Nah, we're just friends."

"Sweet…do you mind if I ask her out then?"

"Go for it," I replied, feeling a pang of jealousy. I knew I needed to keep my attention on becoming a life player, my studies, and I still needed to apply for a job.

"Cool," Robby breathed.

I fell asleep only to find myself repeating the identical dream I had the night before. Eerie visions of Roman Architecture crept inside my head. I fell into the cold river. This time I could breathe under water. In front of me a graceful Lorelei with long, blonde hair was swimming.

She smiled at me, motioned with her hands, and mouthed, "Come."

I awoke abruptly from my dream, just as I had the night before. My clothes felt damp. Crap, I thought, another rotten night's sleep. I rolled out of bed and changed into a new T-shirt and shorts.

The next morning my wake-you-up roomie let me sleep in. My eyes flickered open, I glanced at the clock—9:17 a.m.

"You're awake, awesome. Wanna go shoot some hoops?" Robby asked.

"In a while," I mumbled, and turned over in my bed.

When I got up, Robby and I had breakfast together—Raisin Bran— soon after someone knocked on our door. It was Jared.

"You look much better this morning," I said.

"Thanks, I guess," he responded like he didn't care. "You told me to come back another time, so here I am."

"Hey, bro," Robby interjected, and made hand motions in the air like he was throwing a ball in a basket. "We're gonna shoot some hoops; ya up for it?"

"Sure, sounds like fun," Jared replied.

We grabbed a couple of balls and went out to the courts. Since there were only three of us, we played a game of horse, until other guys asked if they could join us. We ended up with enough guys to play a real game.

Around 11:30 a.m. I announced, "I gotta go."

"Eeww Bladen has a lunch date," Robby teased. "Can I come?"

"It's not a date," I defended. "Julia's mom invited me over. You're the one who wants to ask her out, remember?"

All the other guys started whistling and made fun of both Robby and me. I ignored it and went to take a shower.

❖ ❧ ❖

When I arrived at Julia's door, she opened it out of breath. "Hi, c'mon in; my mom can't wait to see you."

My heart did this weird butterfly flip thing when I saw Julia again. I reminded myself I didn't have time for a girlfriend, not that she was into me anyway.

"Hello Bladen," Julia's mom gushed. "I'm so happy to see you. How are your parents?" Lisa's ash-blonde hair looked like her daughter's. She was the same height as Julia with eyes the same shade of blue. She wore a black blouse and tan slacks. She was pretty and in good shape for her age.

I talked with Ms. Simms for a while and told her about *my* family. I noticed that when I asked *her* questions, she never answered me directly. She always reverted the conversation back to me. I figured it was due to the account Julia gave me about their family the day before. Actually, Julia cast me a warning glare as if to say, *don't you dare bring up what I told you.*

The doorbell rang, chiming to the song of Beethoven's Fifth Symphony.

"Unusual doorbell," I said.

"I know," Julia said, embarrassed. "Adonis liked it so much, my mom bought it."

Julia opened the door and in walked her best friend Gloria. She looked like a goddess and must have been close to six feet tall. She had ebony skin and high cheekbones. Her jet-black hair cascaded around her shoulders in masses of impeccable braids with black and white beads weaved into them. Her cocoa eyes sparkled with silver eye shadow that decorated them. She wore a deep red sundress with spaghetti straps and easily could have been a runway model. If Robby was here, he would have freaked at her beauty.

"Gloria and I are leaving now," Julia called to her mom. "We'll be at the mall. I'll be back before dinner." To my disappointment, she waved and was out the door.

Julia's mom walked in, aggravated. "I can't believe she just left. I'm sorry Bladen I had no idea she had plans to go out with Gloria. I do have lunch ready. You'll stay won't you?"

Before I could answer, the doorbell chimed the great Beethoven once more. Lisa swung the door open, and lo and behold, Adonis strolled in. His looks were striking, with medium-length black hair and black eyes. His physically buff body was a little taller than mine, and he appeared much younger than I had anticipated. I was caught off guard by his strong British accent. Julia never said where he had come from geographically. He dressed in cool clothes, a tight white T-shirt and torn jeans.

"Adonis perfect timing—as usual," Lisa purred.

"Thank you, my dear," Adonis answered. He tenderly rubbed her arm and took a minute to gaze into her eyes. Then he glanced at me and looked me up and down. When our eyes met, he stared long and hard, as if to take the time to read me.

"This is Bladen, I've told you about him," Lisa explained.

"Yes, you have. It's nice to meet you." Adonis shook my hand with a firm grip. It hurt a little, so I gripped back just as hard.

"Nice to meet you as well," I answered in a cool tone.

Adonis chuckled, "You have a good grip."

"As do you,"

"We were just about to have lunch," Lisa told Adonis, "care to join us?"

"Love to," Adonis replied. "Let me help you get things ready." Adonis took one more glance at me—more like a glare before he turned and went into the kitchen.

"Did Julia give you a tour of the house yesterday, Bladen?" Lisa asked.

"Just the main floor."

"Come with me then; I'll show you the basement and loft if you'd like."

I nodded my head, and we descended the stairs into the basement. There were a few game tables, including a full-size pool table in the sizable space. Posters of various locations around the world decorated the walls. A baby grand piano sat in one corner near a bulging, tan couch that lined up against one of the walls. Interestingly, I noticed the room didn't have a TV, just an enormous bookshelf packed with books, and a sword on the wall caught my eye. I walked over toward it.

"Fascinating," I said.

"What?"

"This room," I started, "no TV, loads of books, a piano, and this sword—" I brushed my finger across the sword's sheath.

Adonis startled me. "Don't touch that!" I was unsure of how he had suddenly appeared next to us.

"Adonis!" Lisa exclaimed, and gave him a scolding look. "He's not hurting it. It's fine. Bladen, go ahead; take it down if you want."

The sword appeared similar to the one I had seen in the little shop on Church Street. I took it off the wall and noticed the engraved circular and diamond patterns that traversed down the metal in exactly the same way as the one from the shop. The fact that the Simms had the same sword made me curious. Carefully I placed the sword back on the wall.

"You have an awesome room down here," I said.

"Thanks," Lisa answered. "Would you like to see the loft now?"

"Sure." As I headed toward the stairs, Adonis peered at me, coldly. Lisa and I left and ascended the metal, spiral stairs up to the loft and into the first bedroom—Julia's. An old-fashioned canopy bed ornamented in an assortment of pink stood in the middle of the room against a wall. The walls and carpeting were a rose color as well, portraying the innocence I had observed about her. Scenic, Monet paintings hung from the walls. Her bathroom was decorated like her bedroom—a romantic look.

Then we walked into Lisa's bedroom, an impeccable room with tan walls and matching carpeting. Colorful abstract paintings hung from her walls that matched her businesslike personality. She also had an adjoining bathroom with parallel decorations that suited her style.

"Are you both ready for lunch?" Adonis called.

"We're coming," Lisa answered.

We descended the stairs into the kitchen.

"You made wonderful gourmet sandwiches, Lisa," Adonis said, "but look at the size of the boy. I didn't think that would be enough to feed him, so I ordered a couple of pizzas. You don't mind do you?"

"Um, I guess that's okay." Lisa pointed to the food. "I did make a lot of sandwiches, though; I can't imagine this wouldn't fill him up."

Lisa's comment seemed to go unnoticed by Adonis. He glared at me again and began to drill me with personal questions.

"So you fancy Julia do ya mate?"

I felt tense and ran my fingers through my hair. "Excuse me?"

"I mean do you *like* Julia?" Adonis reworded the question and made sure he annunciated each word slow and clear, like I had just learned the English language.

"I'm sorry," I answered, irritated. "I still don't understand your question. I mean, I spent the day with Julia yesterday, but that was the first time I've seen her in years."

"Do you drink a bit at the bar?" Adonis continued.

Lisa's mouth dropped open. She elbowed Adonis hard in the ribs.

"Ugh," he said, "what'd you do that for?"

"Leave him alone, Adonis."

Adonis stared at me cold and hard. "You better not mess with Julia or our family boy or you'll regret it."

Lisa came to my rescue, once more. "That's enough, Adonis. You bother Bladen again, and I'll ask you to leave."

After that, Adonis behaved–like a normal person. We shot the breeze for at least two hours. I lost track of time, until I heard the front door slam shut, signifying Julia's return.

She dashed into the kitchen like a whirlwind. "Oh pizza, my favorite food. Yum! Thank you to whoever ordered it."

"That would be him," I said, pointing to Adonis. "He's pretty nice once you get to know him."

"Thanks, mate. You're not so bad yourself." Adonis threw his head back and roared with laughter. Strange man.

Julia grabbed my arm hard and said, "C'mon, let's go for a bike ride down by the lake."

I gazed into her eyes. The intensity in them made me say, "Okay."

"Adonis, you don't mind if Bladen borrows your bike, do you?" Julia asked.

"No, go ahead," Lisa intervened. "It's in the garage."

"Thanks for answering for me, my lady," Adonis said. He stood and pretended to walk around drunk. "I think I've had a bit too much whiskeee to make any kind of right decision. You know what they saaay; don't drink and talk at the same time."

Lisa playfully squeezed his cheeks and laughed. "Stop."

I told Lisa and Adonis thank you and goodbye.

Julia and I found the bikes, strapped them to the bike rack on her car, and headed to the parking lot at my dorm. The ride into Burlington on bikes was a little far from her house.

When Julia stopped the car, she jumped out in a flash with her bike ready to go, before I even took mine out of the rack.

"I'll race you," she yelled, as she zoomed past me. "Last one downtown buys the other one an ice cream."

I had to admit she pedaled fast. I knew I could bike much faster, but I figured I'd let her win. Before long, we arrived at Church Street. She pulled up to the little bistro we ate at the day before.

"I won!" She proudly said in between breaths. I wasn't out of breath at all. Sorry to say, she noticed. "Wait a minute. You let me win didn't you?"

"You're fast," I answered, shrugging my shoulders. "I owe you an ice cream." She protested, but then she gave in.

When we walked into the restaurant, I noticed a sign proclaiming, 'Hiring'. We bought our ice creams, and Julia strolled outside. I told her to wait for me, while I asked for an application. I planned to take it with me to fill out and then drop it off later.

Back outside, I sat next to Julia on a bench and asked, "How's your ice cream?"

"Mmmm, pistachio…delicious. How's yours?"

"Good." I had ordered plain chocolate. "I have a question for you."

"What's your question?" Julia asked in between licks.

"Why did you leave with Gloria today, when your mom invited me for lunch?

Julia stopped for a moment. "I knew it would bug my mom. I'm sorry."

"Why did you want to bug your mom?"

"Because she's never around; I already told you that. It was stupid." She grinned. "Why are you asking? Did you miss me?"

I smiled wickedly back at her. "What if I did?"

She giggled and took the last bite of her ice cream, as she moved closer to me—close enough that I could smell her perfume—lilacs, maybe. I glanced down at the sidewalk. I have to say, I enjoyed the heat between us, and so did she.

Julia broke up the moment and had her helmet back on, her bike ready to go. "I'll race you to the lake." I threw the rest of my ice cream away and jumped on my bike, riding right behind her. We swerved around the people on the street, until we arrived at the bike path by the lake. I sped right next to her. Lake Champlain flew past us with the sun radiating on it, splattering crystal beams into the air. Julia's hair blew wildly in the wind. She glanced at me and smiled with her stunning grin. I watched her for too long. My bike hit a rock, and I almost lost it. She laughed.

When the path ended, we came to a small beach embedded with stones. It was isolated, other than a middle-aged couple that was playing with their young daughter. The little girl must have been about four. Her dad's hands were gripping her around her waist. He spun her high up in the air. The girl's head tilted back, and she squealed in delight.

Julia gazed at them wistfully. She looked as though she missed what she had never had. Other than the laughter of the little girl and the lapping of the lake water, it was quiet. My thoughts escaped back to Arcis. I literally ached inside, as I wondered what adventures awaited me there.

I broke out of my thoughts, when Julia waved her hand in front of my face. "Hey Bladen?"

"Yeah," I answered casually, embarrassed that she had caught me daydreaming again.

"Where do you go?" she asked in a soft voice, her eyebrows raised up, arms crossed.

"What do you mean?" I tried to evade her question. I picked up a stone and skipped it across the water. I watched as it sank beneath the surface.

Julia took a deep breath and said, "You've done that a couple of times. I know there's something on your mind. What is it?"

"It's nothing."

"Come on, Bladen. It's me. I told you my deepest, darkest secret yesterday...something I've never told anyone, not even Gloria. You can trust me too, you know."

"I do trust you...but, I don't want to talk about it right now," I answered. Julia looked hurt. "I promise, I'll tell you...just not today...okay?"

"That's fine, but promise me you'll tell me sometime soon."

"I just did, and besides I give you my Scout's honor," I said, with a salute.

"Stop doing that." Julia shook her head. "I'm serious."

I changed the subject and decided to ask Julia about Adonis. "Today...Adonis gave me the cold shoulder. He wasn't friendly at first...why?"

Julia laughed. "He's not overly *nice* to anyone. In fact, from what I could see he seemed to like you, and that's saying something, because he scares everyone else away. Gloria's really my only friend...my only true friend. My family keeps to themselves. When Adonis chases away my friends, he always tells me it's for the best." Julia paused for a moment. "I hope he doesn't scare you away."

"I don't scare that easily," I shrugged. "It's getting late. We should get back. Wanna race again?"

"You're on," Julia darted toward her bike.

"What does the winner get this time?" I asked.

"How about dinner?"

"Now *you're* on," I scrambled toward my bike. With ease, I biked faster than Julia, though I led her to believe she was almost as fast as me. When we neared her car, I sped past her and barely won.

"Nice race," she said, smirking, "though you seem to win or lose whenever you feel like it."

I smiled. "I guess that's because dinner is more tempting than ice cream. But please don't feel like you have to feed me. I want to fill out my job application and drop it off tonight, anyway."

"No, I owe you dinner," she said, firmly. "You bought me ice cream. And I believe fair is fair."

Julia and I sat silently again, as we drove back to her house. I glanced at her out of the corner of my eye, while she curled her golden locks around her finger. She looked relaxed.

When we arrived at her home and walked in the door, the smell of lasagna hit me. I was grateful for a good meal. We had pleasant dinner conversation, and I ate way too much. When it was time to go, I thanked Lisa and wished Julia good luck in class the next day.

I drove back to school only to sit in my car while I diligently filled out my application. A little later, I drove downtown. I made up my mind to find Berard. He had said if danger ever found me, he'd be there, so I thought up a brilliant plan to make him find me.

After I dropped off my application, I walked around town. I wanted to find any strange person on the street. Eventually, I found him—a really dirty old guy, destitute in tattered clothes. He held a brown paper bag wrapped around a bottle of something—alcohol for sure. The smell of his breath hit me from a distance.

"Hey," I called. "You…come here." I terrified the man.

"Leave me alone, boy," he hollered, and shook his brown paper bag at me.

"No, I'm not going to hurt you." I tried to coax him into coming closer to me. "Here take this knife and pretend like you're going to cut me with it."

"You're crazy; get out of here kid."

"Please, I need you to do this for me," I pleaded, and threw the knife toward him.

He picked up the knife, and, as he aimed it in my direction, he lunged toward me. I jumped to the side.

"Stop," I screamed. "I told you; I'm just messing around."

"I don't mess around kid. Get out of here, or I'll hurt you."

I twisted around and sprinted away, only to see Berard. He placed his arm straight out in front of me. When I hit into him, it felt like a brick wall against my chest, the air squeezed out of my lungs.

The homeless man stopped in awe, when he saw that Berard appeared out of nowhere. "You people get away from me," he shrieked, with fear.

Berard calmly walked up to the man and took hold of his arm. They vanished, leaving me on the sidewalk alone. Then he reappeared. "Shame on you. How dare you pick on a helpless man, terrifying him that way."

"And where've you been?" I demanded. "How dare *you* take off and not tell me where you're going. I found your room empty."

Berard stopped for an instant. "And why would I need to tell you where I escape to? Do I need to answer to you? Are you my caretaker?"

"Well...no...it's just that," I faltered.

"It's just that what?" he asked, as he strode toward me. "How does your chest feel after slamming into my fist? When will you get it? You can't win against me. Let's not go through this every time we meet. I'm not the enemy. I'm here to help you, and I suggest that you refrain from terrorizing innocent people like that homeless man."

"I was trying to find you. I'm sorry," I said. "Where did you take him? I didn't realize you could teleport other people around beside yourself."

"To a shelter where he could get a hot meal, and, yes, I can transport others besides myself. Come on; we need to talk." He motioned for me to follow him.

We walked a few blocks, taking in the cooler air before we entered a home—Berard's new place. It was kind of a dump, actually. He lived in a tiny, white house with peeled paint, black shutters, and a covered porch on the front. Another young guy, maybe a college student, sat in a rocking chair on the front porch. He had messy, blonde hair and wore an Aerosmith T-shirt and a pair of blue jeans. I watched him curiously, as we were introduced. I entered the house. Berard took me to their kitchen and offered me a glass of juice.

"No thanks," I said. "I want to know what's going on in my life."

We found a comfortable place to sit. I finally told Berard every detail of my dreams. He watched me as I spoke, attached to every word.

"What do you think? What do my dreams mean? Do you think it has to do with becoming a life player?"

Berard closed his eyes and rubbed his hands slowly together. Eventually, his eyes flickered, and he stared at me. "I think Vorago wants you scared, because you're going to be pulled into the game soon."

"I know Vorago is the king of all demons in Arcis. His objective is to get all life players to lose, but I don't get it; he didn't scare me."

"Do you know where you are in your dreams?"

"No," I answered, honestly. "Should I?"

"Yes…now that you're a life player everything about the game holds special meaning. The sick man who screamed out to you was looking for, Aesculapius, the god of healing. That tells me you were in the Tiber River, which is located in Italy and runs through Rome. You have to analyze everything you experience as a puzzle. Put the pieces together, and you'll know what you need to do when you're pulled into the game."

"Rome—where St. Peter's Basilica is located?" I interrupted. "Funny you should mention that, because when I first started playing the game, I thought the basilica looked like St. Peter's even though the app objective didn't describe it that way. I shouldn't have begun the game there. It's where the game is supposed to end, not begin. How could that have happened?"

"Maybe because the fighting in the game is rather intense right now," Berard answered. "Vorago may have tried harder to intimidate you. I'm sure he doesn't want you there. Don't worry, though. He tries to intimidate most new life players."

"Most of them?"

Berard looked thoughtful. "Hmm...those he feels will become especially powerful."

Not to sound arrogant, but I did play extremely well on my iPhone, so that news didn't surprise me.

"You should also know," Berard explained further, "in Arcis everything appears like somewhere on Earth. It's a mirage. Therefore, if it appears like you're in Rome, you're not, obviously because you're in the game. And the scenery around you can change at any time. It's Vorago's weapon to confuse you. He wants you to be curious about your surroundings to make you weak in the game. If you don't pay close attention, his army can attack you and cause immense harm on Earth, which you already know. I think it's interesting that he placed you in the Tiber River in your dream. It must mean you'll be one of the best players, but we'll have to wait and see."

"So what do I do now?"

"Go and resume life as usual. You're next step will happen just as destiny desires it."

STRAW AUTOMOTIVE

R̲ing ... Ring ... Ring ... My iPhone rang as I drove back to campus. I couldn't answer it until I parked at my dorm – too much annoying traffic. By then the ringing had stopped. I pressed a few buttons on my phone. Simms popped up on my caller I.D. My heart pumped. I need to stop having this reaction to her, I thought, as I dialed Julia back.

"Hello?" Julia answered.

"Hi, it's me," I said. "You called?"

"Yeah," I heard her begin to say. "I just wanted to tell you how much..."

Confusion followed, as the sound of deafening static filled my head like an angry radio. My body began to blow in and out like a balloon. Then I was sucked limbs first through a straw-like portal that appeared to come from my phone. My iPhone devoured me! Well...one of me. When that me arrived at the other end, my body popped out with great force.

"Ow!" I cried. When I played the game with Thorn, he never had pain. Geographically, I was standing at what Berard had thought was the Tiber River. But this time I wasn't alone...and it wasn't a dream. I was floating in a larger vessel with a number of men, each of us paddling our oars on either side.

A scary-looking man acted as captain in the front. "Thrust in your oar," he yelled, urgently. "Paddle hard as ya can. Don't stop!"

I shoved my paddle down, hard as I could—captain's orders. My paddle crushed against the rocks below and moved the vessel forward. The other men groaned in agony, as though they had been rowing for days. The waves beneath the boat trembled, and because of my dreams, I could predict what would happen next—the distorted giant would rise high above the water.

I wish I could've bet a load of money on that one, because, sure enough, he stormed up from below the surface of the water. He towered above us and cried in anguish, "I'm diseased and beg to be healed. Aesculapius, where are you?"

The enormous giant picked me up like a toothpick. He could have easily crushed me beneath his inflated, stubby fingers. And as he threw me effortlessly into the water, I knew I needed to take a deep breath.

As I fell beneath the waterway, my eyes rested on the lovely mythical, Lurlei. Once again, she beckoned to me with her long, elegant fingers. Her nails were doused with blood-red nail polish that matched her rose colored lips. Her long, blonde hair floated around her angelic face, cradling it. Her emerald, scaled tail curled up to the right of her. Her smile welcomed me.

Without warning, I was no longer swimming in the river. I stood on a bank and then began to walk on the dry land in front of me. It was a moonless evening, with eerie, flat clouds that hung in the sky like used-up cotton balls.

My clothes clung to me, wet and uncomfortable. I looked down and drew in a deep breath. I tried not to laugh. I still had my jeans on. That was cool, though, an ugly dark-red belt at least three-inches wide encircled the top of them. The green, long sleeve shirt I'd been wearing had altered into a silver color like household utensils. My shirt, along with my jeans, had transformed into an impenetrable fortress of armor. My head felt weighted. I reached up and felt a steel helmet that gripped securely to my temples and covered most of my face. A sword in its sheath hung from my right side.

"Hallo," said a squeaky voice with an English accent.

I couldn't see where the voice had come from. I searched around.

"Over here ya fool," the squeaky voice went on to say. "Look up."

I raised my head to the sky and saw a miniature, amethyst-colored bird, about the size of a humming bird, flapping his wings. "Uh, hi?" I answered. I wasn't used to talking with animals.

"You Earth people...so trying," he muttered. "You'd think by now I'd get used to it, but no...I still find it so aggravating."

"You talk...with an English accent?" I noted. "Interesting."

"Of course, mate. Are you all right, then? Didn't you know what to expect here in Arcis?"

"I'm in Arcis? Really?" So I was in the game. Sweet, I thought.

"Oh bother, they never train 'em right, the life players from Earth... so clueless. Of course, you're in Arcis. Would you have expected to be anywhere else?"

"Well your accent sounds English," I retorted. "Maybe my phone messed up and sent me to England instead. What's up with your accent?"

"I have always wished to imitate our Lord, obviously."

"Does Lord Spero speak with an English accent?" He didn't in my video game.

"Spero can speak with any accent, but Spero's not the Lord I speak of. Spero's more like the chief. Ya know...the head honcho. The Lord Adonis doesn't nearly hold the power of Spero."

"I'm confused. I thought Spero was the king, not a chief, and who's Adonis? I still don't get the whole accent, and why am I talking to a bird? I've seen mythical animals in my game, but they didn't talk."

The minuscule little thing pulled a short, gleaming, silver sword out of its sheath that dangled at his side. He began dueling with the air. "Okay, okay...it's like this...see. Spero is the king. You're right about that. Adonis is a lord—important, but he doesn't have power like Spero, and my accent I have acquired from my great admiration for the amazing Adonis. I tried a southern drawl, but it didn't work for me. Then I thought I'd talk like someone from Long Island, but I wasn't feelin' that either. To finish, I started talkin' like Adonis. That did it for me. It felt right, ya know. It got me in the battle mood. At any rate, you should know that many creatures in Arcis talk but not all of them. There ya go—all in a nutshell. Have I answered your questions?"

"Yeah you have. Thanks." I thought it was kind of weird that another Adonis lived here in Arcis, especially whose accent sounded the same. I wondered if the Adonis I met was a life player too. "I know someone on Earth named Adonis, you know."

"Lucky you," the little bird answered, dryly, "but this Adonis isn't a life player from Earth. He's from here and only here."

"What's your name?"

"Slaughter," the bird announced, as he strutted his feathered body around.

"Slaughter?" I laughed.

"Laugh all you want. I earned that name."

Right then, I heard an ear-splitting squawk that startled me. In the sky, what appeared to be a crow darted toward us at an alarming speed. It was a heck of a lot bigger than any ordinary crow, and its eyes blazed, as red blood dripped from them. When it opened its mouth and squawked again, huge black worms like snakes spilled out of it and poured like rain on my head.

"Ugh!" I hollered and brushed them off my body.

"Now I'll show you why I'm called Slaughter," he snickered.

The amethyst bird blew up at least fifty times larger and flattened the crow. Within seconds, the crow sounded out its last ghastly breaths and plummeted to the ground.

Slaughter winked. "Told you so," he said. "See ya 'round kid." I watched as he flew away.

Everything grew silent, which gave me a chance to check out my surroundings. Things appeared a little different than my actual video game.

Ancient buildings stood high back to back around me. I couldn't see anyone. It looked like a ghost town, which was strange. There was always someone around when I played on my phone. To my left, a sandy passageway cut through the buildings. Where the path wound around, entire pieces of the buildings appeared as though they had been sliced out. Literally, they were gone.

When I peered further in between the buildings, I saw that the path led to a massive, bubbling ocean of water and fire. The fire flickered on top like the burning flames of a candle. I thought I could make out a sandy beach lined along the ocean's shore.

On my right, another trail cut through the buildings. Along that route, three brilliant, blinding suns shone right next to each other. I covered my eyes with my hand but still couldn't gaze directly at them. They were too bright. Each one pulsated like a beating heart.

Straight ahead, I strolled along further and came upon a courtyard where a giant basilica with three beautifully constructed domes stood before me. St. Peter's Basilica, I thought to my surprise. Everything else had looked so strange. Did this mean I was in the final level of the game? I glanced around and noticed that the largest of the domes had been built in between two smaller ones. Majestic, enormous columns were erected at the front of the building. My heart began to pound inside my chest; fear gripped me.

"Psst," a voice whispered. "Come here." Someone grabbed me by the shoulder and pulled me into a shadowy corner.

"Get your hands off me," I spat, and tried my hardest to shove the person away.

"Are you nuts? You'll get beaten out there," the voice warned.

While my eyes adjusted to the darkness, I saw a bearded man in his thirties. He had thick, auburn hair and warm, brown eyes that smiled. He wore the same silly armor as me.

"Uh...nobody's out there," I answered, like he was crazy.

"Get down," he whispered urgently, and shoved me to the ground.

"Look dude, what's your problem? Man, you better be a life player." He slapped his hand over my mouth so hard that my lips drew blood as they cut against my teeth. "Ow!" I called out.

"Sorry," he whispered. "I'm a life player too, and you would be wise to do as I say. C'mon follow me."

I followed as we darted around buildings. I began to understand why he told me to shut my mouth. He saved my butt, actually. There were a few hundred freakish demons marching and chanting, "Kill...kill." I didn't know where they came from, though their hypnotic chant made me want to walk toward them and give them a big hug. Sick.

The bearded life player I was with gripped my face and pushed plugs in my ears, so I could no longer hear the beasts. I broke out of my strange trance and had to admit, the beasts were a bit scary—even for me. It was a whole lot different seeing them in front of me, rather than on my little phone.

The frightening beings, larger than most men, were standing lined up in rows. They had Medusa hair loaded with slithering snakes, blood red eyes, squashed lips, and noses too large for their faces. The hoods from their pitch-black cloaks fell down against their backs.

Their leader sat perched in the center among all of them. I was sure it was Vorago. He sat high up on the most intimidating black stallion I had ever seen. The stallion had black wings that extended at least six feet out on each side.

Vorago didn't look like a monster either. He emerged human but wicked and enraged. His lengthy, dark hair curled and whipped around his face, covering his night-black eyes. He yelled to the beasts. Captivated, they held still as he shrieked the next plan of attack. I felt sick, as I began to realize fighting here in real-life wasn't going to be as easy as fighting in my video game.

As Vorago spoke, one of the ill-fated demons rudely interrupted. Vorago clutched his sword, and swiped the beast, disembodying one of his fingers. The demon fell to his knees, buckled over in agony. Vorago roared with laughter.

The bearded man urged me on. We left the terrorizing scene and strode to a modest home made out of cement. The man told me to hurry and enter in.

Once inside with the door shut, he turned to me. He extended his hand to shake mine and welcomed me. "My name is Benedict. I'm not from Earth. I live here in Arcis. You'll be safe here."

"I'm Bladen," I said.

"Yes I know. I've been expecting you. I know you're new in Arcis. I'm sure your questions abound, but would you like a cold drink first?"

"How about a shot of something hard to quiet my nerves?"

Benedict smiled. "You have a good sense of humor, but you're too young for such a request."

"Am I?" I retorted.

"How about a soda, instead?"

I shook my head in disbelief. "That's cool. You can drink soda in the game?"

Benedict laughed. He strolled into a small kitchen and poured me a drink. Then he came back. "Here."

"Thank you," I said "Now maybe you can tell me. Why did I land at St. Peter's Basilica? I thought the game is supposed to end there. The same thing happened with my iPhone game."

Benedict nodded his head. "Apparently, Vorago thinks you have power. Only the most powerful life players land there first. If it happened in your game and now, it means you can't play the real game progressing in levels like you should be able to normally. You could be thrown into any level at any time. That's my guess, anyway."

"Your guess?!"

Benedict nodded.

That sucked. I had little to count on in the game. How was I supposed to know how to play?

Forgetting it for the moment, I couldn't help but check out his place. "Nice little house you got," I said. I saw one open room that probably contained everything he owned. The kitchen made it only a little larger than my dorm room. A single bed, covered with only a white sheet sat in one corner, a wooden couch and chair in the other. Bare cement plastered the walls, with only one window.

"Yes, it's all I need. Bladen...you should know that Arcis may have seemed like a game to you on Earth, but Arcis is a real world just like Earth. And right now, anyone who lives on Earth and is playing this game might have the ability to see you. Though, sometimes life players *do* look different in the game just like the scenery."

"You mean people are watching me...right now?"

"Possibly—if they're on this level of the game."

"That's freaky," I said, softly. Benedict had confirmed what I thought about the game. But what about Julia and the angry man that beckoned me into the game? The girl in my game had looked like Julia. "It's like watching reality TV shows on Earth, isn't it?"

"Yes, I suppose it is," Benedict answered.

I scratched my head. "Wait a second. If someone's playing the game right now on this level, can they control me?"

Benedict shook his head. "No, in the game, players can only control their avatar. If someone's playing the game on Earth, and they weren't chosen to be a life player in the real game, they have no control over real catastrophes either. Even though you're a real life player, if you're playing the game on Earth and not here and you lose a level, nothing happens to real Earth. Catastrophes only occur if you lose in the *real* game, here in Arcis."

I thought about my avatar, Thorn. "Does that mean some of the players I run into while I'm here aren't real. They're from the game?"

"Yes. The fictional players are more like robots. They don't speak. You'll know who the real players are, don't worry. You should also know that outside my home Vorago and his troops are allowed to attack, but you can't be harmed once you're inside. We're safe in here and in any life players' home in Arcis."

"Cool, sounds like the safety zone when playing tag," I joked.

Benedict stared at me with intensity. "Hmm," he said, and then asked, "Do you realize the dangers you face now that you've agreed to be a real life player?"

"Sort of," I answered. "Vorago's demons can attack me here in Arcis, but I can't be killed here because it's a game, right? And if I lose in battle, losing the game, Earth pays the price. That sucks, but I doubt I'll lose, so where's the danger?"

Benedict nodded. "You're right. You can't be killed *here*. Vorago's demons can harm you immeasurably, though…even *if* you win the game. And the more injured you become in Arcis, the more evil power that'll be spewed on Earth. It's of the utmost importance that you fight with immense strength here. Then *we* hold greater influence and power on Earth. You understand this don't you? Whether you win or lose, Earth is affected by the game."

I walked over to a table and set my drink down. "Yes, I understand that, but I don't get how the danger here relates to *my* life in particular. I mean, I have no worries about being killed. It doesn't faze me a bit."

"Now it's my turn to laugh," Benedict said. "Your life can easily cease to exist. Maybe not directly by Vorago and his troops, but by the death players."

"Death players? Who are they? There are no death players in my Arcis game, at least I've never seen any." Then it occurred to me that Berard didn't tell me everything. He only said that I'd meet beings to assist me.

"It's my understanding that you haven't owned the game for long. You have a lot to learn and must have not come across them yet. Death players exist like you. They live on Earth, but they follow Vorago not Spero, just like all the demons here. They adore him on Earth and offer sacrifices to him there. Death players don't play the video game, and they can't engage in battle here. Most of the time, they fight on Earth. Here you find them frequently in what looks like the Coliseum or any other arena. They sit in the stands and seek out life players in battle. If you gaze at them eye-to-eye, they have the ability to make a computer-like image of every thing about you, called tagging. If a life player becomes tagged, the death player will go back to Earth, send that image out to all other death players that exist, and then seek to assassinate that life player. Rarely, does a life player survive this. My advice, be extremely cautious never to look a death player in the eye while in Arcis."

"How will I know if someone's a death player?"

"They're the only ones who sit in the stands and watch the battles. They can't tag life players on Earth, but they'll kill any, if they're able to find out who they are."

"How can they find out?"

"Well, they can't see Spero's emblem behind your left ear like you can see theirs. Rather, they find out when life players meet at an Assembly."

"An emblem?—you're right I haven't heard about a lot of this. Death players have an emblem also?"

"Yes, also behind their left ear. Theirs depicts Vorago. It's a bloody emblem, literally. Sometimes real blood drips from it, even on Earth. Whereas, life players have the ability to see their emblem, death players can't see a life player's or even their own, for that matter."

"So, on Earth, if I think someone might be a death player, I can check their ear—for the emblem."

"Yes," Benedict answered.

"Okay I get it, so now what's an Assembly?"

"You'll need to talk to your patriarch about that one. Ask him when you get back to Earth."

Of course, Benedict wouldn't tell me everything. Berard had told me I couldn't learn too much at one time. I had to learn to be forbearing. I was stunned that Earth and Arcis were so connected, and I was beginning to understand, though, I still had a few questions. I looked at Benedict. "So tell me. Who made this game and who chooses the life and death players? They can't be the same person."

Benedict nodded. "Spero made the game. He chooses the life players. You already saw where his home is, near the three suns. Spero allows Vorago to choose the death players."

"Then why can't death players battle here just like life players?"

A melancholy expression emerged across Benedict's face. "Spero made both our worlds. Death players…are…sons and daughters of Spero…like you and me, but they've chosen Vorago over him, and Spero thirsts for their return. He wants them to know they're always welcome back home with him. He—Spero—is merciful and forgiving. This rejection causes him immense pain."

"Amazing…I didn't know that. I mean…most people don't know that." I began to feel the weight of this new quest I was chosen for, and I had to admit, I was scared.

Benedict nodded then left me alone with my thoughts for a while.

Later, the aroma of onions sautéing, waft by my nostrils. I found Benedict in the kitchen cooking a steak dinner.

"Mmmm, that smells good." I said.

"You are welcome to join me, if you're hungry."

"No thanks, I'm really not hungry. But it does smell good."

In case you don't already know, if your parallel body on Earth ate, then you wouldn't be hungry in Arcis. But please remember to eat a little something while you are here. You will need it to sustain your strength.

I had forgotten my body had sliced in two and had no idea what was going on back at school. "What am I doing on Earth right now?" I asked

"You don't know?" He was taken aback.

"No."

"Nothing at all?" Benedict continued.

"No, absolutely nothing. Should I know what I'm doing there?"

"Yeah," he remarked. "Try to imagine traveling back to Earth into one body, without being able to remember anything. The end result — complete confusion."

"What do I do about it?"

"You'll have to focus on both bodies while you're here, until you get it. Let's start now. Sit down, close your eyes, and concentrate on what you think you might be doing on Earth at this moment. What's happening back on Earth should be like a mini-television in your mind."

I squeezed my eyes shut and focused hard. "Sweet. I see Robby and the phone...I think Julia's calling...not sure...now I see her face. Man, this is confusing."

Benedict spent hours with me day after day for what seemed like forever as he trained me to use my somewhat broken mini-TV. It should've been cool, but it wasn't. It was frustrating. I lost track of time and couldn't understand the importance of it anyway. Benedict explained that Vorago could use my amnesia against me. Maybe even help him blast Earth somehow! I wasn't sure how a little amnesia would cause that, but eventually my TV skills improved. A visual picture of my life in Burlington came into focus, except it seemed more like bad TV reception.

Benedict taught me about all the weapons I could use in Arcis, too. I was happy to find out there were lots of them, just like when I played the iPhone version. I especially liked the knives, tomahawks, daggers, bow and arrows, slingshots, and catapults. They didn't allow guns in Arcis, just like in the game. I gathered blowing away the demons with guns would be too easy.

"I think you're ready to go out," Benedict informed me one morning.

"Go out where?" I asked.

"Outside my door," he answered.

"Out there?" I hesitated and pointed to the door.

Benedict laughed. "Yes, out there. When you leave, you won't know where destiny's grasp will take you. You'll be teleported and could land anywhere in Arcis, maybe at the basilica, maybe somewhere else. Make sure you stay alert and concentrate on home and Arcis. Okay? Oh and don't get killed."

Benedict's sarcasm failed to amuse me. "Funny, Benedict. Yeah. Real funny."

Benedict chuckled again.

I was kind of scared. I wasn't surprised I could teleport, but it bothered me that, like my avatar, Thorn, I had no idea *where* I'd be teleported. "What if I need to find my way back to your house, and I can't do it?"

"You won't be able to, but don't be afraid." Benedict reassured me. "Your body holds greater strength than you know. I'm sure of that." I shook Benedict's hand and stepped toward the door. When I opened it, I saw nothing but a gray blur, just before the straw sucked my body through it again.

Teleporting felt exactly like when my iPhone sucked me in. I landed on the sandy beach near the ocean of water and fire, the abyss. The blaze above the lapping waves was beautiful, yet precarious at the same time. Let's just say, I didn't exactly feel like going for a swim.

I bent over and picked up a shell with unusual lettering on the side. It vibrated in my hands. When I turned it over to examine it more, I heard a sound. I brought it to my ear and listened. "Die," it whispered. A slimy, green tongue whipped out and lashed my face.

"Sick," I yelled and threw it to the ground. I swear I heard the ocean laugh at me.

"Do you need help?" A voice asked.

I peered down the beach. Sitting high up in a lifeguard's chair sat a good-looking, young guy who looked about my age with a deep tan and shaggy, white-blonde hair.

Sprinting toward him, I yelled, "Hello." As I grew closer, he altered into one of the demons I had previously seen in the basilica. Honestly, Medusa hair seemed to be the fashion in Arcis. He smirked while a few snakes fell from his head and slithered toward me at an alarming speed. I grabbed my sword and hacked them in half. I listened to their violent squeals and watched as they dropped dead at my feet. I breathed a sigh of relief. My heart thumped in my chest. Blood pulsated to my head and throughout my body in an adrenaline rush.

When I sat down on the sand to catch my breath, the ground transformed into quicksand. I began to sink, until I saw a stick in front of me.

I looked up and saw my new friend Benedict. "Take a hold of the stick…hurry," he yelled.

I grabbed it with all my might. He heaved me out with great force. The quicksand disappeared and changed back into ordinary sand.

"Are you okay?" Benedict asked.

"Yeah, thanks for saving me. Who was the lifeguard? He called out to me in a way I thought I could trust, but then he turned into this…demon. Man, I swear he was…sick looking." I blinked my eyes and shook my head. I was pumped.

Benedict glanced around frantically, before he replied, "It may have been Vorago. He possesses the ability to shape-shift into anything he wishes. You have to be careful out here. The dark one can appear as anything or anyone he pleases. Now, I must be off…Godspeed." As quickly as Benedict appeared, he disappeared. Apparently he, too, could teleport and vanish into thin air, except he looked like he had control over it.

As soon as he left, a colossal-size octopus crawled out of the water. The twenty or so legs on it numbered more than any average octopus I had ever seen in pictures. Dark, gray grit coated its body. Massive, crimson eyes shone from its head. Ivory horns bulged from the top of it. I backed up, hesitating.

"Where you going pretty boy?" The thing jeered. "Don't ya wanna dance? My tentacles are dying to squeeze the breath out of you."

As I fumbled with my belt, it opened, revealing various gadgets and weapons. I found a poisonous dart wedged against the side. Scrambling, I placed the dart into the slingshot and pulled back before I let it go. I barely saw it. It flew at supersonic speed. Then it slammed into the octopus, forcing it to the ground. Its putrid eyes rolled back into its head.

Feeling panicked, I dashed up and drove my sword repeatedly into it. When I felt sure it wouldn't budge, a sense of immense relief like a blanket covered me. I dropped to the ground, overwhelmed and fatigued. The game was over. I must have won the level, so why hadn't my phone pulled me back into it yet?

STRIFE'S FROM THE HEART

My body lay saturated in sweat. One end of the tangled, white bed sheet wrapped around me and squeezed my waist. The other end dangled near the floor. I tossed and turned immersed in a muddled, sleep.

A veil of darkness as black as obsidian stone enveloped me. All my senses were heightened. Echoes resounded in my ears, as a shadow leisurely edged toward me. Its legs scuttled against the granular ground beneath us. The pungent smell of perfume filled my nose. It held the scent of springtime lilies. My mouth watered with a burning desire. My blood pulsated, until...

The shroud obstructing my view was drawn back. Flashes of mirror images bounced off the glass cage surrounding us—the reflections revealed two, black spiders with blurry red spots. Black widows? Was I one of them?

The one reflection showed a female that moved toward me to devour me as the main entrée, no doubt. At my feet, a double-bladed knife called to me. I curled my leg around it; beads of sweat dripped from my forehead. And as the other spider drew nearer, I stabbed her.

Then I watched in revulsion, as she melted into human form and cried out my name, "Bladen, save me."

"Bladen, wake up...you're going to be late for class." Robby griped and shook my shoulder. "Wake up! Wake up!"

"Wh...what?" I asked, wholly out of it.

Robby continued to shake me. I was disoriented when I closed my eyes and thought I saw Benedict's cement house.

"That's it, Bladen. I'm leaving. If you're late for class again, it's your own fault, man. This is ridiculous."

When I heard that, I woke up fast, feeling startled from my sleep. I was panicked. "What do you mean late, again? What day of the week is it?" I couldn't remember when I was sucked back through my phone—no recollection at all.

"Dude, it's Friday. No, maybe it's Tuesday. If you're that out of it, figure it out yourself," Robby grumbled. I'm sick of it. You've been such a jerk lately."

It was too late for me to ask him the date. He had left the room. I jumped out of bed, no time to dwell on my bizarre dream. I grabbed my clock. *Shoot*, 8:30 a.m. I threw on my clothes, grabbed my schedule, and raced out the door.

I asked the first person I saw, "Dude, what day of the week, is this? But he gave me that Dude-you're-partying-too-hard look and just laughed at me.

I figured no one else would tell me, so I ran to my car and sped to the nearest convenience store to buy a newspaper. It was Wednesday—the second week of class. Wednesday? How could that be? Hadn't I been in Arcis for more than two weeks?

The time in Arcis raged by like a blur. Benedict had helped me stay in tune with my parallel body, yet I felt so confused.

I looked at my schedule...Chemistry. I had already thrown the books I needed into my car, and class started at 9:00 a.m. I wouldn't be late. I drove and parked my car close to the chemistry building. I found my room. I took a deep breath and entered.

I decided to be inconspicuous and take a seat in the back. As I flipped through my notebook, I realized I had taken notes from Monday last week, all the way up until yesterday...weird. I had no memory of doing that. I had chemistry class on Mondays, Wednesdays, and then a lab on Fridays, but I had no memory of being in class at all.

The classroom filled up, but the professor hadn't arrived yet. I looked at the guy next to me and recognized him from the cool trinket shop in town, where they had sold the unusual swords.

"How ya doing?" I asked. "I recognize you from the store on Church Street."

He stared at me like I was crazy, but then nodded his head before he turned away.

I continued to talk to him. "You're name's Anthony, right? How long have you worked at that cool store?"

He whipped his head toward me and retorted in anger, "This is like déjà vu. We had this same conversation last week and on Monday this week, you freak. Why are you doing it again? I told you before, I don't like talking to people. Not only that, we were given assigned seats, remember? You're supposed to be sitting in front of me, not next to me."

"Sorry," I mumbled. I picked up my books and sat in front of him. Sure enough, another student walked by and took the seat I had been in.

My memory sucked. I felt like a complete moron, and knew I needed to work on my life player skills. Now I understood why Benedict had warned me about the importance of my mini-TV. I had already made two people angry with me—Robby and this not so new guy, Anthony.

I finished my morning classes and drove back to my dorm. When I got there, I sank deep into a chair, with one arm slung across my eyes.

I thought of Arcis and its evil demons. I couldn't wait to play more of the game, so I could slay them—drive my sword deep into them.

Being in two places at one time made me feel like half my soul exited my body. In the morning when I woke up in one body, I felt whole again. Unfortunately, I had no control over when I'd play Arcis again. I took out my iPhone and turned on the game. I watched as two players mutilated a demon with horns. Its large pig-like body lay shaking on the floor. One of the players looked toward me and gave me the thumbs up. I pulled back, surprised. Could he see me?

"Bladen, what are you doing? You're supposed to be working at your new job, remember?" Robby asked, as he entered our room.

"My new job…of course," I said, as though I knew what I was talking about.

Robby was unconvinced. "At The Bistro, on Church Street—right?" he asked. I stared at him, my face blank. "You're schedule's right next to you on the desk."

I sat up and picked up the schedule and read the 'Congratulations on your new job' notice, with my hours right under it. I was scheduled to work Wednesday at 2:00 p.m. until closing.

I grabbed the stuff I thought I'd need at work, told Robby thanks for keeping me straight with my agendas, and ran out the door. I hoped it was my first day on the job. The thought occurred to me that I could screw up, if I'd worked there already but couldn't remember.

When I arrived at work, I put on my uniform—a red T-shirt that read THE BISTRO in white, bold letters. Another guy was assigned to train me. It was my first day after all. I breathed a sigh of relief. I had been hired as a waiter—a breeze after I had worked as a waiter back home.

Several hours later, close to 9:00 p.m., I saw Julia saunter in with Gloria. They sat at a table I was assigned to.

I walked up to them, wondering if my loss of memory had made me mess up with Julia, too. "Hi girls," I said. "Can I get you something to drink, while you look at the menu?"

"Hi, Bladen?" Julia asked, unsure of herself.

"We'll have a couple of diet colas, thanks," Gloria said.

"Sure," I answered and walked away to put in their drink order.

"I'll be right back," I heard Julia tell Gloria. Then she strutted up to me and tapped me hard on the shoulder. "Are you acting like you don't know me, again?"

"Again?" I answered, puzzled. Great here it comes, I thought.

"Uh, yeah, like you have been for the last week," she said, hurt and irritated.

"I'm sorry, Julia. I don't know what you're talking about," I said, like I really felt bad, because I did. Okay…so I messed up big time with the cute girl I liked. Now, I understood why Benedict had warned me about the importance of my mini-TV. Vorago could mess with my life, weakening me as a player.

"I see, so, it's going to be like that," Julia said.

"Like what?" I whispered, leaning toward her. "The last few days have been busy, Julia. I sincerely don't know what you're talking about. Look, why don't you come sailing with me this weekend."

My boss, Alfredo, shouted at me. "New boy, no flirting with the customers!" Alfredo—that's a pretty funny name for a guy who owns a restaurant. And he's getting on me for flirting? I'm not even flirting! He's this Spanish-speaking Costa Rican who thinks he's so smooth. He's the flirt who definitely loves women, not just likes them … *loves* them, though he hasn't had the best luck in the past. He's been married quite a few times. Not that all men from Costa Rica have a bad rap like him, but to see this fifty-something guy with a big potbelly, who likes to eat and drink way too much, make advances toward practically every woman that walks through the door, is rather sickening. And yet, he moans and groans that none of his ex-wives appreciated him. Ugh! Whatever! "Get to work!" Alfredo continued. "It's always like that here. You new boys think this job's a way to pick up girls. Let's go, before you lose the new job. Okay?"

"She's a friend boss," I defended.

"Whatever kid, just get to work."

"Call me…before Saturday, okay?" Julia smiled.

"I will," I said "Now I better get back to work, so I don't get fired and lose the *new* job."

Julia went back to her seat, and the rest of my shift was smooth, no mess-ups. Tonight, The Bistro closed at 11:00 p.m. By the time I finished cleaning up, it was midnight.

I was walking in the dark to my car, parked a block away, wishing I had brought a flashlight when someone grabbed my shoulder. Startled, I twisted around and pulled the person by the shirt collar.

"Hold onto your pants! It's just me," Berard chuckled.

I let go of him. "You know I'm glad to see you." That idea shocked me. "I played the real Arcis game, and there are some things I'm not sure about."

"I'll ride in the car with you. You'll have time to ask me a few questions then."

In the car, I remembered how Berard had told me he would show up if I was ever in trouble. The thought prompted me to ask, "Why did you find me, tonight?"

"You weren't safe walking lad. There were a couple of dudes waiting to attack you for money."

"Lad…Dudes?" I rolled my eyes, which I hated because I thought it was a girly thing to do. That was Berard, though, talking freaky again, like some Irish dude.

Berard shrugged. "I'm trying to talk normal."

"Keep tryin'" I said, nodding my head nice and slow. "I could've taken them on, you know, but how did you end up getting rid of them, anyway?"

"I appeared out of nowhere and gave them my best scary face." Berard scrunched up his face real tight.

"Eww, you're best scary face. Does it look like that?" I asked, imitating his expression.

"No…you don't want to see it. It looks like something out of a horror movie. I'm serious. You won't be able to sleep, boy."

We had already pulled up to the parking lot at my dorm by the time we finished our conversation. "I'm too tired to talk more now. Do you mind if we talk about it tomorrow?" I asked, rubbing my sleepy eyes. My body felt disoriented, like the adjustment that's needed when traveling to another time zone. I was dying to talk to Berard, but I could hardly keep my eyes open.

"When can we meet tomorrow?"

"I have classes. Then I'm working the same schedule at The Bistro."

"And when do your studies take precedence?" Berard asked.

"Take what?" I asked, confused.

"Take priority." Berard chuckled.

"Whenever I can fit it in," I answered, annoyed.

"No," Berard said, firmly. "Change your work schedule and ask for less hours. You won't get a handle on Arcis if you're too busy, and your studies will take a toll."

"Okay. I'll talk to my boss tomorrow. Right now, I gotta sleep." I shook my head to stay awake.

"I'll see you tomorrow," Berard said, and vanished.

The next morning, Robby didn't wake me up. I set my alarm. When it went off, I took a quick shower, got dressed, and ate a bowl of cereal—Frosted Flakes, this time. Robby danced around, as he celebrated his second date since he arrived on campus. He told me he felt like a kid at a candy store. Later, I headed to my biology class.

When I got there, the class was almost full with only a few seats empty in the back. I sat in one of them. The professor hurried in a little late. She put her books and papers down, and went swiftly to the front of the class. She was a heavyset, fifty-something woman with gray hair pulled back into a tight bun. She wore a goofy-looking, jean dress with a white, scoop-necked shirt underneath. Her pale, blue eyes sparkled with a drop of insanity. Yeah. She looked crazy.

But then a beautiful girl almost floated into the class. She had ebony hair, with just the right amount of curl, that flowed down to the middle of her back. Her jade eyes sparkled with mischief, and she was rather tall. Her red t-shirt and cream-colored miniskirt showed off her slim figure. Every head in the class turned and gawked in her direction. There weren't many seats left to sit in, so she came and sat next to me. I didn't realize it, but I was holding my breath. When she sat down, I let it out a little too loud. Crap, I bet she heard me, I thought.

She flipped her hair back away from her face and whispered, "Hi, I'm Angelina."

"Uh…uh…hi," I stammered. I was comfortable with Julia, but Angelina made me squirm in my seat.

"What's your name?" She asked, softly.

"Bladen," I blurted out. Yeah. I felt stupid.

She smiled, but never said anything after that.

I had the same crazy work schedule for the rest of the week through Saturday. My boss told me I could work fewer hours the next week.

I wanted to meet with Berard, but he told me he was too busy. Doing what, I had no idea. I figured he was being a jerk, teaching me patience again.

All my classes during the week were pretty cool. On Monday and Wednesday, I took pre-calculus after chemistry, and on Tuesday and Thursday, I had introduction to psychology after my biology class, with my science labs on Friday. On Saturday morning, I studied the material I missed during the week. Then, I cruised off to work at 2:00 p.m. again. The restaurant was crazy busy just like it had been the night before.

I was working my tail end off waiting tables, when I caught sight of Berard as he relaxed at the bar, drinking a soda. He appeared from out of nowhere. Julia walked in with Gloria. I couldn't believe I'd forgotten to call her. I wasn't assigned to wait on her table, so I didn't get a chance to talk to her. Our eyes met, though, and she looked super angry.

Ignoring the problem with Julia for the moment, I walked up to Berard. "Am I in danger?" I asked, wondering why he was hanging around again.

"No, but we still need to talk. I'll be here later tonight when you get off work. Don't make any other plans, okay," he ordered, as he nodded his head toward Julia.

How does he know about Julia? I thought. Honestly, he could really get on my nerves. "No problem, I'll see you later," I said, and rushed off to wait on another table. I had no time to argue with him.

I was so busy I never said hi to Julia or got the chance to explain why I hadn't called. I waved, but she didn't wave back. I picked up a napkin and scratched a message on it with my pen. "Sorry, I didn't call. I've been here every night. I'm off tomorrow. Sailing then? Call you in the morning." I handed my note to their waitress and asked her to give it to Julia, who took it, read it, but still wouldn't look at me. She and Gloria left after their meal without saying goodbye.

Later that night, Berard came just as he had promised. "It's time to talk about Arcis," Berard said. I know you'll be pulled into the game soon, and you need some assistance before you go. Let's stroll to my place and chill there for a while."

I knew he was trying to act cool again. I didn't say anything this time.

When we went to his house, it was empty. "Where's your roommate," I asked.

"He's never here. That's why I picked him as a roommate. It's like having my own place."

"Oh...that's cool. I'm glad you're happy with that," I said.

"No small talk, Bladen. You had a hard time keeping track of Arcis and Earth simultaneously while you were in the game. You have to know what's going on in both worlds. We need to work on that."

"How did you know?" I asked, surprised. "And how did you know your roommate wouldn't be around much?"

Berard hummed the theme song to the old show "The Twilight Zone." It was a far out sci-fi my grandparents had watched when they were young.

"Cut it out," I said.

"Never mind me...sit down."

I sat on the couch in the living room and leaned back, placing my feet comfortably on the ottoman in front of me. "How are you going to help me? I'm not in Arcis playing the game right now. I'm here. Besides, I trained for this already when I was in Arcis. I don't understand why I came back so confused."

"Close your eyes," Berard said. I peeked at him and didn't close them right away. "Now!" he shouted.

"Okay, okay," I said. Geez. He can be so demanding, I thought. I grit my teeth and closed my eyes, mostly. I did still peek a little. I watched as his body began to tremble. His face turned a deep shade of purple, almost plum, as he stepped toward me. Man, he creeped me out. Then when he placed both his hands on my head, I felt immense heat like fire come from them. The pressure forced my eyes closed. My body began to shake like my brother's Ford truck when it broke down the previous summer. And that's all I could remember until the next morning.

The phone and the sound of Berard's voice woke me up. "Yes he's here, Robby, don't worry. He was tired and crashed…that's okay…I'll tell him…bye." I heard Berard hang up the phone.

Panicked, I jumped off the couch and went into the kitchen. It was 9:00 a.m. "Berard, how could you let me sleep so long?"

"I didn't think you'd want me to get you up." Berard was standing by the refrigerator. He turned to look at me.

"What did you do to me last night—the heat thing?" I asked, sitting down in a chair at the table.

"I bestowed a gift upon you. Now when you play the game, you'll have knowledge of what's happening in both worlds."

"How is that possible?"

"You had a problem focusing on your life on Earth when you were in Arcis, but now the mini TV in your mind will work. You'll be able to see what's going on with your earthly self while you're in Arcis. I mean…it won't be to perfection. You'll have to work on it a little, but for the most part, you're all set."

"No," I explained, "what I mean is…h…how could you do that for me? Benedict, a man I met in Arcis, couldn't help me in that way, and he spent *days* training me."

"Benedict? He's a great friend of mine—powerful player. I'm glad you met him. He'll be most helpful to you in Arcis. Make sure you always listen to him. However, he couldn't give you the gift to see both worlds, because we can only pass on the gifts Spero bestows on us. Anyway, don't worry about it. Your roommate called. He was concerned about you. How did he get my number?"

"I gave it to him. Is that all right?"

"Sure," Berard said. "Just make sure he doesn't know anything about me, or about the game. These are secrets. You understand this... right?"

"Yeah, are you kidding. I wouldn't tell anyone. They'd think I was crazy." I stood up and walked to the living room, grabbed my shoes, and went back into the kitchen.

"Are you hungry for breakfast, or are you in a hurry?" Berard asked, while frying some eggs on the stove.

"Dude, I'm starved, but I told my friend Julia I'd call her last week, then I forgot. I told her I'd call her this morning."

"Why can't you call her and have breakfast?" Berard asked, confused.

"Oh yeah. I'll do that." I couldn't believe I didn't think of it myself. "Sometimes I forget I have my cell phone on me." I didn't actually forget I had my phone, I just forgot that I could use it as a phone, not a game.

Berard shook his head and smiled. "I'd even let you use my phone if you asked."

"Yeah. Right. Thanks." I felt nervous about calling Julia. Maybe that's why my brain felt scrambled like the eggs.

"You want some toast too?" Berard asked.

"Sure," I answered, absentmindedly. Thinking about Julia and the game got my mind going. "Hey, Berard, there's something I forgot to ask you. When I first played Arcis on my phone...the creature I fought...its head did this...like weird thing...and then...it completely transformed into a blonde girl...it looked just like Julia, but she doesn't even like video games." I used my hands near my head to show Berard how the creature had changed. "Can you explain what happened to its head and why it looked like her?"

"Julia?" Berard asked, surprised. "Where was your avatar fighting?"

"The basilica," I said.

Berard took a deep breath and turned away from me. His head dropped down. I edged around to the front of him and watched him with his eyes closed, deep in thought. I tapped him on the arm.

"Sorry," he said, startled and turned off the stove. "When a creature transforms its head, it's called clone-imaging. Vorago's demons normally alter into someone you care about. It's a feature of both the iPhone game and the real-life game. In the video game, you shouldn't know who the person is, though, only in the real game. That way it's harder for you to fight them. You wouldn't want to demolish someone innocent, especially someone you care for...see? Why Julia? Did you know her before you came here?"

"Yeah, when we were kids. And Benedict already told me we can watch the real game, but that doesn't explain why I wouldn't recognize a real-life player? I mean, let's just say that Julia is a life player. Why wouldn't I be able to watch her on the screen? What's the big deal?"

"You could watch her on the screen, but you wouldn't know it was her, because players' looks are supposed to be altered to those viewing the game. It gives the life player privacy."

"Are you sure about that?"

Berard took a drink from his glass. "Pretty sure."

I ran my fingers through my hair, disbelieving. "You're not totally sure? You gotta be kidding me. Let me ask you this. I saw an angry man in my game wearing black clothing. He seemed to be glaring at me like he could really see me. Is that possible?"

Berard's jaw dropped. "What? Where was your player fighting?"

"Again, in the courtyard—near the basilica."

"Was that before or after the clone-imaging?" Berard's eyes looked like they were going to pop out.

"After." For some insane reason, I was enjoying the fact that I seemed to shock the heck out of him.

Berard shook his head. "That shouldn't have happened, unless...do you care a lot for this girl Julia?"

"That's kind of personal," I retorted.

"With that answer, I would say yes, though, your avatar was still at the basilica. That's where we think the great pearl filled with power and peace is guarded just like in the video game…you and Julia…either there's a very special connection between the two of you, or it was a fluke. That's very unusual. I've never heard of anything like this before…and the man…I didn't think anyone in the game could see us, but I don't know. Vorago's power can alter the game, allowing for new rules. Let's get back to Julia, though. I did sense something between both of you. It was tumultuous. You're relationship is heated so soon? Is it not?"

"I guess being nosy and knowing what's going on in my life without me wanting you to is another gift of yours. Is it not?" I mocked him dryly. "And I thought you and I were getting along so well."

Berard chuckled. "Don't be angry. I'm here for your own good. Don't forget that. You're patience seems to have improved a bit over the past couple of weeks. You're a quick learner. I'll try to find out more information about your questions for you…now call Julia and have some breakfast. That's an order."

I called Julia, but no one answered. The ringing felt like a repetitive echo in the mountains. She probably didn't want to pick up the phone. She probably had caller I.D. and didn't want to talk to me after the way I acted this week.

I gave up and ate breakfast with Berard. He made a mean omelet, literally. The eggs looked like they had eyes glaring back at me.

When I was back in my car, I thought about Julia, again. My stomach kinked up like a bundle of nerves that made me wish I hadn't eaten quite so many eggs. Thinking she was upset with me made me anxious during the short car ride. I tried to convince myself that I didn't like her that much, but as soon as I pulled into the parking lot at school, I called her again. My car clock showed 11:00 a.m.

"Hi," Julia answered, with a frosty voice.

"I'm sorry," I began.

"Don't worry about it," she interrupted, sounding gentle. "I know you had a busy week…forget it."

"I tried to call you earlier this morning," I explained.

"Yeah, I know. I checked my phone. I was taking a shower. Sorry I didn't call you back."

"Why didn't you?"

"I wasn't sure if you still wanted to go sailing, or whether or not I felt like going…myself." Julia sounded careful, choosing her words.

When she said that, I knew I had offended her this week. I tried to coax her into going. "Look, I'm sailing today. I'd like it if you went, too."

There was silence on the other end of the phone until she gave in. "Sure…why not…it sounds like fun. What time to do you want to go?"

"How about I pick you up in a little while?"

"Sounds great," she said, and hung up before I said goodbye.

I sprinted up to my room to change clothes and brush my teeth.

When I walked into the room, Robby greeted me. "It lives." He dramatically fell to the floor, raising his hands and arms and feet up into the air.

"Funny," I replied, shaking my head.

"Seriously," he began. "Tell me you're gonna be around a little more, bro. I've barely hung out with you in the last couple of weeks. I like you when you don't act like an idiot. With you gone, it's been just me and Jared. You know the more we guys hang out, the more babes we attract."

"I will," I laughed. "Right now. I'm going sailing with Julia, though."

"Oh sure, the lady always wins. I should've guessed. If it were me, I'd be hanging out with you…not the girl."

"Yeah right, wild-about-girls Robby would always pick the girl first."

"I don't know if I like that title," he said. "You should call me, girls-are-wild-about Robby. Yeah. I like that much better." He told me he had a third date planned already. Lucky guy.

When I was ready, I ran out the door. I revved my car engine and drove a little too fast to Julia's.

"Hey, c'mon in. I just need to grab my bag," Julia told me, opening the door before I had a chance to ring the doorbell.

"You didn't let me ring the great Fifth Symphony?" I asked, pretending to be shocked. "Either you couldn't wait for me to come, or you didn't want to listen to your ingenious doorbell."

"I'd rather listen to the doorbell than you," she replied, with a coy smile, showing off her dazzling white teeth.

"Ouch, that hurt," I teased again.

Julia threw her bag over her shoulder. "After ignoring me this week, are you trying to flirt with me?"

"I'd rather not have you mad at me," I said.

"I'm not mad at you…anymore," she smiled. We stepped outside. Julia turned to lock the door to their house and set the alarm. "I'm excited to go sailing. I've never been before."

"You'll love it. It's really cool. It's not too windy today either, so the waves should be calm, always a good thing when you sail the first time. If you like it today, I'll take you out on a windy day, when the sailboat tips on its side, and you feel like you can barely stop yourself from falling in the water. Now that's fun."

"Sounds like it."

As Julia and I walked to the car, I sprang ahead of her and opened the door.

"Oh, now I *know* you were rude this week. Are you sucking up?"

"No," I laughed. "I'm trying to be a gentleman for a lovely lady."

She rolled her eyes and smirked.

When we arrived at the lake, I signed in for the catamaran. When we walked outside, I saw a small group of guys getting ready to ride on a motorboat. A couple of them checked out Julia when we passed by. I glared at them to intimidate them, but they didn't seem to care. Julia didn't even notice.

"Did you see that?"

"See what?" she answered, with innocent eyes.

"Those guys." I nodded my head in their direction.

She glanced toward them and shook her head.

"Never mind," I said, feeling annoyed by my jealousy.

At the catamaran, Julia unzipped her shorts and began to take them off. She was wearing underwear.

"What are you doing?" I asked, in horror.

"I'm taking off my clothes, so I can put my bathing suit cover on," she answered, with more blameless confusion on her face.

"That's your swimsuit? It looks like your underwear," I retorted, without thinking.

The group of guys we had just passed began to whistle.

I grabbed my towel and covered Julia's body.

"What are you doing?" She asked, disgusted and pushed me away.

OVER AND OVER, JOKES ON ME

heard the other boys laughing at us while Julia continued to take off her shirt. I died of embarrassment, when I saw she was only wearing a white tankini. She slipped on a pink, dress-like swimsuit cover over it.

"Is this okay?" Julia scorned. "Do you approve of what I'm wearing?"

"Uh—u—" I stuttered. "If you had taken your shirt off first, I would've known that you had on a swimsuit."

She laughed at my discomfort. "Are you trying to act like you're my father? What's your problem?"

I felt bad. "Um…let's forget about it. Okay?" I threw my bag onto the catamaran and unlocked it from the dock. "Come on up." I extended my hand to Julia.

So things weren't going so hot in the Julia department. I proved to be a total mess-up again and began to wonder how much more she would take.

Out on the water, the catamaran sailed like clouds in the sky. It felt weightless on this Indian summer day. The blazing sun beat on our bodies and faces. I gripped the rudder with my left hand and slipped my shirt off with my right.

"What are you doing?" Julia asked.

"I'm taking my shirt off because it's hot?" I said, in a questioning tone.

"Here," She threw a towel at me. "You should cover up with this."

89

"No thanks," I said, and threw the towel back on the deck.

"You don't get it do you?"

"Get what?" I asked.

"You covered me up with a towel," she said, disgusted, "when I had a perfectly modest swimsuit on, yet you think nothing of hanging out in front of me with your shirt off."

"I'm a guy," I shrugged my shoulders.

She let out a frustrated shriek.

At that exact moment, I felt my body being sucked in and knew what was about to happen—Arcis, here I come, I thought. When half my body popped out at the other end of the straw, I found myself on the beach by the ocean of water and fire. Down the shore in the familiar lifeguard chair sat another lifeguard, but he looked older this time with fairer features.

"Do you need help?" he yelled.

My body went forward involuntarily, as I listened to myself yell back, "Hello?"

It was like reliving a bad nightmare. The lifeguard rushed toward me. Snakes dropped from his head like mini-bombs. When they hit the ground, the sand flew up like puffs of smoke around them, making it hard to see. I grabbed my dagger and sliced them into bits and pieces. Brown and red, blood-like crap oozed out of them.

I glanced at the water. Sure enough, the giant octopus came out skating en route for me.

"You wanna dance?" I yelled out, before it had a chance to say the words.

The octopus swore under its breath. Once more, I pulled out my poisonous darts and fired them at the hideous creature. It dropped to the ground. I thrust my sword through it several times until it no longer moved.

I fell to the ground panting. A voice yelled, "Do you need help?" I stared down the beach and saw the same lifeguard. This time he appeared younger and had darker features. I blinked my eyes and shook my head in disbelief. I felt my body, yet again, be thrust forward. I listened to my voice scream a hysterical, "Hello!"

I tried with all my might to pull away and run in the opposite direction, but I couldn't. Fate dictated to me that I had to quarrel with the slimy snakes and over-sized octopus once more. At least I wished it had only been once more. I fought them over and over again.

As I was losing the level in Arcis, some of my attention went to what was happening at the same time with Julia back on Earth. My mini TV worked fine, thanks to Berard. I was amazed at how much slower the time on Earth crept by in comparison to Arcis. Julia had raked me over the coals for being a chauvinistic hypocrite. She actually used the word pig instead, if you can believe that. She was ripped I didn't apologize for thinking she would disrobe in a public place in her underwear in the first place. Girls! I should've been more upset about what she had said, but I was blown away by how much more time passed in Arcis than on Earth. I'd fought for what seemed like an hour in Arcis, yet on Earth Julia had only said a few sentences. Besides, I was panicked by my continuous struggle with the octopus. I watched my earthly self from my mini TV in Arcis and opened my mouth to defend myself against Julia's wrath.

"Hello," I heard a beatific voice utter back in Arcis. I looked up and saw a lovely woman with coffee-brown, curly hair in her early thirties. The flowing, white gown she wore extended down to her ankles. A serene expression shone on her face. Her ruby lips curved slightly upward on each side, revealing a welcoming smile.

I didn't have time to respond. I had to relive my seemingly endless encounter with the unaccommodating lifeguard and anomalous sea creature that wanted to dance to destruction. After I killed the venomous snakes and the sickening octopus, still another time, I heard the woman's pleasant, angelic voice again, "Would you like some help?"

I was beat from my continuous battle. "No," I said, sarcastically. "This is so much fun. Why would I want to stop?"

The woman laughed. "I'm sure with how long this has gone on, you're ready for it to end. Now—watch me closely, so you'll know what you need to do in the future."

She wore the same silly red belt as me, although, it looked much more fashionable on her. She unclipped it. As it opened, she pulled out a long cable and wrapped it around the motionless octopus. "Ego postulo vires," she uttered under her breath. Gusts of wind blew her hair. With unearthly strength, she pulled the creature into the ocean. What appeared to be rubber gloves, grew on her hands. She picked up the bits from the torn snakes and threw them into the ocean. This task was effortless for her. When she finished, she looked toward me, smiling with satisfaction. "There," she breathed. "Now they'll be rendered powerless."

On Earth, I had just begun to express my sincere apologies to Julia. I had only said a few words.

"Thanks," I said to the pretty lady, "I'm Bladen. You must be a life player."

The gloves on her hands disappeared before my eyes. "Yes, my name is Gianna. I know who you are. Benedict sent me to help you. He would have come himself, but he was too busy with other things."

"I guess this unsightly belt *can* come in useful. How do you use this thing?" I tried to yank the silly thing off. "I found some poisonous darts in it, but I didn't see anything like the cable you used." I continued to tug at the belt.

Gianna smiled, amused. "Benedict told me that you were pleasantly entertaining. I see what he said about you is true."

"I'm so happy you find me amusing—no really—I'm here to play the game, rip apart the bad guys, and help Earth." I glared at Gianna. "But I suppose the fact that I'm clumsy and left to learn much of this on my own *would* be quite funny, hysterical I'm sure."

"We were all trained the same way, Bladen, and you've had a lot of help just like the rest of us…" she said, her smile fading. She showed me how to unclasp my belt. It had a long cable like the one she used. Several poisonous darts hung from the side. There was one slingshot, several daggers, and other gadgets attached, too. I didn't recognize all the weapons.

"I suppose I'll need to figure out what these are on my own—right?" I challenged, still annoyed, pointing to the ones I hadn't seen before.

"Only some of them. If you need help, others on our side will show you how to use them."

"How did you stop the snakes and octopus?" I asked dumbfounded. "I slayed them over and over."

"As you may know," Gianna said patiently, "all evil beings that live here are already dead — they're immortal. That's why they continued to assault you. Their power won't be relinquished until you throw them into the abyss." She pointed to the ocean of water and fire.

"Is that what you call this…this creepy ocean?" I asked. The prank caller's words came back to me, have fun swimming in the abyss. "How will this abyss crush their power?"

Gianna nodded. "When you seemingly slay here in Arcis, you must throw all remains of any creature into this sea. The gloves that appeared on my hands acted like magnets. They picked up any pieces I might've missed. It's the only way to eradicate their authority. Once that's taken away, they'll never get it back. Now how do you feel? Would you like to see where I live and get a refreshment?"

"Do you live here?" I asked in surprise. "On this ocean?"

"Not on the abyss. This ocean's full of poison. It's a wicked stew brewing. The flames on top are caused by the potent evil from all those on Earth and in Arcis who follow Vorago. If Spero's army loses the game, this sea will erupt like a volcano and spew its sickness throughout all of Earth, and everything will die…but enough about that. Now we must go. We're not safe out here."

Gianna gripped my hand and pulled me toward her. She ran with unbelievable speed. I tried to keep up, following with my legs extended in my fastest sprint.

Flying above my head, I saw Slaughter—my little bird friend. He squawked a high pitch repetitive, "You better hurry, or you'll be attacked. You better hurry, or you'll be attacked. You better hurry, or …

"Or I know, I know. I'll be attacked," I finished glumly. "Slaughter… are you a tiny bird imprisoned in a hummingbird's body?" I grumbled, bothered by his chant.

"No time for humor," he screeched. "I'm outta here!" He sure could be a speedy little bird. I barely saw him fly away.

As we ran, dark-gray, ominous clouds charged across the sky, along with unrelenting winds. The sand flew up in tiny tornado-like spirals, making it hard to see and hear.

Three distorted-looking Minotaurs charged at Gianna and me. They had the body of a human, the head of a bull, and lips that were not really lips at all. They were thin lines that made an O-shape where their mouths should've been. Their eyes sagged, as though they were one hundred fifty years old. And their fur was nothing more than a scanty mass of greasy sprouts placed sporadically here and there on top of their heads. Their noses lay squashed up against their faces like pigs rather than a bull. The clothes they wore were gray and fit as poorly as the Hulk's. They didn't utter normal words. They muttered garble.

"You bastards!" I screamed, terrified. I charged toward them with my sword aimed outward ready to plunge deep into their grotesque bodies.

They reacted with what seemed like laughter that ended as my sword drove acutely into the first being. Brown jelly-like crap splattered onto my face from the Minotaur. I watched it plummet to the ground.

I spun around and charged toward the second Minotaur. I twirled around my sword and gazed into the being's eyes. They were empty—without a soul. As my sword sank into it, I heard its body pop and tear like a huge hot dog with natural casing. It met the same fate as the first one, lifeless on the ground.

When I searched for Gianna, she had already taken care of the third Minotaur. She was wrapping it up with the cable, ready to drag it into the abyss when I ran up to her.

I removed my long belt that I now appreciated and pulled out my cable. I wrapped it tightly around one of the motionless Minotaurs and tried to yank it toward the water, but I couldn't make it budge. I glanced desperately toward Gianna.

"Help!" I yelled, hoping she could read my lips above the chaotic noise from nature.

"I can't help you," she yelled back. "Ask Spero."

"How do I do that?" I hollered over the sound of the whirling wind.

"Look toward the three suns," she called. "Spero's home."

I turned my head to the suns and was blinded by them. Out of nowhere, words that held no meaning to me emerged from my mouth, the same words I heard Gianna use.

"Ego postulo vires," I spoke softly, but when I tugged on the cable, nothing happened. "Ego postulo vires." I said, louder this time. As I chanted the words, I gained the strength needed to pull the Minotaur into the fiery waters. I chanted the phrase a fourth time and bound the cable around the second repulsive monster. With one swift movement, I threw it into the abyss. The water sizzled like grease on a stove as the Minotaur sank.

Gianna motioned to me to follow her. She said something. I saw her lips move, but I didn't hear any sound. The wind was too wild, thrashing about as though it were its own monstrosity. I dashed out-of-breath after her for what felt like forever, until we came up to a modest cabin with a front porch. She unlocked the door. We both sprinted inside.

It took our combined strength against the wind to shut the door behind us. At last the lock clicked. We both breathed a sigh of relief, end of game. We both won, yet I was still in Arcis.

"Good work, Bladen," Gianna said. "That was excellent for a beginner. You vanquished the power of two of the three Terras."

"Terras? Is that what you call those things? I thought they were Minotaurs. That was a lot different than my video game."

"Yes, they're Minotaurs called Terras." Gianna took off the white jacket she was wearing and draped it on a rack that hung from the wall beside the door. "We call any wicked ones that fight on land Terras. And the real game *is* different from the app."

"What about the sea creatures? Do they have a name also?"

Gianna gestured for me to have a seat on her couch. "Haven't you learned this, yet?"

"No," I said, and sat down.

"The beings that come from the sea are the Undas, and the ones that fly in the air are called Aers. When we refer to all of them, we call them demons. Even though they have different names, that's really what they all are. And I'm an old life player that lives in Arcis, not on Earth. Do you know about the death players?"

"Yeah, I've had a lot explained to me already. I didn't know some of the particular names, though."

"That's good—well you must be hungry and tired after all that fighting. Would you like something to eat and drink?"

"Yes, thank you, but wait…Gianna. I'm not sure what level of the game I'm on. Benedict told me I could be thrown into any level at any time."

"Oh…you began the game at the basilica then. Benedict said he thought you'd become powerful. But you've won only one level, I'm afraid. Benedict told me about the first time you fought the octopus. It didn't count as a win, because you didn't throw it into the abyss. And even though you won't know what level you'll be pulled into, you'll still have to win ten levels before you can try to restore the pearl of peace."

"Really? That sucks." I had some choice words I wanted to say, but not in front of Gianna.

"I'm sorry," Gianna said, before she walked into her kitchen.

I laid down and put my feet up on the arm of the couch. I realized for the first time that my body ached—a lot.

Gianna's log cabin was about the same size as Benedict's, although lovelier. It felt like a vacation home with a tiny wood stove that sat in one corner. Cozy furniture and various flowers were placed all around on plain wooden tables. The fragrance that came from them smelled unusual, like an exquisite perfume. I took in a deep breath. The scent made me feel relaxed and sleepy. The vibrant shades of the flowers suddenly burst into the air like the aurora borealis. They looked like new secondary colors, with a strange mix of violet, indigo, and lemon. My body felt more relaxed than it had in months.

Gianna interrupted my thoughts when she returned from the kitchen. "Here's a special loaf of bread, and this hot herbal tea will give you strength."

I took the tray of food and thanked her. I bit into the spongy bread and sipped on the syrupy, hot tea. It tasted delicious, and, again, it was like nothing I had ever experienced on Earth. Gianna stood and stared at me while I ate.

"What is it?" I asked.

She cupped my face in her hands and studied my eyes with keen awareness. "Hold still," she said, softly. "Hmm—I see that you're with a girl—sailing."

I pulled away from her in surprise. "You can see what I'm doing on Earth?"

"Yes, I can. May I take another look?"

"Oh…okay." Once again, she held my face and stared straight into my eyes. I watched her, curious.

"I see that you're both having fun and smiling, but the girl has a sadness about her. She's had pain in her life. I also see a connection between the two of you. There's something unique and special about both of you, yet there's also turbulence." She let go of my face and stepped back.

"How could you know that?" I asked.

"It's one of my gifts—the gift of sight," Gianna said, in her angelic voice. "Spero gives us all different talents to assist us. We're given the things we need to accomplish the tasks he sets before us. You'll also receive talents, if you haven't already."

"No, I don't have anything special about me. Not like what you just did," I said.

Ah, but that's not true. I heard you say 'Ego postulo vires'. Do you know what that means?"

"No, I don't. It surprised me when it came out of my mouth. What does it mean?"

"You asked for strength, and Spero gave it to you." Gianna spoke in a motherly way. "Spero doesn't always give what's asked of him. A life player's heart needs to be in the right place, but sometimes he *does* give words that are needed whether a player knows what they mean or not. That's what happened to you. That's a gift. Now you could use some sleep, but first finish your tea."

I took her advice and finished my drink. Soon after, I fell asleep.

I tossed and turned restlessly and began to dream. A dense fog rolled aimlessly around me. I felt winded as I ran; my breath pounded loud and steady. Nervously, I glimpsed behind me and saw eight, humongous legs that looked like sticks chasing after me. It was a blur of black and red. That crazy spider again?

In front of me, a giant hourglass was filled with red sand that dropped like rain from the top to the bottom. "Time is running out. Time is running out," an evil voice screeched, followed by a wicked, sneering laugh. The dream played like a never-ending horror movie for what seemed like the entire night.

I awoke startled and didn't recognize my surroundings right away. I was groggy. I tried to find the bathroom, but to my surprise, I slowly realized I was no longer in Gianna's house, I was in Benedict's. What the heck? I thought. I searched for Benedict but couldn't find him anywhere. My stomach grumbled. I opened his refrigerator for a snack and found some odd looking meat. I took a piece of it and ate it. Mmm…it tasted so good, I finished the rest and laid back down for more sleep.

I dozed in and out. In my vague dreams, I stared at my stomach in amazement. I watched it blow out like a bubble. It looked like some pregnant lady's bloated gut. A voice split through my dream like an ax splits a piece of wood. "Wake up!" My body shuddered. I felt like I was going to throw up bricks. When I woke up, I saw that my stomach had grown to the size of a large water balloon. Panicked, I rushed to the bathroom just in time to puke everything I had just eaten into the toilet. I was relieved when my stomach shrank back to its normal size.

I walked into the living room, just as Benedict was walking into the kitchen. He opened the refrigerator, shook his head, and laughed. "What did you eat?"

"Some kind of meat in your fridge," I answered, still feeling kind of queasy.

"You ate my wormale," Benedict explained. "Wormale is a delicacy in Arcis. In fact, one bite is enough food for one entire day—looks like *you* ate enough for more than a few days, no wonder you were sick. You're lucky you threw it up, or you could've been sent to the infirmary for days.

"Infirmary?"

"Yes, we have hospitals here also. Sometimes life players stay there for a while to heal…if they need to, or they heal in a hospital back on Earth."

We were interrupted by a low singing chant. I became mesmerized with the tune playing outside. My body lifted a couple of inches off the floor and floated on air toward the window. I felt *really* happy, like I had chugged a can of beer or two. A dopey smile must have emerged on my face.

I gazed out the window and saw distorted-shaped men marching around Benedict's house, demons for sure. Multitudes of them lined up around the house. They all looked the same with o-shaped mouths and pig-like noses. These were Minotaurs too, but their heads looked more human with venomous scorpions for hair. Their tails shook and their black, beady eyes glared at me, large and more pronounced than normal scorpions. I couldn't tear my eyes away. I didn't want to. I felt drugged.

Benedict came to my side and put earplugs in my ears. As soon as he did, I fell to the ground. "Ow," I cried, and rubbed my left ankle where all my weight had fallen.

I was sure Benedict asked me if I was okay, although I couldn't hear him. I only saw his mouth move. I nodded my head and hobbled to the window. I watched for what seemed like an hour, until the army marched away. Then Benedict and I removed our earplugs.

"Are you okay?" he asked.

"Yeah my ankle's just a little sore, thanks. What was that all about? I thought they couldn't hurt us in your house."

"They can't, but when they sing their song of enchantment, they try to hypnotize you. They want to penetrate your soul and convince you to join their side. Their voices sound beautiful in an eerie sort of way. It makes you desire to listen, but you can't. If you do, you might step right out the door and into their arms. That's what they wanted today. When they realized their plan wouldn't work, they departed."

That evening I slept on Benedict's not-too-comfortable couch. The icy chill in the air made me pull the warm, wool blanket Benedict had given me up to my chin. I tried to breathe heavy into it to make myself warmer. It didn't work. I nicknamed this place Benedict-and-his-house-of-discomfort. Seriously, this place sucked...worse than my dorm room. Eventually, I did fall asleep and began to dream, yet again. What else? I guess life liked messing with my head while I slept.

In my dream, I was lying in my bed in my dorm room, feeling that same creepiness I had experienced before. The room began to close in on me. At the same time, hundreds of tiny, black widow spiders swarmed on the floor next to me. Just as they were about to crawl onto my bed, the room narrowed in, until it swallowed me whole.

A beeping sound echoed like an alarm. I opened my eyes and saw Benedict. "Have you found out what an Assembly is yet?"

"No," I groaned. "Get lost." I put the pillow over my head.

Benedict yanked it off. "Get out of bed. We need to go. You're about to experience an Assembly in Arcis."

I stood up. Benedict grabbed two brown cloaks and handed one to me. They each had an immense hood that more than covered our faces. I looked at Benedict like, what's up with the red riding hood cloak?

"It's best if nothing and no one can see your face," he explained, when we slipped out the door.

As we secretly crept through the streets and past all the aged-looking buildings, I became aware of my time with Julia on the catamaran.

I concentrated hard on my conversation with her. I had been telling her what activities I liked. "…and playing the guitar is awesome. It's one of my favorite things to do. What about you? What do you do in *your* free time?"

Julia looked thoughtful. She took a moment and twirled her hair with her finger. "I dance—ballet is my favorite—and the piano—I absolutely *love* to play."

"Who's your favorite composer?" I asked, curiously.

"Bach, Beethoven, and Mozart—you know the usual. But I like Yiruma the most."

"Yiruma? Who's he?"

"He's a fairly new and young, Korean composer."

"Will you play for me sometime?"

"Only if you'll play for me first," she answered, with a smile.

"Sure." I shrugged my shoulders.

The catamaran sailed smoothly over the water—like a skater on ice. The warm, late summer breeze brushed our faces.

I placed my hand on top of Julia's. "Here," I said, "take the rudder, and I'll put my shirt back on. I know it bothered you earlier."

Julia shook her head timidly. "I can't do that. I don't know how to sail." She took her hand away.

"You'll be fine," I reassured her. I took her hand again and placed it on the rudder. "Try not to move it…okay?"

When I jerked my shirt back on, Julia's hand slid off the rudder, which made it go around toward the sail, causing the boat to take a turn I hadn't anticipated. I lost my balance and struggled to stay on the boat. I ended up rolling off the canvas into the cold water.

"Bladen!" Julia cried out.

SECRETS UNFOLD

Julia panicked and screamed. I free-styled and threw my body back onto the boat. I watched my shirt float away.

"Are you okay?" I glanced toward Julia and shook my wet hair.

With wide eyes, she nodded her head.

"I'm sorry I don't have another shirt to wear. I hope my naked chest doesn't bother you too much," I teased, and pointed toward my lone top that disappeared along with the hurried current.

"I think I can *endure* that," she added in a saucy tone. "Just don't make me sail the boat again, not unless you want to go for another swim."

"No problem," I mused.

We sailed in silence for quite some time. Julia was easy to be with--easy to talk to, when we did talk—and definitely easy on the eyes. She sat hunched over with her arms cradled around her legs; her chin rested on the top of her knees. She gazed out at the water and didn't notice me studying the rays of sunlight that exploded down on several locks of her golden hair. As the strands gently floated up and down in the breeze, I noticed the ones weaving throughout that had been highlighted by the summer sun. I studied her, until she glanced up and caught me staring.

Her lips curved in a generous smile. "What are you doing? Watching me or sailing the boat?"

My female gracelessness erupted. "Um…um I couldn't help but notice how pretty your hair looks in the sunlight." My face felt like it had turned three shades of purple.

"Thanks," she said and turned back to gaze out at the water.

I changed the subject. "So…since you like to dance and play the piano, have you been in a lot of recitals?"

Julia didn't respond.

"Julia?"

"I heard you," she said. "It's just that—I've never been in *any* recitals. Adonis—well you know he's—he's unbelievably protective. He always tells me that it's best for me to be out of the public eye. It *has* caused contention between us, but he's the closest thing to a father that I've ever had. Besides, I did have lessons. I had a private teacher for both ballet and piano."

"You could have a performance in your house with your family and friends," I offered. "I'd love to see you."

"Maybe."

The thought of Adonis struck me like a hammer over my head. Who *was* he? Slaughter had said he lived *only* in Arcis, but *come on*. The Lord of Arcis had the same unusual name as Julia's sort of step-dad who also spoke with an English accent, and he made life like a semi-prison for Julia. Something didn't ring right here, and I planned to find out what.

In Arcis, Benedict and I had been in a monotonous council meeting—the Assembly. Talk about dull. To be exact, we'd been there for more than three hours, and I still had no idea what they were discussing. It took all my strength *not* to fall asleep.

I did learn a cool new trick while I sat there, though. My watch told me the time in Arcis *and* back on Earth. When I concentrated on Earth, my watch showed me that time of day. And when I zeroed in on Arcis, my watch switched to that time. I sat there bored stiff and spent way too much time goofing around with my wristwatch.

The life player seated beside me, Gregory, looked amused and must have been new to this life just like me. He asked what I was doing and wanted *me* to show him how to change the time on his watch. We sat there like a couple of little kids with a new toy.

In this meeting, ten people were seated at an oval-shaped table in the middle of the stage. They all wore the same brown cloak as me. A shadow cast in front of their hoods hid their faces. They seemed to be having a heavy discussion they hadn't shared with us yet.

I sat in the audience where hundreds of us waited in silence for any orders that might be given. When I thought I couldn't stand to sit there any longer, a man finally stood up from the oval table. He put his fingers to his mouth and whistled loudly. The large crowd of people sat up erect and alert, waiting for instruction.

The man yelled out in an inhuman voice. "It's time for us to share with you our conversation and new plan of attack."

"What's wrong with his voice," I whispered to Gregory.

"The man that's speaking is Adonis. I heard he disguises his voice here because he still lives on Earth. He's not only one of the new life players, but he's also Lord of Arcis."

Slaughter *was* wrong. Adonis still lived on Earth? "I heard that Adonis was the lord here," I replied. "But why did you call him a new life player?"

"Life players that no longer live on Earth, therefore they've died and only dwell in Arcis, are called the old life players. Life players, like you and me, who are still living between here and Earth, are called new life players."

"Oh," I said, surprised. "I thought there was only one kind of life player."

Gregory shook his head. "Even though we differentiate between life players, calling them old or new, we still give them all the same name in conversation. We refer to them as simply life players."

Adonis clapped his hands. He moved to the middle of the stage. "Thank you all for waiting so patiently–soon, we'll all meet in what will appear to be Myndos, Turkey—in the bathing houses. It will be there that we'll catch the enemy off guard when they're soaking and relaxing. It will happen during their annual Nawt Festival, otherwise known as their festival of desire. An abundant number of demons will be gathered there, giving us a great opportunity to force Vorago to relinquish an immense degree of his power. Our enemies are growing in number, and it is of the utmost importance to remove them from Myndos. When it's time, most of you will be teleported there. Please…I beg all of you to do whatever you can to train for this. After Myndos, we *will* meet here again to discuss our position. You'll have at least one or two Assemblies on Earth to discuss this matter ahead of time. And, if you all win the battle in Myndos, miracles will happen on Earth. Thank you."

Deafening cheers went out from the crowd, as people discussed what a huge success that would be for us. Adonis extended his arms and hands outward toward all of us. Beams of light that spun from his fingertips encircled our entire group.

I turned to Gregory. "What's going on?"

"In the Assemblies in Arcis, we all gain strength from Spero. That's where the white light originates. Can you feel its warmth? It's comes from the three suns. Hereafter, we'll all partake of the same bread. This, too, will give us strength to fight. We need the Assemblies to live, or we can't do our jobs with much power."

After everyone ate, Adonis spun around and strode away. The audience clapped and cheered again in a deafening manner, until he was out of sight. I knew I had to find out if *this* Adonis was the same Adonis I knew on Earth. The thought seemed somewhat crazy and insane, but I needed to know for sure.

After the council meeting, Benedict and I went quietly back to his house. He didn't speak to me whatsoever. He knelt on the ground in deep meditation, his head bowed low and eyes closed. I rested on his couch and daydreamed about Julia. Her long hair and incredible smile…

Sometime much later, Gianna awakened me. I was at her house near the beach again and not at Benedict's modest home in the city.

"Good morning sleepy head," Gianna said, beaming.

I grumbled, "Leave me alone."

Gianna laughed. "I so enjoy having you around—rest for a while longer. Later, it'll be time for you to rise. I have something I want to show you."

Gianna made me curious. I jumped up and found her in the kitchen. She saw me and told me to sit down. "Would you like something to eat?"

"Depends on what you have. If it's wormale, no thanks."

She laughed just like Benedict had about the wormale. "You must have already experienced it, then?"

"Regrettably, yes," I answered, not wanting to remember.

"Did you have too much?"

"Obviously."

Gianna took a steaming dish out of the oven. It smelled amazing. "I don't like wormale myself," she mentioned, as she made my plate of food. "You don't *ever* have to worry about having it here. Benedict lives quite simply and doesn't eat much more than that one delicacy. My life here is a tad more extravagant. This is a baked omelet with cheddar cheese, vegetables, and melted butter. I thought you might like something more earthly. I also have fresh, squeezed orange juice and toasted wheat muffins for you."

My stomach grumbled. "Thank you," I said graciously. "Remind me to kiss you later." Gianna smiled.

My table manners failed to serve me as I wolfed the food down. My face reddened when I burped a little loud.

Gianna placed her hand on my cheek. "Your mother must thoroughly enjoy feeding you. Are you finished? I have something special for you to see."

"Yeah, thanks again for the food," I said, wiping my mouth with the back of my hand.

I followed Gianna out the door onto her covered porch. The only place to sit was on a tiny wicker loveseat that had been pushed up against the house, next to the door. Everything about Gianna's home was perfect and looked recently renovated. The log cabin had been stained a beautiful, brown chestnut color.

Gianna took out a long, golden key and pushed it into the air. When she turned the key, I heard a series of loud clicking noises. Whatever lock she put the key into was invisible to my eyes.

"Come on," she told me. "This is a secret pathway that leads to the beach, the only spot I enjoy because it's not part of the abyss, but be careful, if you step out of the path, you could get attacked."

I stared in amazement as we walked down a trail, lined with smooth, yellow cobblestone. "This is so cool," I said. I saw the sand on the outside of the path but heeded Gianna's warning and didn't dare step into it. The walls and ceiling that surrounded us were transparent, allowing the outdoor light to stream in. They must have been magical. I had never seen anything like them on Earth.

When I raised my head, the three suns, Spero's home, spun and pulsated like a heartbeat in the backdrop. They threw brilliant rays of light that danced and radiated their warmth throughout the path and onto Gianna and me. Gianna gazed at them in a state of ecstasy.

We reached the water. Gianna took my hands into hers, sighed, and gazed into my eyes again. I knew she wanted to see what I was up to on Earth.

"You're still on the sailboat with the girl," she smiled, "interesting." Then she turned her gaze away from my eyes. "Bladen, you need to know, numerous battles will be fought. I feel you'll be a part of many of them." She looked back at me. "Spero asked me to bring you here today, so you can rest and gain strength. You'll spend a short time on Earth, before you'll play the game again. So, that means goodbye for now. I hope to see you again soon."

"Bye Gianna. Thanks for everything," I said.

Gianna hugged me, then leisurely walked up the path and out of sight.

I bent over, grabbed a handful of sand, and threw it into the water. Each morsel glistened like snowflakes in the winter sun. They floated down, until the water swallowed them up. The view before me was otherworldly—like nothing I'd ever seen on Earth.

"Cool," I said, stunned when it echoed back to me from the water, "Cool, cool, cool."

Several rocks surrounded my feet. One in particular caught my eye, a flattened stone, gray in color, and perfect to skip across the water. I threw it. It skipped once, twice, three times, and rested at the surface for a few seconds. Ringlets that originated from where the rock had dropped ebbed outward one after the other. A distinct voice in my head said, "The ringlets are your life. Everything you do, every choice you make will profoundly affect others. Make your choices well." I stared around me to see where the voice had come from but didn't see anyone.

I swam in the ocean and sunbathed. It felt like a sweet vacation. I fell asleep until I began to feel the, now familiar, straw feeling when I traveled through my iPhone. My body blew in and out and then popped out at the other end.

Ah, once again, whole—one person instead of two. I blinked my eyes from the glare of the sun. It felt good to know I'd get a break from Arcis and the real game for a while. Julia squinted. "What's with your wicked grin?" she said, with a toss of her hair. "Penny for your thoughts."

I watched another catamaran sail out on the water. "Nothing really... I'm happy to be here...sailing...with you."

"Thanks," Julia said, disbelieving. "I think there's more on your mind than that, but you never tell me where you go in that head of yours, anyway. I suppose I'm getting used to it."

I glanced at my watch, disappointed when I noticed our rental time was almost up. "Comin' about," I said, and turned the boat around to head for shore.

We arrived back at the docks. I took our life preservers and gear and handed them back in at the shop. Julia and I walked slowly to my Saab, where I had an extra T-shirt in my car. I slipped it on before we headed back to her house.

I didn't have a lot of time before work, but I wanted to find Adonis, look behind his left ear, and see whether he was a life player or not. My anxiety grew so much as we neared Julia's house, beads of sweat began to form on my face.

"Are you okay?" Julia asked, concerned. "You're sweating profusely, Bladen, and it's not that hot."

I wiped the sweat from my face and rolled down my window. "I'm fine. Profusely, huh?" I smiled at Julia. "Big word…even for a college girl."

She rolled her eyes. "Not really."

"Are you going to the bonfire tomorrow?" I asked Julia. The next night a massive bonfire had been scheduled down at one of the beaches for all the local college students.

"As a matter of fact I am," Julia stressed. "I have a date, and it's *not* your roommate."

"What are you talking about?" I asked, surprised.

Julia glared at me. "Oh, I guess Robby and I both forgot to tell you. He told me that *you* said he should ask me out."

I glanced at Julia out of the corner of my eye. "That's *not* what I said. He asked me if it was okay to ask you out, and I said sure because you and I are just friends."

"Uh…yeah…big difference," she replied, her voice dripped in sarcasm. "Did you stop to think maybe I wouldn't want to go out with him?"

"So…you told him no?"

"*Yeah*, I told him no. You and I are friends. I thought that would be a conflict of interest."

"How would our friendship be a conflict of interest?" I mused.

"Never mind…I wouldn't expect you to understand."

"Well, did he take it all right?"

"Don't worry…I let him down gently."

"Sooo…who ya goin' with?" I teased, just before we pulled onto the street where Julia lived.

Julia punched my arm. "Wouldn't you like to know."

"Cut it out, I'm driving," I joked and swerved around her driveway before I parked.

Julia rolled her eyes again and looked especially cute. She gathered her belongings. Before she stepped out of the car, she leaned toward me and gave me a quick kiss on the cheek, not exactly what I had daydreamed about, but close enough for now.

"What was that for?" I asked, trying to act cool and not show I was psyched.

"For taking me sailing, and because…well…you're like a brother to me, except that we don't live in the same house." Julia blushed.

I raised my eyes. *Brother?* I thought in disappointment.

She jumped out of the car before I could respond.

I yelled after her. "Wait! Where does Adonis live? I need to see him."

Julia's face pinched up in confusion. "Why? You're not going to talk to him about me are you—the whole recital thing?" She shrugged.

"No, my question has nothing to do with you." I stepped out of my car.

"What do you want him for then?" she asked, as I followed her down the sidewalk.

"Tell me who your date is, and I'll tell you why I want to see Adonis."

"You're a brat, you know that?"

I bowed toward Julia. "One of my better qualities." She punched my arm again. "Hey, you're gonna give me a bruise."

"I thought you were in a hurry because you have to work," Julia said, ignoring my bruised arm.

"My question for him is quick…I hope."

"Tell me what you want him for," Julia pleaded, with her hands together.

"For me to know and you to find out," I chuckled.

◈ ❧ ◈

Our teasing ended the moment we arrived at Adonis's door. He lived next door to Julia in a tiny house that looked like it had been built in the 1800's. It was tan with green shutters and had other various shades of paint peeling down the sides. There was a tiny porch in the front with an old rocking chair in one corner.

Julia knocked with the rusty, metal knocker that hung from the front door—no one answered. She knocked again, still no response.

"Hold on," Julia said. She rummaged through her bag and pulled out a key. She unlocked the door. We went inside. Everything in the house looked dingy and well used. Some of the furniture had rips in the fabric.

"Hello," Julia yelled out, but still there was no response. She shrugged her shoulders. "I don't think he's here. Let me go look in his garage."

I followed Julia and passed by a door with five, huge dead bolts that kept it locked. "Hey Julia," I called. What's with the locks on this door? Does Adonis have some cash stashed here or what?"

She stared blankly at me. "I have no idea what's in that room. It's the *big* family secret. Believe me, when I was younger I tried my hardest to break into that room. For as long as I can remember, no matter where we lived, Adonis always had a room just like this one."

"Do you want me to bust down the door for you?" I asked, with a sly grin.

Julia laughed. "You could try. It's—like it's magical, though. I know that sounds weird, but I couldn't make a scratch on the door. And you know what's even weirder? Adonis seemed to know I'd tried, even though he wasn't around when I did it."

"How could you tell he knew?"

"Because…the night I tried to break in…after dinner…he told me to mind my own business and stop snooping around his things. He never saw me, so he had no reason to say that to me."

"Really? Well maybe *I* can help."

Julia shook her head. "No, if you make him angry, he may not let you come around here anymore."

"Oooh, I'm scared."

"I mean it," Julia warned. "If he told me I couldn't see you, I'd miss you. So, forget about it. Come on, let's see if he's in the garage."

I followed Julia, and to my surprise, I saw a-far-from-ordinary garage. It was a business. "You're kidding me," I remarked. "Adonis is a middle-aged, hippy mechanic? Cool."

Julia searched around for Adonis. "Yeah, this is a good business for him. He makes enough to live on, and he can keep an eye on me when my mom isn't around. Hey, here's a note."

Julia pulled a taped piece of paper off one of the doors. "It says, 'I had to go—be right back'. He probably left this note for my mom."

"Too bad, guess I'll try to find him later." I glanced at my watch and noticed it was getting late. I still had to get to work on time, so my boss, who loved to yell, wouldn't freak out on me. That man was *not* the coolest guy to work for.

Julia and I left toward her house.

"By the way," I called to her, as she headed toward her door, "I plan on going to the bonfire tomorrow, too. Guess I'll find out who your date is after all." She turned and spit her tongue out at me just before she stepped inside.

Later, I strode down Church Street to The Bistro and saw Berard flash around. He didn't stop long enough for me to talk to him.

At my job, it was a busy night even for a Saturday. All twelve tables and the bar in front had filled up. The deafening noise made it hard to hear the radio in the background. I waited on tables and went through the monotonous motion of taking care of the needs of all the customers, not always how I felt like spending my Saturday nights. Sometimes it was a serious drag, but the cash was cool.

I saw Berard flash around a few more times. He annoyed me as usual. I wanted to yell, what's your problem, dude? He must have sensed my anxiety. When I turned to wait on a new table, he appeared in front of me.

"There's someone around you tonight who used to be dangerous," Berard whispered. "That's all I know. I don't know who it is." Then he vanished.

At first, I didn't pay attention to what Berard had said. I still questioned whether or not he had a full deck of cards upstairs in that brain of his. Later, though, I thought twice when I went to wait on a new table and saw the blind man sitting there. He looked harmless enough. I walked up to his table where he sat staring at a menu. I did think *that* was kind of strange, considering he was blind.

"Hello," he said, darkly. "I'd like to order something to eat. What do you recommend for a poor, blind man?

DANGERS UNDERLYING

"**W**e have a Saturday night pizza special," I answered, like I didn't care. "You can have all the pizza and soda you want for only $9.99."

"I'll have that," he answered, staring down at the menu. If he's blind, I thought, then what's he looking at the menu for?

I put in his pizza order and later brought him his food. While I waited on other tables, I noticed him wolf down his meal. Pepperoni grease dribbled down his chin, as though he hadn't eaten in months. When I handed him the check, he already had his money out, eleven dollars. He told me to keep the change.

Just when I thought he was ready to hobble out the door, he turned and gestured for me to move toward him. I leaned my head near his.

"When life is amiss, blow it a kiss, but be careful what lurks behind," he whispered. "If you look there, you *will* care, because you'll be facing a pair of knives." His breath smelled like he hadn't brushed his teeth in months. I held in my gag, turned away to breathe, and moved to wait on another table. I turned back toward the blind man, but he vanished. Annoyingly, I felt bad I hadn't offered to pay for his meal.

"Hey can we get some service?" Julia's familiar voice resounded. It was Julia. Her face had become a comforting sight.

I shook away the bizarre feeling I had felt with the blind man. "Hey," I said with a wide grin. "Long time no see. Can I start you off with something to drink? A soda?" Julia had come in with her friend Gloria, as usual.

"Diet," both girls said in unison, giggling.

I brought the girls their drinks. At almost the same time, they both stared toward the door of the restaurant. They weren't the only ones. Angelina from my biology class strolled in, carefree. She threw her head back to move her lengthy, black hair out of the way, a determined, set smile upon her face. Everyone gawked at her beauty.

Angelina stopped for a second. When she saw me, she made a beeline in my direction. I acted like I didn't see her and went to wait on another table. I couldn't dodge her, though. She walked up behind me.

"Where're you going?"she breathed. "You can't avoid me you know."

I stopped. My feet felt like they had super glue on the bottom of them. I couldn't resist her. I turned and faced Angelina with an uncontrollable desire for her that I didn't understand.

"Kid," my boss yelled out. "Get your food for table four."

I snapped out of my daze and pulled away from Angelina. It took all my strength.

Around 10:00 p.m. on most Saturday nights, one corner of the restaurant, a place up in the front near the bar, was sectioned off for dancing. Tonight, couples stood up and leisurely moved toward the dance floor. I watched several guys ask Angelina to dance, though she appeared to refuse them all.

By the time 11:00 p.m. rolled around, only college students were left. Most of them were dancing or eating appetizers. The Bistro closed at 1:00 a.m. on weekends, anyway.

I was leaned over, clearing some dishes from a table, when I felt someone's warm breath on my cheek. "Too bad you're working and can't dance." My heart began to pound when I felt Angelina's hand touch my chest. She laughed, quietly.

Strange, I thought. I mean she was a knockout, but I knew I didn't like her. She seemed normal in class, but now her behavior was…creepy. So, why did I have this uncontrollable desire for her? My spine tingled.

I stuck my face in hers. "Leave me alone. I don't know what weird thing you have over guys, but I don't want anything to do with it."

She picked up my hand and brushed her lips against my fingers. "I promise you. You'll change your mind." I yanked my hand away from her.

My boss screamed out again, "Romeo, back to work."

I walked angrily back toward him. "I don't want anything to do with her, boss. She keeps bugging me."

He threw his head back and cackled. Yeah. Some laugh. "Somehow, I doubt a girl as attractive as her is bothering you," he continued, in his deep Spanish drawl.

"Believe it or not, she is," I countered.

It didn't matter at that point. Angelina had left, and I had Julia to deal with.

"Wow, looks like you were the popular guy tonight," Julia said, putting her hand on my back. My heart started to pound again, this time for Julia. I brushed her hand away.

"Whatever," I frowned.

"Bladen. Seriously. That girl stared at you the whole time she was here. She obviously has a thing for you."

"I barely know her, Julia," I replied, thinking Julia was the girl I wished had been staring at me instead. "And, I need to get back to work before I get in trouble again. I'll see you later."

"See ya 'round then," Julia said. Gloria gave me a wave and a smile goodbye.

I started to clean the empty tables and scooped up a few nasty utensils covered with leftover pizza and what looked like someone's spit, when I cut myself on a knife. "Ow," I muttered under my breath. As blood trickled down my finger, the blind man's words rang in my head. He had warned me about knives. What did that mean? Did it mean I should stay away from any trouble and ignore it, or did he mean it literally, since I had just cut myself on a knife? I didn't have time to think about it. Alfredo stuck his face in mine and screamed, "Move faster boy!" I glared at him and growled. I couldn't help myself. He threw his head back and cackled again. Strange man.

By the end of the night, my muscles ached. I couldn't wait to get to sleep. I entered my dorm. As I walked closer to my room, I heard a lot of people talking. I opened my door and saw friends Robby had invited over. Party time, I thought. All my need for sleep evaporated.

Robby's hair was gelled back, his bangs spiked up. He had a tight, white T-shirt on and faded, ripped jeans. I had to admit he looked cool. A cute girl standing next to him was gazing, enamored up at his face. Her mousy hair, tinted with a shade of auburn, was cut just below her ears. She looked petite next to him and had to crane her neck to look up at him. She was *totally* checking him out, let me tell you. Lucky guy. I swear, he's a chick magnet. The dorm room light that glowed on her face made her deep, cocoa eyes flash against her pale skin. She looked super girly with a pink, lace shirt and a faded, jean mini-skirt.

"Dude, you're back...awesome. We're headed downtown. Wanna come?" Robby asked.

"Count me in," I said, eagerly.

We headed to the parking lot and drove to Axe's Place to shoot some pool. There were three girls with us, Jared from down the hall, Robby, and me. The girls, Brooke, Alicia, and Kaitland were all friends. Brooke and Alicia are sisters, and Kaitland is their cousin. The two sisters had long, strawberry-blonde hair and hazel eyes. They both wore tight jeans that showed off their long legs. Their colorful button-down blouses were cropped at the waist. They looked hot, but I was too shy to talk to either girl much.

Kaitland, the short one infatuated with Robby, was easygoing and down to earth; the kind of girl a guy could easily be friends with. She had slipped on a gray, hooded sweatshirt over her pink shirt. She seemed like a tomboy.

At about 4:00 in the morning, when I felt like I needed toothpicks to keep my eyes open, I recommended we call it a night.

I dropped the two sisters off first. Then Jared and I went to our dorm. Robby offered to drop off Kaitland, and since he didn't have a car, he borrowed Jared's.

I went to my room and pulled out my iPhone. When I turned on my Arcis game, I felt that obsessive feeling return. I had to look. It didn't surprise me when the game skipped to St. Peter's Basilica. It did surprise me when I saw the same angry man pacing inside the basilica. He looked up and pointed his finger at me and mouthed the word, "you." I wondered why he looked so angry. I swear he could see me. I quickly shut off the game and crawled in bed. Soon after, I fell asleep.

In my dream, I saw Gianna's sweet face. "You need more rest for what lies ahead," she whispered in a song-like voice, as melodious as a morning dove. The caress of her palm reminded me of my mother's. The concern in her eyes darkened like the tranquil before the storm, yet they radiated with love and care.

After a time, my blissful dream ended, and a sinister shadow was cast in its place. My breath quickened to that equal of a horse's trotting hoof beats. I ran as fast as my legs would carry me through a narrow, black channel, where a greasy liquid dropped from the ceiling onto my face. I brushed the back of my hand against my cheek to clean off the foul fluid. I could hear someone behind me. The hammering of their feet echoed in my ears. The sound of their breath grew louder than mine.

I glanced back, panicked when I heard and saw a pair of knives slicing against each other. They made a sound that sharpened them for a kill. A kill, I was pretty sure, intended to be me. The knives held in the hands of the shadow hung only a couple of feet away from my face. Glimmering light bounced off them. They appeared eager to bloody up my body. Seriously, the knives curved up slightly like a sinister smile. I shuddered and let out a scream of terror.

I snapped awake and found myself in what I thought was my bed, until my room slowly began to close in on me. The two knives I had just seen came slicing through the wall. When it seemed like my room was going to chop me up like a piece of hamburger meat, I screamed again.

This time, I *did* wake up panting like a dog on a summer day. I realized that I *was* in my room…in the dark…alone. I felt like such a girl for screaming, though I figured anyone else in my shoes would have done the same thing. They'd be stupid not to.

I had a difficult time sleeping for the rest of the night. I wanted to know what the heck was up with my room. Something terrible must have happened in it. I felt it deep in my body, unless maybe that was only my stomach grumbling with hunger.

In the dark, I racked my brain. My imagination went wild as I thought about the shiny, steel knives and what kind of stabbing frenzy they could've accomplished, if they'd been real. The high-pitched noise they had made when they sliced together sounded like nails scraping on a chalkboard.

By morning, I felt numb with fatigue. I hadn't been in touch with my family in a while. I felt guilty. I jumped on Facebook to send them a message. I wrote to my parents first and told them I had a decent job, had settled into my classes, and life was good. Blah. Blah. Blah. I was about to log off, when my brother Nicholas logged on.

"Hey bro how's school?" he wrote.

"Great u?"

"Awesome it's way hot in more ways than one if u know what I mean."

"Haven't talked to u in a while u meet a girl?"

"Yeah Stephanie. I miss u 2 wish we were in the same school. talked to mom and dad?"

"Sent em a message just now. gotta go things to get done we'll talk soon. I wanna hear about stephanie okay?"

"Sounds good take care of urself"

"Bye"

Facebook was an easy way to keep in touch, even though my grammar and spelling on FB sucked and always drove my parents crazy. What can I say? You have to type fast to stay in a conversation. I shut down my computer thinking I hadn't asked Nicholas enough about Stephanie. My life…these dreams…the game…were consuming me.

◈ ◈ ◈

After I showered, I headed down the hall. I wanted to find Berard, then go to the library archives and look up old newspaper articles about Freefall. I turned the corner toward the stairs when a tiny body shot out at me. "Boo!" Berard yelled. I jumped, surprise, only to see Berard laughing, all too pleased with himself.

"You're an idiot." I spat. He continued his donkey sound for a laugh. "You think you're so funny, but you're not. I bet you haven't made new friends, because you're such a freak. I'm right aren't I? You really don't belong in this world."

Berard stopped and stood still for a few seconds. "You're mean," he retorted. "I could call you a lot more…"

I laughed at the whacked expression on his face. Then I felt bad. "Look…I guess I'm not used to you trying to bug me all the time, and I had another lousy night's sleep. Forget it all right? Why are you here, anyway? Did you know I wanted to talk to you or something?"

"Remember, I can be around you whenever you need it."

"I need it now," I said. "There's something…about my room. Something bad happened there. I need to find out what it was." Berard pulled me out of the way and told me to keep quiet. We went back to my room to talk.

"Look, I'm one step ahead of you," Berard said. "I know something bad occurred in your room. That's why at first I stayed across the hall from you. You know, I thought *you* were in some kind of danger. Then when I realized you weren't, I moved. It's not safe for a patriarch to live too close to its subject. Later, I started to do some research, but I couldn't find out anything. It's weird…when I went into the school archives, there were a few years of news missing with no explanation."

I was deep in thought when it occurred to me...Adonis. I felt like he had the key to unlock some of my questions. Berard, as usual, knew my thoughts before I could say them.

"After you see Adonis, let me know what he tells you."

I shook my head in disbelief. I was still getting used to Berard knowing things about me in advance. "How did you know I was thinking about Adonis, and why would it be unsafe for you to live too close to me?"

"I shouldn't live close to you, because death players might identify you more readily—if we hung out a lot."

"Hmm...I guess that makes sense," I answered, thinking I definitely wouldn't want to hang out with him a lot, although I was beginning to like him...a little more.

"I'm going now. Talk to Adonis, and I'll see you later." Berard vanished just as Robby walked in.

My head jerked up. My mouth dropped open. I wanted to ask Berard, again, how he knew about Adonis.

"Hey bro, who you talking to?" Robby asked.

"Uh, I'm here by myself," I answered.

"Weird, man. I thought I heard you talking to someone."

I grabbed my car keys, ran out the door, and yelled back to Robby, "Gotta go. See you later."

I drove maybe a little too fast to find Adonis. When I passed Julia's house, I saw her mom inside their garage. As luck would have it, Adonis was home. As soon as I pulled into his driveway, he opened the door for me like he was expecting my visit.

He stumbled out to greet me. "C'mon in, mate. I've been waiting for youuu. Will you have a shot of Whiskeee with me?"

I peered at him. "You're kidding, right? You're not actually drunk on a Sunday morning, are you?"

"Of course not...honest, smell my breath," he bellowed and blew on my face. "I like teasing ya, mate." I turned my face. His breath smelled bad, though not like alcohol.

"You're kind of—odd," I said.

Laughing, he threw his arm around my shoulder and invited me in. As I walked inside, I saw the door that had been bolted against all of kingdom come. I had forgotten about it. There was a lot I wanted to discuss with Adonis.

He read my mind and asked if I'd like to sit in a chair. "Go ahead, it's time for you to interrogate me with all of your curiosities," he said.

I sat and watched him. His face and body became slightly illuminated. At first, I thought it was from the sun streaming in through the window. I looked around, confused. Adonis studied me, his mouth widened into an understanding grin. His eyes grew gentle, the brown, almost black in them took on a majestic look, like he was someone else, an entirely different person.

"I'm waiting," he said, patiently.

I felt frustrated, wanting to know who he was. I stood up and put my hand on his shoulder. I tried to look under his hair to see if he had a life player's emblem.

Adonis's warm eyes took on a sterner look. "What is it that you seek?"

"Who are you?" I blurted out, abruptly pulling up his hair on the left side of his head.

Adonis grabbed my arm, twisted it behind my back, and flipped me to the floor. In a fraction of a second, he had one hand at my throat. I cried out in pain.

"You need some serious work," he said. Once he loosened his grip on my throat, I coaxed him into letting go. I whipped my hand up and yanked his hair back. My heart stopped in revelation. He had an emblem like mine all right, but it was red, unlike my brown one. I never saw anything like it before.

"You need work, but you *are* strong." Adonis looked pleased.

"Are you going to tell me who you are now?" I demanded.

Adonis shook his head like he needed to clear it. Then he released me nice and slow before he stood up. He extended his hand toward me to help me stand up as well. "I know you're a life player, Bladen. I've known for some time."

"Are you a life player, too?"

"Yes…but I'm more than that. We both sat down, me on the couch, while he took the torn chair.

"What do you mean?" I asked

"I've been watching you since you came to Burlington," he answered. "I know I can trust you." Adonis turned away from me, his face full of emotion. I studied him, searching.

"Tell me," I prodded.

Adonis took a deep breath. Even the way he breathed didn't seem entirely human. "I'm…the Lord of Arcis. That's why my emblem is red."

I laughed—and I laughed again. I knew it. He *was* the same Adonis that Slaughter had talked about.

"Maybe you can tell me what's so funny."

I explained to him how I had first heard about him and how I suspected him to be more than he seemed, especially with Julia's strange upbringing.

When I brought up Julia's name, his facial expression changed. "How do you feel about her?" he asked.

"She's a friend?" I said, caught by surprise.

"Are you sure?"

"Yeah I'm sure."

We were both quiet for a few moments.

"I haven't had this much contact with another life player in years. My life…the path I'm on…it's been a lonely one," Adonis muttered, almost talking to himself.

I didn't know what else to say.

He looked up. "Is there anything more you need?" he asked.

"I have a lot of questions. I just can't think of all of them right now." I couldn't stop staring at Adonis, amazed by who he was.

"I told you before that you need some work, and you do Bladen. I tackled you down with ease. I've mastered all martial arts. If you come here each week, I'll train you to become one of the deadliest life players that has ever existed."

"I'd like that," I answered. "You know—I could use some help. That'd be cool."

"Good," he agreed, with approval. "Humility is the first step to success."

Finally, it was like I woke up and remembered my questions. "Adonis, I believe something terrible happened in my room…my dorm room. I've been having nightmares ever since I moved in."

Adonis stood up from his chair and walked more closely toward me. "What dorm and room are you staying in?"

"Tanner 222."

He whipped around with a sick look on his face. "What? You're in room 222?"

"Yeah, why?"

"Someone was killed in—that—room," he revealed, annunciating each word. A life player was murdered there, body parts everywhere."

"Who was he?" I asked, desperate to know. I didn't get to find out. Our conversation ended. I felt the transition take place as my body was pulled through my phone into the game.

I landed in the courtyard again, the one in front of St. Peter's basilica. Where else? Coal-black air surrounded me, except for the rays of light from the three suns. The suns were dimmed and appeared more like a nightlight.

How unfair, I thought. I land at the basilica, the place with the fiercest fighting, and if I win this level, it only counts as two levels won out of ten.

I felt a safe presence next to me but couldn't tell who it was right away. One of the demons I saw earlier at the basilica emerged. It gradually strutted out of the shadows. The hood of its blackened cloak was down, revealing its repulsive face. Its mushy, distorted lips curved into an evil smirk. This one didn't have a huge nose. On the contrary, the absence of its nose, through which I couldn't believe he could breathe, made ghastly snorting sounds. The slithering snakes atop of its Medusa-like head was hissing obscenities at me. "Die, bastard, boy." At least twenty other sickening demons just like it hobbled out from the corner behind the massive columns of the basilica.

The presence next to me materialized. I felt relieved when I saw Adonis. We stared at each other with somber eyes—a knowing look, both of us understood the enormity of our mission.

Adonis sprinted forward, striking down two of the demons with a single punch to the face. He fought with moves I had never seen before. He spun around, slammed his foot into one demon's head, put it in a headlock, and tore a knife down its throat, deep into its skin. Blackened crud squirt out from it. Its beady eyes popped right out of their sockets. It dropped to the ground, lifeless. I thought it was sick how Adonis could pulverize demons like that. I felt humbled, like a weakling, unprepared for what came next.

FEELINGS EMERGE

At least ten of them charged toward me. "Get the new one," they hissed, in a high-pitched whisper, snickering in sinful delight. "Torture him!" The creatures scrambled about, waddling like drunken nightmares. Some of them bent over on top of me. Some surrounded me. Fish-smelling spit dripped out of their mouths onto my face. Their threadbare clothing brushed against my armor. Rock-hard fists crashed down on every part of my body. I moaned in pain. Their hits penetrated like magic through my armor, as though I wore none. Their giddiness grew louder with each punch. They chanted, "Kill. Kill." Hypnotized, I couldn't move. Their dull eyes twinkled with amusement. Their vicious grins revealed soiled teeth. Pound. Pound. Their fists were the only crafty way they had to fight, but they outnumbered me and covered me with their repulsive forms like a swarm of killer bees.

One of them with freaky red hair appeared. Her pink lizard tongue rolled around, moist with more drops of spit. Her lustful eyes gazed at me with pleasant surprise. "It's him," she breathed, "the one I've always wanted. Leaning over me, she licked me with her repulsive tongue.

One of the other ones pushed her away. "No, he's mine." Another, seething with anger, pushed them all away.

A shaft of light blinded my eyes for a moment, and I no longer saw any of the demons. I felt my body absorb their punches, as I listened to someone chant softly, "Flee vos hostilis creatura." I heard it again, more loudly and with authority. "Flee vos hostilis creatura. Leave, hostile creatures."

To my relief, the demons stopped punching. They had scared the heck out of me. I thought they were going to rip off my armor, yet they all had turned and were gaping with dread at a spinning object that looked like a mini-tornado. I watched it make contact with each one of them and spew them violently into the air. They cried out in anguish. Their body parts twisted and turned in ways–unimaginable—arms yanked back, legs bent in a way that would break a twig. Their necks twisted and spun around and around like a screw. When I scrambled to my feet, I saw Adonis. Like a tornado, he annihilated the demons.

Then the atmosphere turned gray and morbid. The wind whistled and another storm began.

"Put your hand on my shoulder," Adonis yelled. His voice screamed faint in the distance. I could only see his lips move in exaggerated motion. He tapped his shoulder vigorously; his dark hair blew wildly in the wind.

I grabbed his shoulder. We took off with unbelievable speed to a place where tormented humans hung captured in individual, transparent bubbles. The enraged look on their faces emanated from their inner selves. I didn't have time to reflect on it, as I sped to another place and time. I landed with Adonis in an area that looked like the Assembly I had attended in Arcis, but everyone there wore regular street clothes, not armor.

Finally, yanked through my phone, I landed back at Adonis's house, or more accurately, on his frayed burgundy futon. My head flew back against the top of it. My neck barely endured the powerful thrust caused by gravity.

My head ached and felt like I had finished a night of some serious partying. When I woke up, I saw the room spinning around me. A fan blew cool air onto my face.

"Lad are you okay?" I heard Adonis's concerned voice. I heard him again and again and again until it quit. My head throbbed like it never had before. Something or someone encouraged me to drink some nasty tasting liquid. Gradually, I felt more conscience and mildly aware of my surroundings.

"Am I dead?" I croaked.

Adonis chuckled. "No."

"What's wrong with me then?" I demanded. "I feel like I'm dying. The pain...the numbness."

"You took some hits in Arcis and traveled at mock speed to a variety of places. Your body's not used to such travel," Adonis said. "It's okay. I promise you'll be fine."

I fell back into a cavernous sleep and woke up much later. The traveling had left me with more questions for Adonis. After I ate the turkey sandwich he had set on the table in front of me, he came back in the room and sat down across from me. We began to talk.

"Let me see if I have this right," I said. "You must split into two and travel through your phone like me."

Adonis smiled, "Mate, I *am* a lord. I travel all right. I can be in four different places at one time. I'm *always* divided into two bodies, one in Arcis, one on Earth. I live in both places, simultaneously. I'm never in only one world. When you see me stumble and question me as to my sobriety, I'm not in two worlds, but typically in three or four."

"Awe-some," I said, nice and slow. "I've never heard about that."

"Most life players don't know."

"Is that where you took me—to *all* the worlds?"

Adonis nodded. "First, we traveled to Arcis, as I'm sure you already know. Then I took you to another world, but I can't reveal all the details about that world until you've been a life player longer. I *can* tell you that the entrapped humans you saw there are death players we've been lucky enough to catch. It's their bloody prison.

The next world we traveled to will be a secret for you until you've been a life player for at least one year. If your year's successful, you'll travel there to fight as well. Then we came home—back to Earth. I wanted you to experience all of that, so you realize how important it is for you to train with me. Are you willing to work hard?"

"Yes."

"Do you have any other questions?"

"Yeah…of course. How do you plan on training me?"

"I'll teach you every form of martial art I know. I'll instruct you in all the ways they fight in Arcis — with archery, slingshots, swords, cannons, catapults and more. Granted it is an old-fashioned way to fight, but," Adonis continued, "it is the only way to fulfill the old legends. I also want you to be present at the weekly Assemblies that take place on Earth, because they will give you great strength. But," he forewarned, "the Assemblies on Earth are different than the one you attended in Arcis."

I began to feel overwhelmed with school, work, and my duties as a life player. I rubbed my eyes and gazed up at the heavily locked door with all the dead bolts. "What's in there?" I asked. The curiosity had been killing me.

"I can't tell you now," Adonis said, looking leery.

"Julia…does she know all of this?"

Adonis grimaced in pain. He shook his head and looked like he chose his words carefully. "I've needed to protect Julia and her mother. That's one of the reasons why I'm here."

"Does Lisa know who you are?" I asked, incredulous.

Adonis nodded yes.

"That's wrong," I protested. "Julia should know! She's not a little kid anymore."

Adonis's face flashed in anger. "Julia has always been in grave danger. That hasn't changed."

"In danger from what?" I demanded, and walked threateningly toward him. "Tell me now."

Adonis snickered, swiped his leg behind my foot, and in one swift move had me on the floor. "Until I've trained you, don't bother trying to fight me lad. You'll lose."

"Don't you trust me?" I asked, through clenched teeth.

"Yes I do, or I wouldn't have told you so much."

"Then I want to know why you haven't told Julia and why she's in grave danger."

"You *do* care for her more than you're letting on, don't you?"

"Sure, but as a friend."

Adonis's voice dripped with sarcasm. "Right."

"Tell me about the locked door. I need to know," I changed the subject.

Adonis loosened his grip on me and let me up. "Fine, you win. I know you won't get off my back until I tell you. I know your kind."

Adonis went to the kitchen and searched through a drawer. He pulled out a large set of keys and flipped them over until his hand rested on one. He rubbed it for a moment and then walked to the bolted door. Strangely, he used only the one key to unlock every bolt, yet none of the locks appeared to be the same shape. The door creaked open. I eagerly headed for it. I never could have guessed its contents.

Adonis turned on a light. I blinked a few times, allowing my eyes to adjust to the room. I saw walls lined with shelves that meticulously held knives, tomahawks, axes, spears, swords, daggers, bows and arrows, rifles, machine guns, shot guns, and pistols. You name it. It was probably there. Weapons hung from the high ceiling. I didn't even know what some of them were.

"Are these yours?" I stared at Adonis.

He looked amused by my expression. "No," he said. "They belonged to Julia's father."

I was stunned. "Julia's father?"

"Yes."

"Why are there so many guns? How can they be his?"

"Life and death players are allowed to use guns on Earth."

"What do you mean? I...I've never heard that."

Adonis's face took on a somber expression. "Look...we need to talk more." Adonis and I left the room and sat back down in his living room. As soon as we were seated, Adonis began. "Julia's father is one of the most dangerous death players that has ever lived, and...Julia has a twin sister. I don't know if she's ever told you that or not."

"She has...but is her sister a death player?" I asked, and then explained to Adonis about the clone imaging I saw when I first bought my app, and how the girl looked exactly like Julia.

"It's possible you saw Jessica, Julia's sister, in the game. Sometimes Spero gives us the gift to see things others normally can't see. And Jessica does look exactly like Julia, but she's as evil as Julia is good. We also don't know where Jessica or their father lives now, but because of their hatred and rage, Julia and Lisa have always been in constant danger for as long as I've known them. Somehow Jessica and her father, Shamus, have gone undetected. We almost had them. That's why I have most of Shamus's weapons, but since that night—." Adonis sat and wouldn't say anymore.

"What night?" I implored.

"When Julia and Jessica were little, Shamus knew that Jessica would follow in his footsteps and that Julia would not. He tried to sacrifice Julia to Vorago and kill her, but his attempts were futile. Spero sent me to stop him. I was more powerful than Shamus, but not by much at the time.

Since then, my strength has grown, and Spero has given me more gifts, including being a lord. I *was* strong enough to confiscate most of Shamus's weapons, and now here they are, in my house...hidden where no one can touch or use them. If they did, terrible things would happen." Adonis told me this story, but he looked as if he was retelling himself, lost in his own thoughts.

"Adonis?" I asked, snapping my fingers in front of his face.

He blinked his eyes and smiled. "Sorry, I get a little carried away sometimes."

I thought about the man in the basilica and how it looked like he could see me. The life player that had given me the thumbs up came to mind also. I asked Adonis about it.

He told me, "If you've been given the gift to recognize players in the game, then, yes, it's possible for players to see you sometimes too, not always though."

I pointed to the locked door. "It's nothing personal, but that door sticks out like a bad song. How do you honestly expect people to come into your house and not notice it, and you only used one key to open every lock. Don't you think it'd be easy for someone to break in?"

Once more, Adonis smiled at me with patience. "Mate, the beauty of what we do, that of fighting evil, is that great miraculous things can and do happen."

Adonis turned and pointed to the bolted door. "No one can see that door but Julia, Lisa, selected life players, and me. Not a single death player or any other person can set their eyes on it, and you're the only life player I've ever allowed to enter my house. And, yes, the key *is* only one key, you're right about that, but watch." Adonis went over to the locks and put the key into one of them. He told me to move closer. As he put his key into every one of the locks, the key magically changed shape to fit each of them. "I'm the only one who can use this key It won't work for anyone else."

"No way," I breathed, "That's amazing...I'm the only life player that you've allowed in your house...and you showed me this? Why?"

Adonis continued his story. "Julia and her mother, among others, have some large role in helping the world achieve everlasting peace. They don't know it yet, and I'm not even sure what part they're going to play, but I know Shamus and Jessica want them both dead. They've been following us for years. That's why we've traveled from place to place and lived inconspicuously. Now we haven't heard from them or seen them. It's uncanny. Then strangely you come along. I know your mother knew Lisa from younger years, but you never played a big part in Julia's life. Yet, here you are, and Julia seems quite fond of you … plus you both happen to be the same age. I can't help but think you have an important link to her. I don't know what that link is, but…I trust you… like a son."

A smile crept across my face. It felt good to have someone think that highly of me. "Thanks, that means a lot to me."

"All right," Adonis said, "enough stories, you need to go study I believe."

"Yes, I do."

"When you're done studying, I want you to find Berard, and ask him to take you to the Assembly tonight. We meet in secret. You'll have time before you go to the bonfire."

"How did you know I was going to the bonfire?"

Adonis lowered his head. "I know many things. Let's leave it at that. I'll see you later."

He showed me to the front door. "Wait," I said, "my room…who was killed there? Who did it? Do you know?"

"Maybe," he responded. "I'm not positive. When I am, I'll let you know. Hold still for a moment. There's one more thing I need to do." Adonis stared at me with intense eyes. After that, he blew on me. His breath transformed into swirling specks that appeared like glowing, silver confetti. The specks floated in the air encircling me, until they hit me with immense warmth.

"What was that?"

"An early Christmas present. Usually learning martial arts takes years, but I just helped you. Now you'll be able to become a master in just a few months."

I thanked him for the amazing gift and knew we'd become great friends. Before I left, I thought about Lisa. "It's none of my business, but how do you feel about…Lisa?"

He choked before he answered. "My friend, I've made the life player's promise, a vow to live the life of a lord and player alone. Unless we win this battle, reach an era of peace, and my job is finished, I'll never know real love with any woman."

"Then you must love her already." I dared to say.

He laughed and glanced around the room. "Now you owe me. What *are* your true feelings for Julia?"

"I honestly don't know," I answered, without hesitation.

He nodded his head. "Fair enough."

As I was walked to my car, thinking about what Adonis had said, I bumped into Julia.

"Hey," she shouted.

I blinked, feeling absentminded. "Sorry," I said, and looked shyly away.

"Your head's in the clouds again, isn't it?" she asked, but I didn't respond. "I wish I understood you. I wish you'd let me in." I still didn't answer. "Forget it." Julia gave up and threw her arms in the air.

Our conversation broke up when one lonesome, tiny dove swooped down and flew near the top of Julia's head. I chuckled when it took a crap on her hair.

"What's so funny?" she demanded.

I walked over to Julia and began to wipe her hair. "That bird just relieved itself on you."

"Gross!"

"Don't worry. I think I can get most of it out," I said, as I gently cleaned it up. I saw her staring at me out of the corner of my eye.

The dove swooped back down at our heads with persistence. I threw my fist out to scare it away and accidentally slammed it to the ground.

Julia and I stooped over to look at it. "I think you killed it," Julia said, giving it a shove with her foot. She was right; it was dead. Julia went into her garage and came back with a shovel. I picked it up. We walked into Adonis's backyard and buried it.

My head began to ache in unbelievable pain. I clutched my forehead with my hand and groaned. Then a loud voice shouted, "Get her inside as quickly as you can".

"Did you hear that?" I asked Julia.

"Hear what?"

I heard it once more. "Run! Now!" A blustery gust of wind blew and rain began to sprinkle down. I put my hand on Julia's back and gently pushed her toward her house. She resisted me at first until black, menacing clouds rolled in. We ran to her house. As soon as we were in, the wind slammed the door shut behind us.

Lisa came up to us, startled. "Are you both okay? What happened?"

My hand was still holding onto Julia's arm. She shook it free. "Nothing Mom…we're fine. We were outside when the storm came in. Did you sleep well?"

Julia's mom wore her pink, terry cloth bathrobe and probably came home late in the night. I was surprised to see her. "Yes, I'm going back to sleep, though." Lisa glanced at me. "Make yourself at home, Bladen. I hope you don't mind me being rude, but I'm exhausted."

"No, you're not being rude. As soon as the wind dies down, I need to go anyway."

Lisa kissed me on the check and told me to come back for dinner another night. When she walked out of sight, Julia whispered, "How did you know to bring me inside *before* the wind blew?"

I cradled Julia's cheek with my hand. She grabbed it like she wanted to move it but then decided otherwise. The warmth of her touch sent a tingle down my spine. "I'm not sure," I replied. I thought to myself that we couldn't have been in danger, because I didn't see Berard, but I couldn't tell Julia *that*. We stood for a few moments in the foyer—without words, until the wind died down. I brushed my lips against Julia's cheek and said goodbye.

I sprinted to my car in the pouring rain and raced away. I drove too fast with my foot like a rock on the pedal, trying to escape my growing feelings for Julia. I knew deep in my heart I wanted to protect her—from her father I knew—from what else I wasn't sure.

I drove back to my room, feeling in awe that a courageous life player had died there, although it did creep me out. I glimpsed around, wondering what exactly had occurred, but I needed to study. I grabbed my books and darted off to the library to cram in some homework before the bonfire.

A song by Yiruma started to play on my car radio. Julia had said it was her favorite composer. The beautiful music matched her perfectly.

I arrived at the library and dove deep into my studies. I forgot everything and even lost track of time, until I heard someone clear their throat.

"Time to go."

I looked up and saw Berard. "How did you know where to find me?"

"Adonis," he whispered.

I smirked. "So, you knew about Adonis all along didn't you? You just didn't tell me."

He nodded, waved his hand, and urged me to follow him. I grabbed my books in haste and did what he asked. As soon as we went outside, Berard started to walk up into the air in a step-like fashion.

"What are you doing?"

Berard checked around. "Don't move yet, someone's watching you. No one can see me right now, but they *can* see you." I stopped as though I was waiting for something or someone. "Okay…now take your right leg and step up into the air."

I hesitated for a fraction of a second.

"Do it," he commanded.

I lifted my leg as he had requested. As soon as my foot landed on a step, a short staircase appeared that led to a long, yellow school bus. I ascended the stairs.

"You're okay now," Berard explained. "No one around you can see you anymore, except for all of us on the bus."

"Really? Nobody can see us? Can they see the bus?" I asked, intrigued.

"No, we're completely undetectable."

I entered the school bus and was caught by surprise when I glimpsed around.

DARKNESS WELCOMES

I sat in the front of the bus that was empty except for the bus driver, Berard, and me. Yeah that's right—empty! No big excitement here. I self-importantly sat back and stretched out my legs, even though they were still cramped in front of me. I folded my arms and stared at Berard, with my eyebrows raised. "So…dude…the bus is empty. Why was it so important for no one to see us?"

"You still have a lot to learn kid, don't you?"

"I've learned plenty."

"Well," Berard answered, sarcastically. "First you walked up in the air. I think if anyone saw that, they might freak. How's my English on that one? Second, if hundreds of life players are at an Assembly and death players catch wind of it, they bomb the Assembly and afterward go party, drink champagne, and celebrate because of the big win. Make sense?"

"Okay okay, I catch your drift," I said, sitting upright in my seat.

"You still have some things to learn, eh?"

I ignored him but knew he was right. "So, what's up with the big, yellow school bus? It reminds me of the Magic School Bus cartoon show my little sister watches on TV."

"The yellow school bus is to remind life players they're always learning, should remain humble, and stay focused. It's a chosen life of sacrifice."

I *did* wonder why we were the only ones on the bus, but I didn't feel like asking Berard any more questions.

The ride to the Assembly was quick. Berard and I eagerly stepped off the bus. I watched as the driver sped off.

We stood out in the middle of nowhere, high up on an area of land, overlooking Lake Champlain. The scenery was beautiful. The darkness from within a group of dense trees contrasted with the sunlit leaves on the outside. Lake Champlain shimmered in the backdrop. Only one house, a tan colonial, nearby could be seen, and whoever owned it was just now pulling their Toyota truck into the driveway.

"Hey dude, I just robbed your house," I yelled, to the man and woman when they stepped out onto their driveway.

Berard told me to stop being a jerk.

I laughed. "I'm not being a jerk. They can't hear me, and you told me no one could see us. I was just checkin' it out. It's pretty cool, actually."

Berard ignored me and walked over to a spot on the grass. He held his hand palm down just above the ground. "Aperio…open," he whispered. A covered opening in the grass appeared out of nowhere. It looked like the kind of door that belonged on a ceiling, leading to an attic. Berard walked over to it, pulled on the rusty handle, and descended the stairs. I followed. There was a musty, damp smell that penetrated my nose and caused me to sneeze.

At the bottom of the stairs, we came to another entrance and entered a most exquisite room. The walls were adorned with icons painted with startling detail. The images in them seemed real. I reached out and touched one, taken back by how pliable and warm it felt. The woman embracing a child in it stared at me with lustrous, smiling eyes. Goose bumps formed on the surface of my arms.

We entered another room, a large auditorium with seats and a stage. An enormous, golden box was placed in the middle of the platform. A man wearing the same cloak I had seen in Arcis paced back and forth on stage. I would've bet money it was Adonis.

"Hey, how are you? I recognize you from chemistry class." A familiar voice from behind me interrupted my thoughts.

I spun around and saw Anthony in front of me with a wide, hospitable grin. "Hey," I greeted him with uncertainty, "why are you here?" I remembered that in class, Anthony was anything but friendly.

"I'm a life player too, of course," Anthony explained. "C'mon let's sit down." Anthony told me he wasn't friendly in class or on campus because he didn't want to draw attention to himself. He was a serious life player who understood the dangers of being exposed and had no idea that I was also chosen to play in the game.

Berard came and sat with us. "Quiet," he whispered, "we're about to begin."

I thought I saw Gregory, the guy I met in Arcis, from a distance. He stood against the wall by himself. I wanted to say hello. I told Berard and Anthony I'd be right back. When I approached Gregory, we slapped high-fives. It was a little hard for us to recognize each other, since we had been wearing our cloaks in Arcis. I asked him why he wasn't sitting, since there were so many empty seats. Gregory had been to several Assemblies on Earth and knew what to expect. He explained: "My friend, this auditorium is full. There are hundreds of life players here. You can only see life players that you've met or seen before. If you think it's empty, then that tells me you haven't encountered many players, yet."

"Seriously?" I asked.

He nodded. I watched him greet other life players I couldn't see. Now I understood why Adonis had told me Assemblies on Earth were not the same as the ones in Arcis.

"What's with the golden box on the stage?" I asked.

"If you open the door, you can see what's going on in Arcis," Gregory explained.

"Cool," I said, then felt pain as my head hit against a metal object behind me. When I turned, I saw a silver, metallic sword hanging from the wall with a number of engravings etched into it. The engravings formed a language I couldn't understand. I lightly traced my fingers over them and then felt my body change, readying itself to biplace and enter the game.

I was sucked again like dirt through a vacuum into my phone, and while one of me stood next to Gregory, the other me landed in front of the basilica, yet again. This time the courtyard shone bright like daytime. Not a soul could be seen. I dared to walk into the center of the courtyard.

"Hello," I yelled. My voice echoed back. I hoped this would be my opportunity to win my third level.

Adonis crept up next to me from out of the shadows. I wanted to ask him about the voice I'd heard in my head near Julia's house. When I opened my mouth to speak, he put his fingers to his lips and said, "Don't say a word, just focus most of your attention here, not on Earth. You're going to need all your strength."

After a few moments, a massive black stallion with huge wings galloped up to me. The man sitting on top was the same man I'd seen when I first met Berard. His long, night-black hair blew slightly from a soft breeze—a breeze I couldn't feel myself. His penetrating, raven eyes peered at me briefly, before he began to talk to Adonis in a language I couldn't comprehend.

I knew it was Vorago, and because I knew of his merciless reputation, I was astounded by his striking good looks. Not that I'm into checking out other guys, but if I didn't know of him, I would have thought he was humane and respectable. I should've wanted to tear him to shreds and squeeze his throat, but I couldn't move. He mesmerized me.

After the two finished their conversation, Adonis said, "Have a crack at him. If he agrees, he's yours."

I couldn't believe it. It sounded like Adonis had offered me to Vorago. Vorago spun around on his horse and trotted closer to me. "Hello my friend," he said in a voice laden with honey. "I'm here at this moment to graciously ask you to come and follow me. Close your eyes for a few moments, and I'll show you all that you may possess and all that you could aspire to, if you join me."

My eyes closed, forcibly. I had no control over them. At first, I saw nothing but gray. Then I watched myself like I was an actor on a movie screen. I was playing baseball in my backyard with ten-year-old Nicholas, my brother, and the neighborhood kids.

I was up to bat with two strikes and two balls. "No batter, no batter, no batter," the kids on the opposite team screamed. The pitcher, a huge, fat kid, wearing an undersized blue T-shirt wound his arm up and threw the ball. He looked at me with cruelty. "You're a geek, Bladen."

I shot the kid back a glare and stuck my tongue out at him. The kid threw the ball. I swung at it but missed. The kid yelled, "THREE STRIKES."

"YOU"RE OUT!" The other kids hollered and then chanted, "Bladen is a loser, Bladen is a loser."

I ran home crying. Nicholas, who always felt bad for me, ran after me.

I still had my eyes closed, when I heard Vorago's voice inside my head promising, "You were nothing. I can make you something." I tried to rip my eyes open, but they were sealed shut like they had been lined with super glue. Then I saw myself in a mansion with super hot girls surrounding me, a red Porsche outside, a closet full of expensive clothes, autographed pictures of me with sports legends hanging on every wall, and a private jet that would take me *anywhere* in the world. Vorago's gentle voice continued, "This *and so much more* than you can ever imagine will be yours, if you join me. And so much more, so much more" he carried on in a sing-song way. I shook my head and tried my hardest to tear open my eyes but still couldn't. I saw a beautiful seashore and an enormous yacht. "And this too could be yours," he announced with the excitement in his voice as a game-show host.

I fell to the ground on my knees and clutched at my eyes, trying to break them open. "No!" I screamed. My imprisoned voice finally released. I felt bathed in his wickedness. "I will *never* join you!"

"Suit yourself," Vorago said through gritted teeth. I unlocked my eyes and saw him in front of me, his face fueled with anger. His hair flew wildly in the wind and altered into vipers. His stallion reared up and roared like a lion. His tongue transformed into a lizard's that flashed in and out of his mouth several times.

Not so good looking anymore, I thought sarcastically. He swore at me with rage, spun around on his horse, and charged off.

"Destroy him!" he ordered without looking back and before his stallion flew up into the sky.

The demons with Medusa hair and beady eyes came out to fight us again. This time I felt more prepared for them. When the demons charged toward me, I hit one of them directly in the chest with the heel of my foot and knocked the wind out of it. I watched sadistically as it hit the dirt. Its holes for a nose made a raspy sound. I rolled out my cable and wrapped it around the demon. I threw it into the abyss, which was at least five hundred feet away. I felt breathless with my new strength, thanks to Adonis.

The next one came at me. I kicked its head and watched its pathetic thing for a mouth wince in pain. I struck its chest with my fists, right then left, pummeling it down to the ground. I wound it with the cable and threw it into the abyss. I struggled this way for what seemed like a couple of hours. This time I fought alone, though, without Adonis.

One last demon charged at me. Its snakes for hair screamed obscenities at me, until it's head altered into that of Julia's. The clone imaging technique didn't throw me off. It made me fight harder. I struck it down, hitting it repeatedly in the face. It grimaced in agony, with a pathetic, deep sounding moan.

Before I could think, I traveled through my phone back into one person again, still attending the earthly Assembly. Only a little while had gone by with Adonis still speaking on stage. "It's time to eat. Come and share the supper," Adonis waved his hands toward the food, proud to feed us. I gathered our mouths were fed at the Assemblies on Earth in the same way as in Arcis. We all walked up to the stage, ate, and drank a sip of liquid from an extraordinary golden chalice. Then it was time to leave.

Berard came and found me. We entered the school bus that had more life players on it than I had first presumed. The bus dropped me off by my car in the library parking lot, and I drove back to my dorm and entered my room.

Robby was jamming to tunes, getting ready to go to the bonfire downtown. He turned down the music and asked, "Dude, good to see you. You're barely around. You going to the blazing fire?"

"Yeah," I said. "Wanna go together?"

He came over and put his hand on my shoulder. "Normally you know I'd want to go with you, but tonight I have a date. You know, duty calls."

"A date with who?"

"Oh come on, can't you guess?"

"Kaitland," I answered, with one word.

"That's right, bro. I'll see you there," he said, and splashed on a little aftershave and darted out the door.

I took my time getting ready and couldn't believe I planned to go by myself, yet Julia had a date. The thought of showing up alone made me feel stupid, but I continued anyway.

I drove down to the bonfire, parked my car, and strolled down to the group on the beach. Music played from a car stereo, while the murmur of indistinguishable conversation and the occasional roar of laughter filtered through. At first, I didn't see anyone I knew. After a few moments, I saw Robby with Kaitland and her friends next to the booming fire. I joined them, and we all talked and joked about nothing in particular. I glanced across the fire and drew in my breath…Julia. My breathing quickened, and I figured I probably had a goofy smile on my face. Robby elbowed me awake and laughed as he saw me staring at Julia. I didn't care. I wouldn't have cared, even if he caught me drooling. I'd stare all the more at her.

She looked shy as she talked with her date, a medium-sized guy with brown hair, wearing a green parka and blue jeans. She glanced up at me and waved. I wanted to bug her and say hello to her date, but I didn't have time. My fantasy bubble burst.

Angelina came up to me with her hypnotizing skills and drew me toward her like a magnet. I felt like a half-dead carcass, trying to pull away. I was sure my facial expression was screaming, no!

Instead of spending even a fraction of a second with Angelina, I decided to leave. I yanked myself away from her and told Robby I had to split. His disappointment showed, but he thought maybe we could all meet up later in our room. I agreed.

Almost halfway to my car, Angelina sauntered up next to me again. "Can you give me a lift?" She asked, her voice sweet as honey. It reminded me a little of Vorago's. She used whatever magic she possessed to draw me closer to her. Our faces moved together, and she slipped her arm tightly around my waist. I glimpsed back, surprised to see Julia still watching me. I couldn't withstand Angelina's power, though.

"Of course," I drawled like a ladies' man, placing my arm around Angelina's shoulder.

"Oh, a Saab," she cooed. "One of my favorite cars."

I drove her to her dorm. After I parked, I turned off the ignition. "There you go see ya," I said real quick, hoping she'd hurry up and get out, but she lured me to her again. I couldn't figure out how she had the power to reel me in like a fish. Our faces almost met in a kiss, but I had the strength to pull back the slightest bit.

"How can you resist me," she murmured, "when most guys can't? Why can you?" Her eyes probed mine deeply as if trying to hunt down the answer.

I summoned every bit of strength I had to break her spell and blurted out, "I don't know what strange power you have, but I don't want to be here with you Angelina. Please leave me alone." She looked shocked and hurt and turned away. "I'm sorry," I continued. "I don't mean to be unkind, but I barely know you, and the way you act is…well…kind of weird."

"I...I get it." She opened the door and stepped out with her head held high. She tossed her hair back and pretended like she didn't care. I felt terrible driving back to my dorm. But what was I supposed to do? I didn't feel like kissing some psycho girl no matter how beautiful she was.

I needed to study for chemistry the next day, anyway. The professor had said we were going to have a quiz on Monday, and I wasn't ready. Lousy grades came easy for me. If I didn't work hard, the big, fat D or F in red on my papers didn't exactly make my day. So I immersed myself in my pile of chemistry notes for quite some time and didn't notice the soft tap at my door, until it became a BANG.

I stood up, opened the door, and to my pleasant amazement, it was Julia. "Um...what are you doing here?" I asked. "I thought you were on a date."

"Can I come in?" Her cheeks were flushed cherry red from the cool September air.

I moved aside and held the door open wider. "Sure. Are you going to tell me why you're here? Are you okay?" I was beginning to sense something was wrong.

She sat down on a chair. "I asked my date to drive me here."

I couldn't help but grin. "Do you mind if I ask why?"

"My date Josh was a jerk, too touchy, you know. I told him I wanted to leave."

"Uh...Okay." We sat for a few moments in uncomfortable silence. I couldn't wipe the smirk off my face.

"What happened to the girl you were with?" Julia asked me. "You know—the dark haired, incredibly gorgeous one?"

It clicked for me then. Julia came here because she saw me with Angelina and must have been curious. "She asked me for a ride home. I gave her one."

"That's all?" Julia asked. "It looked like there was more to it than that."

"You sound jealous," I had to say.

"No," She said, as she nervously pulled her hair on top of her head.

"So...how're you getting home?" I asked, certain I sounded amused by now.

"I was kind of hoping you'd be here to give me a ride." Julia twirled her hair around her index finger.

I was increasingly enjoying the moment. "What if I wasn't here?"

"Then I would've taken a taxi," she retorted, yanking her hand away from her hair.

We were interrupted when Robby, Kaitland, and their friends bounded in. "Dude, it's awesome you're here. You guys wanna party?"

"I was just leaving. Sorry." Julia faked a smile.

"Do you want me to take you home now?" I whispered to Julia.

"You don't have to. I didn't mean to put you in an awkward position," she whispered back.

"I don't mind, I promise." Are you kidding, I thought, psyched.

We told Robby and his friends goodbye and walked to my car. Julia remained quiet the entire ride to her house, as usual. I wondered what it was about riding in my car that almost always made her silent. I didn't dare ask her—guess the answer scared me a little. Maybe she didn't feel like talking to me. Maybe she didn't think I was cool enough. What was I thinking? Ideas that sucked, so I pushed them out of my mind.

When I pulled into her driveway, she placed her hand on top of mine and asked me if I wanted to come in. A wave of electricity pulsed through every nerve in my body. My face flushed. Maybe she does think I'm cool, I thought. I *did* hesitate at first but then agreed to follow her inside. What guy wouldn't? For a guy who's typically a klutz with girls, I was having a pretty good night.

Her house was dark except for the outside light. She pulled out a key and unlocked the door. We both found our way into her kitchen. She turned the light on and asked me what I wanted to do.

"Where's your mom?" I asked, looking around. "I thought she might be here."

"No, she's in New Hampshire this week. She leaves on Sundays when she works in that branch. Do you want to make some popcorn and watch a movie?"

"Score," I muttered under my breath.

Julia glanced at me shyly but said nothing. She took out the popcorn popper, bowl, and butter. I melted the butter in the microwave and dumped it on the popcorn when it was done. Neither one of us spoke, though I felt the sizzling voltage between us. I couldn't help but notice how pretty Julia looked, her lips soft and inviting.

We both grabbed our popcorn and a cola out of the fridge and sat on the couch. Julia rummaged through the DVDs near their big screen TV. "What kind of movie do you feel like watching?"

I was curious as to what Julia liked. "Anything you want. Surprise me. How 'bout you put in your all-time favorite?"

While Julia was getting the movie ready, I sat on the couch and opened my cola. It spilled over onto the carpeting and made a small mess. I rubbed it up with my foot. Julia went into the kitchen and came back with a dishcloth in her hand. I shrugged.

"Here, let me help you." When she bent over to wipe up the soda for me, her hair cradled beautifully around her face. I sat back down on the couch and stretched out my left leg. Julia didn't notice and tripped over my sneaker after she stood up. I reached out to stop her from falling. I held my hands around her waist and pulled her toward me. She ended up half on me and half on the couch—go figure. Luck was on my side again. I brushed her hair out of her face.

"Sorry," she whispered. I felt her breath on my face.

"It's okay," I said. Neither one of us moved. I stared at her face and glanced at her lips. She let out an uneasy laugh and stood up. She straightened her shirt as she moved off my lap. Bummer, I thought.

Julia put the DVD into the player and started the movie. I brought the dirty dishtowel back to the kitchen and placed it in the sink. I ran my fingers through my hair, feeling anxious, wanting to talk to Julia rather than watch a movie. Yeah, right. Just talk. I wanted to do more than that. I mustered up the courage to tell her what I wanted—the talking part, of course, not the part where I was dying to see how her lips would feel on mine.

"Um, Julia...do you want to just hang out instead of watching a movie? I'd rather talk, how about you?"

"Y...yeah sure."

"Are you disappointed? Because if you are, we can still watch a movie or play a game," I said. I found her nervousness *really* attractive.

She shook her head. "It's just that," she started to say, "what kind of game do you want to play? We got rid of most of our games long ago. It's not that fun playing them alone."

"I'm sure we can think of something," I answered, hoping she didn't mean a board game.

Julia's eyes widened; a smile formed on the corners of her lips. "We could play the questions game. It's something I've always played with Adonis and my mom."

"The questions game...what's that?"

Julia revealed a broad grin and cute giggle. "That's exactly it. You just asked me one question, and I'm answering it. Then I get to ask you one question in return. The game continues that way, but if one of us asks a question the other one doesn't want to answer, then you still have to answer indirectly. Does that make sense?"

"Yeah sure, but how do you win the game?"

"There's no winner. It's just for fun to help us get to know each other better."

"Is that why you played with Adonis and your mom, so you could all get to know each other better?"

Julia laughed. "No, that was their way of being nosy about my life. I didn't always tell them much. Besides, you're cheating. You asked me three questions already. Now it's definitely my turn."

Julia sat on the couch next to me, twirling her hair with her finger—an adorable habit I kept noticing. After a few seconds, she lifted her head. She flipped her hair out of her face and asked me her first question.

FIRST KISS

"Okay here goes." Julia tilted her head to the side. "Do you like that beautiful girl you gave a ride home?"

"Angelina?" I choked on my soda. "Are you kidding?"

"Uh, no you can't ask me a question in return. That's not how the game works. You have to answer my question. If my question made you uncomfortable, you can answer it in a different way—remember? It doesn't have to be answered directly."

I stared at Julia, disbelieving. "I don't know Angelina that well. I gave her a ride home. Why are you so curious about her?" I was really thinking, Lighten up on the rules will you.

Julia sat, her face expressionless. "I'm curious because I want to know if you like her, or are you attracted to her? That's not the first time I've seen her close to you, and I'm a girl, so believe me, the look on her face when she sees you screams total attraction."

I laughed, surprised again by Julia's choice of bold statements, until I noticed a wave of hurt pass across her face. "I'm sorry," I said. "I wasn't expecting such personal questions. I thought you might start with…let's see…a question like what's your favorite color? Why are you so serious about this? It's just a game, right?" I brushed a few strands of hair away from her face.

Julia pulled away defensively. "That's okay we don't have to play."

"No no—I want to play," I insisted. "I have to answer the question, but I don't have to go into detail, so to answer your last question…no. I'm not attracted to her. Now it's my turn. Are you attracted to Josh?" I figured, if she could ask me, I could ask her.

"No," she answered, looking pretty darn happy I asked. "My turn… would you want to go out on a date with Angelina?"

I found Julia's jealousy flattering. "Look, how about we go into a little more detail, so this particular conversation doesn't drag on."

"Okay, but you still need to answer my question," she reminded me.

I ran my fingers through my hair. "No, I wouldn't want to go out with Angelina on a date. Honestly, I realize she's good-looking, and I've noticed heads turn when she walks into a room. Something about her bothers me, though. Besides, I could only be attracted to someone who's nice, not just beautiful. There are a lot of things that attract people to each other, not just their looks."

Julia stared at me for a couple of seconds, looking a little surprised by what I said. That's when I thought, Oh crap. She probably thinks I find her ugly. Trust me, I have sisters. I know well enough *never* to call a girl ugly or anything remotely close. That was like an instant death sentence. I ignored it and asked my next question. "Now let's see…my turn…why did you go out with Josh?"

I couldn't tell what Julia was thinking at this point, but she leaned back and looked more relaxed. She moved her body sideways, closer to me.

I thought my heart was going to pound right out of my chest. I slowly brushed my fingertip along her forearm. She smiled and took in a deep breath.

"I told you before, Adonis doesn't let most people get near me, but for some reason, recently, he told me I could date if I wanted to. Josh asked me to the bonfire. I said yes, and he turned out to be a jerk."

I leaned against the couch and sat like Julia, just opposite her, our faces only about one foot apart. "Why was he a jerk?" I broke the rules of the game by asking another question in what I thought was a soft, sexy voice. You have to give me some credit. I wasn't Robby, but I was trying *real* hard.

"That's two questions," Julia counted, "and it doesn't matter anyway, forget it. I don't want to go out with him again." Julia moved her head closer to mine.

Okay almost there, I thought as Julia asked her next question. "Have you been out with anyone on a date since we started school?"

This time *I* moved my face toward hers, and now our lips were only a few inches apart. I felt Julia's breath on my face. "I haven't asked anyone out on a date in months," I answered, in a low voice. "You seem to be very interested in my love life though."

Julia smiled, took my hand into hers, and put it over her heart. "Can you feel how fast my heart's beating?" She laughed, softly.

"Yeah, I like the way it feels," I said, "but it's my turn for a question." I knew what I wanted to ask her, but my brain felt jumbled. Every ounce of blood pulsated inside my veins with the heat I felt between us. I began to trace her lips with my finger. They were the perfect shape and rose color. They looked moist and inviting. Julia breathed in and looked eager like me to have our bodies so close. "My next question is...do you want me to kiss you?" My body shuddered.

"Yes," Julia murmured, closing her eyes.

I took her face into my hands and gently placed my lips on top of hers. Her lips felt soft, wet, and incredible. At first our warm lips moved slowly, until I felt like the soda inside of a shaken can, bursting to get out, feelings unleashed. She placed her hands at the nape of my neck and entwined her fingers through my hair. I tilted my body back on the couch. She pressed her body into mine. I guess kissing someone I liked so much came naturally. I felt like a pro. We kissed like that for a long time. Then I brushed my lips down the side of her neck, and my hands tightened around her waist, until I felt her hesitate. I moved my face back away from hers. Our breathing sounded erratic, like we'd just come back from a long run.

"Are you okay?" I asked.

"Yeah, why?"

I moved back on the couch and pulled my hands from around her waist. "You seemed fine…now…uncertain."

Julia stood up and turned toward the kitchen. "I just need a glass of water. Do you want one?"

"No thanks," I answered, disappointed.

Julia took her time filling up her drink then sauntered back into the living room. Her glass clinked when she placed it on the table, before she sat back down.

"Let's see," she said, "I have a new question."

"Technically, it's my turn," I interrupted her.

"No you're wrong, it's mine," she insisted.

"You asked me if I wanted a glass of water. That was the last question, but I'll be a gentleman and let you have a turn, anyway," I teased.

"Thanks because I really do want to ask the next question."

"What do you want to ask me?" I murmured, our faces inches apart again.

"How do you feel about me?" she asked, and then looked timidly away.

I held my hand under her chin and turned her face back to mine. "I think it's kind of obvious."

"No, I need to hear it." She turned away a second time.

"Look at me, and I'll tell you." She brought her gaze slowly back toward mine. I shifted my body, allowing more space between us and took a deep breath. "I think you're amazing…what I mean is…when I talked about being attracted to someone…whose beauty's more than skin deep, I was thinking of you."

"So you don't think I'm *that* pretty." She looked ripped.

"No no, I meant—" Julia shoved me away and dumped half her water in my lap on purpose. "What the…Julia!" I couldn't believe she did that.

"I should've known you'd be a jerk too."

See, I told you about girls and looks. Man, was *I* in trouble. "Julia. Hold up. I think you're hot all right? I meant you're nice *and* hot, not just nice."

Julia stopped and stared at me. She let out an uneasy giggle. "You *do* think I'm pretty then?"

"No, I think you're beautiful."

"Sorry," she laughed again, before taking a sip from her water glass.

"My turn for a question. How do you feel about me?" I asked, mocking her.

She smirked at me before she began. "You're a nice guy," she answered, nonchalantly, twirling her hair with her finger.

"That answer won't do," I scoffed. I took the rest of the water in her glass and dumped it on her.

Julia shrieked. "Okay, you're hot and nice too!"

"Yeah, that's better. Now we're even."

We made out for a while after that, our lips felt like they were made for each other. I felt like I could easily fall in love with her. And it was a much better feeling than my obsession for my phone. It was getting late, though, almost midnight, and I wanted to be rested for my chemistry quiz. Julia begged me to stay for some of the movie. I liked the begging, *a lot*, so I stayed.

"Popcorn?" she asked, handing me the bowl. She started the movie and sat down.

"Thanks…what movie are we watching, and what's it about?"

"The movie's called Becoming Jane. Have you seen it?"

"No."

Julia finished chewing her bite of popcorn. "You've heard of Jane Austin, right?"

"Yeah, I had to read Pride and Prejudice in high school. It wasn't my favorite book. I'm not into romance novels."

"This movie's about Jane Austin's life as an author. Her life's as interesting as her books, I think."

"How so?"

The movie was just starting. Julia paused it to answer my question. "She fell in love with someone she inevitably couldn't have."

"That sounds depressing. Are you sure it's good?"

"Yeah," she sighed.

I started to watch the film, munch on some popcorn, and gulp down my soda. I rested my head on the back of the couch. Julia's head leaned against my arm. The flowery scent of her hair and perfume flooded my nose–in a good way. Unaware of how drained I felt, I fell into another turbulent sleep and barely watched any of the movie.

I wasn't sure if it was a dream or if I was pulled into my phone for the game, but I found myself walking along the beach near Gianna's house. The protective plexiglas cover that kept her safe from the demons surrounded me. The heat that generated from it warmed me. Feeling dead tired, I sat on a plush coach loaded with pillows. Gianna walked toward me, her dark hair flowing in the breeze. Her smile grew wider as she came nearer.

Neither of us said a word. She leaned over me. Her hands embraced my face, as she stared intensely into my eyes. She nodded her head. Her eyes beamed when she used her gift of sight. But then she shook her head, and sadness crept into her eyes.

I woke up, disoriented, with something heavy on my chest. I fumbled around in the dark. I had forgotten where I was. When I reached down, I grabbed onto a handful of hair. What? I thought. Where am I? Still groggy, I rubbed my eyes and remembered...Julia. She was asleep on my chest. A blanket was covering both of us.

The room was quiet and shadowy. I pressed the light on my watch to check the time—3:08 a.m. I couldn't believe I fell asleep. Panic gripped me when I thought for sure Adonis would be ripped at me if he found out. I slid out from under Julia, carefully placing her head on one of the couch pillows. I adjusted the blanket to make sure she stayed warm. I wondered if I should stay or go. I sat on a chair and rested my legs on the accompanying ottoman. I thought about this new dream and wondered if Gianna was trying to send me a message from Arcis. I felt too tired to care and soon fell dead asleep again.

All too soon, my alarm went off. I shut it off right away so as not to awaken Julia. I stood up, crept to the kitchen, and opened the refrigerator. At the same time, my stomach grumbled. The packed fridge indicated that Lisa had probably shopped over the weekend. She knew how infrequently Julia would stop at the supermarket for herself. The sight of eggs, bread, and butter on the shelf in front of me made my mouth water. I took them out, along with the gallon of 1% milk from the bottom shelf and set them on the counter. I found a large frying pan in the cupboard above the stove. After I cooked my food, I wolfed it down in a hurry to get to class. I left a plate of food for Julia and cleaned up my mess, including any dishes. I found a yellow, sticky note pad and black pen. "Enjoy your breakfast," I wrote and left it beside the plate.

As I walked toward the door, I couldn't help but tiptoe near Julia. I caught a glimpse of her asleep and noted the peaceful expression across her *deeply tanned* skin. I wished I could brush the few strands of golden hair away that were resting across her lips. I sighed and reluctantly walked out the door, gently closing it behind me.

When I walked into Chemistry class, I noticed Anthony with his usual antisocial glare that I now understood and had grown accustomed to.

The class began to fill up. The professor, a fairly young man in his thirties, wore another bow tie attached to his jade-colored, button-down shirt and tan slacks. He started to pass out our quiz papers.

My hands were sweaty. Tests and quizzes had that affect on me. I could always envision those big, red D's and F's, even if I didn't get one. Once I saw today's quiz, however, I realized I'd studied enough and finished rather quickly. Yeah, one for the good guy, I thought. After the professor droned on about balancing equations, he let the class go. I sprang out of my seat and headed for the door.

I had pre-calculus next, which I enjoyed more than chemistry. I had a hard time paying attention. My mind kept wandering back to Julia—her smell, her taste—the way she looked when she threw her head back to get her hair out of her face. Just thinking about her made me feel confused. As my thoughts continued to creep back to Julia, it finally dawned on me—the realization of my choices in life. I could choose Julia and skip my role as a life player, but if I continued as a life player, it would be hard to date Julia—kind of like Spider man trying to date M.J.

When I finished my classes for the day, I went back to my room to study and send messages to my parents and Nicholas on Facebook. Neither of them were available to chat, so I left them messages in their inbox, making sure my note for my parents was sort of grammatically correct.

> "Hey Mom and Dad,
>
> School's great, and everything's going well. Talk to you when I come home for our yearly hike to Little Rock Pond. Tell all my little buddies I miss them.
>
> Love,
>
> Bladen"

I didn't have much to say to my brother.

> "Hey Nick, how's Steph?"

I didn't have to work in the afternoon, so I took advantage of the time to study, feeling good about staying on top of what I had learned so far. I turned my phone on vibrate just in case someone called—you know who—but nobody did.

Later Robby came in. "Dude, good to see you."

"You too," I said, and threw a pillow at him. We took a few minutes to catch up. He'd been hanging out *a lot* with Kaitland, her friends Brooke and Alicia, and Jared. He hoped to have a guys' weekend at his house in a few weeks with Jared and I. Normally I worked on the weekends and had to make sure I found someone to cover for me.

Even though Robby sidetracked me, I waited in anticipation to see if Julia would call, and as fate would have it, she did. My phone vibrated. The caller I.D. announced Simms. My out-of-control heart sped up. I hoped Julia didn't regret our night together.

"Hello," I answered.

Julia's apprehension resounded on the other end. "Hi…um…Bladen?"

"Obviously," I teased. "Who else would answer my phone?"

"Um…" she said, with such increasing nervousness. It made me wish I could hug her to let her know everything was okay. I understood her awkwardness, something I had often felt myself.

"Do you have to work tonight?" she asked. I envisioned her twirling her hair.

"No."

"Well…do you want to study together?"

I had already studied, but I wasn't about to say no. "Sure, do you want to meet at the library?" I knew we could've met at her house, but I wasn't sure how she'd feel about it.

"Yeah, does three work for you?" she asked, breathing a sigh of relief.

"Sounds good. See you then," I answered, and hung up the phone.

Wanting to look good, I went and took a fast shower and threw on a pair of blue jeans—my favorite. The outside temperature was cool, so I wore a long-sleeve, dark-blue T-shirt.

Robby caught me as I dabbed on cologne. "Whew, what's the smell, bro? You tryin' to attract one babe or a whole litter of 'em?"

"Funny," I said, shaking my head.

"Oh, I get," Robby didn't let up, "you're trying to make her jealous aren't you? You know, using the smell to get the other hotties to check you out, like the animal kingdom."

I laughed, grabbed Robby's arm, and twisted it behind his back. I carefully shoved his face up against the wall so as not to hurt him. "Whoa, man. I didn't know you had strength like that. Where'd you learn how to do that?"

I saw Berard flash around and figured my display of strength made him angry. I made sure he saw me glare at him. Otherwise, I ignored him. I let Robby go, and told him I guess it was just luck. He didn't believe me, but he dropped it.

At three, I waited in front of the library. I didn't want it to be difficult for Julia to find me. I was sitting on the front stairs, when I saw her blonde hair, radiant in the sunlight. She wore tight, blue-jeans and a dark-blue sweater. Funny, I thought, the colors she chose match mine.

She waltzed up to me and saw the similarities in our choice of clothing right away. "Uh, wow...we look like twins."

"Yeah, real cute" I laughed. "You ready to study?"

She fiddled with her hair, still uncertain how to behave around me, and I have to admit, I felt the same way—butterflies in my stomach.

We stepped inside the building and sat in my favorite place—a spot right beside a window on the second floor, behind a bookshelf. It was so hidden, even the janitor skipped cleaning there. The windows by our table were smudged with dirt and the bookshelves were tainted with dust.

We took out our books and pored over them without talking. Meanwhile, I was tapping the table with my finger.

"You're being kind of noisy," Julia said.

"Sorry," I said, and stopped.

Julia leaned toward me and went on, "Thanks for breakfast, by the way, it was delicious."

"I'm glad you liked it," I said, thrilled she had mentioned it.

That broke the ice.

We both talked more at ease after that. In between our attempt to study, we discussed everything from the weather, to which class we hated the most, who was our favorite author, and our favorite music, until Julia asked me to be quiet. She placed her finger across her lips, rolled her eyes, and pointed just behind me. I turned around and saw Josh, Julia's date from the night before.

"Hide me," she mouthed, her voice almost inaudible. My attempt to block her didn't work. Josh bounded up next to her. I wondered how he had found her.

"Hi, Julia. Can I talk to you for a sec?" Josh asked, in a brusque tone, glancing my way briefly.

"Sure," she answered, halfheartedly.

He took her by the arm and led her behind one of the bookcases. I moved my body closer to them to listen.

"No!" Julia responded, to something Josh had asked.

"I don't take no for an answer," he spat.

"Ow," Julia cried.

"Julia are you okay?" I asked, walking behind the bookcase–my hands gripped into fists ready to take care of him if necessary.

Julia's face looked like she was about to burst into tears, but she nodded her head.

I glared at Josh. "Why did you tell Julia you wouldn't take no for an answer? Did you threaten her?"

"It's none of your business. Get lost!" I turned away briefly, shook my head in disbelief, and turned back to put my face in his. "You and me outside, now!" I said in a husky voice.

"Let's go."

I almost laughed to myself as I followed the idiot outside. Humorously, when we exited the library and descended the stairs, he spun around and dove toward me. I stepped aside and watched him take a face plant into the cement sidewalk. He sprang up and reached for my face. I grabbed a fistful of his sweatshirt around his neck and held him up in the air with a single hand. I strolled over to the nearest maple tree and shoved his body hard against it.

"Ugh," he grunted, the wind knocked out of him. "Put me down!" His garbled words spilled out of his mouth.

Berard began his usual flash routine. I ignored it again. I knew he'd be ripped at me the next time I saw him, but at the moment I didn't care. I wanted to scare the heck out of this idiot for upsetting Julia.

"You get near her again, and you'll regret it," I threatened under my breath, shoving him harder into the tree.

Julia screamed at me to stop, her voice filled with alarm. I let go of his writhing body and watched him drop to the ground and sprint away. I felt satisfied when he continued to glance back in fear.

A small group of students that witnessed the commotion gathered around us. I pushed passed them and took Julia by the elbow. We strode back into the library to pick up our books, as quickly as we could. Without talking, we strode to my car and ignored the students that were still hanging around outside.

"Get in," I ordered, when we neared my Saab.

She made an exasperated sound and climbed into her seat. I stared at her with fiery eyes. "Okay, what happened between you and Josh? Did he hurt you? I want some answers."

TRUTH AND TEARS

Julia stared angry and stone-faced out her passenger door window. "I don't want to talk about it. It's embarrassing. And what right do *you* have telling me to get in *your* car? I can get in my own car and drive home. Besides, *you're* not normal. How did you lift Josh up like that?"

My teeth were still clenched, but I softened my voice. "Julia, that guy threatened you. That's more important to me."

"I can take care of myself," she muttered.

I threw up my hands. "Whatever. You don't have to tell me, but I'd like to help."

Julia didn't seem to want to fight. "It's not that...he wouldn't keep his hands off me on our date, and he kept pressuring me to have sex with him."

"What?" I bellowed angrily, but then quieted my tone. "I'm so sorry. Are you okay? Did he hurt you?"

"He didn't hurt me at the bonfire, but he grabbed my wrist and twisted it hard just now at the library."

"So when he said he wouldn't take no for an answer back there, did he mean sex?"

Julia nodded.

"Okay...that's totally frickin illegal, Julia. You need to report this." I wanted to scream some choice words, but not in front of her.

She gaped at me with innocent eyes, her arms wrapped around herself. "I'm kind of scared," she choked.

I hugged her and stroked her hair. "Adonis should've given you some tips before deciding to let you date." Julia let out a feeble laugh.

I drove her to the campus security office and let her tell the officer what had happened. They took Josh's name down and said they'd take care of him. If any similar problems occurred, she promised to let them know.

Julia wanted me to drive her back to her car. I was supposed to train with Adonis, but I didn't want Julia to know. I hoped Julia wouldn't see my car when I went to Adonis's house.

As chance would have it, when I pulled into Adonis's driveway, Julia walked over. I rolled down my car window.

"Hey," she said, smirking, "Whatcha up to?"

"Not much. Thought I'd visit Adonis today."

"Again?"

"Yeah I like him. We're becoming friends."

"You can't fool me Bladen," Julia scoffed. You have some explaining to do."

"Like what?" I asked, playing dumb.

Julia placed one hand on her slim hip and tossed her head back irresistibly. "Gee, let's see…like why you had some kind of super strength going on back at the library, why you're here to see Adonis and didn't let me know, and why you're head sometimes seems so lost in the clouds, you forget what's going on around you."

I signaled to Julia to come closer. She came up to my window and held her face just inches from mine. My heartbeat quickened. "Okay, I'll explain, but not right now. I need to see Adonis first. Afterward I'll come and talk to you. Sound good?"

"Keep in mind, I told you my deepest secrets and trusted you with them. You can do the same with me," she offered in agreement.

"Deal. I'll see you later." I opened my car door and walked away. I didn't allow myself the luxury of one last glimpse at her. I went up to Adonis's door and let myself in, uninvited.

Adonis jumped when he saw me. "You startled me. Why didn't you knock, mate?"

"Sorry, I'm here to train remember?"

"Yeah, I remember. Next time knock first, though, and remember your manners."

"Yes sir," I promised.

Today we worked on the art of Karate, punching and kicking, and Aikido, throwing and pinning. I had to know how to fight on Earth and in Arcis, especially if I was attacked without warning and didn't have time to pull out one of my weapons. On Earth, I never carried a weapon, anyway. After Adonis spent an hour with me, he asked if I felt ready for more training in a real life situation.

I didn't know exactly what he meant by that, until I felt gravity suck my body in, and I traveled through my phone, landing in unfamiliar territory in Arcis this time.

On Earth, Adonis and I relaxed and watched television.

In Arcis, I landed in an amphitheater. If my memory of history served me correctly, it was the theatre from Pompeii, Italy. History had always been one of my better subjects, B's and C's. Anyway, the arena was shaped like an ice skating rink, with shadowy grass that lined the inside wall. Utterly fascinated, I stared in awe around me, until I remembered Berard's warning: in Arcis all places were a mirage and something to distract me. I had grown familiar to landing in the courtyard of the basilica or on the beach near the abyss. Being somewhere new made the hair on my arms stand on end in anticipation.

I thrust my hands out and carefully circled around me. The arena was empty. I had no weapons readily accessible, only my wide belt that held my cable and gadgets. Without warning, an unknown life player stood next to me, clothed in heavy armor.

I peered into the life player's helmet and heard a gruff, familiar voice. "Pay attention!" he ordered.

I knew it had to be Adonis next to me again. I turned away. Suddenly, five Terras, land demons, charged at us. They all materialized into attractive human forms, something I had never seen before. It was like the clone imaging, except *everything* about them appeared human, not monstrous at all. Even though I knew they were already dead, I had a difficult time attacking them in their human form. I defended myself with some martial art moves, a kick here or there, but other than that, my body felt immobile.

"Don't let them trick you. They're not human," Adonis shouted. "Attack them, and don't look into the stands. Death players are watching."

The demons multiplied with too many of them for us to handle alone. Soon a few more life players emerged. One of them stood next to an enormous catapult, large enough to throw something equivalent to the size of two adult humans.

I clutched the arm of one of the demons and spun it around. With great difficulty, I grabbed its neck, twisted, and cracked it just like killing any human being. The cracking noise seemed eccentrically loud and real. Even though it didn't kill it, the demon laid limp long enough for me to toss it to the life player with the catapult. I quickly seized another demon and repeated the same technique, making it motionless. I cast it to the life player and watched as he catapulted them both into the abyss.

I peered at the life player, wondering if he was real or not, but I only saw gleaming metal when I looked inside his helmet—a fake. He was a robot. That meant someone was playing the video game and could probably see me. I turned my face up toward the sky and gave the thumbs up.

I glanced around and searched for Adonis but didn't see him anywhere. I did notice one life player, struggling in a fight. Too many demons descended on me for me to help him. The life player screamed in agony, as he was beaten to a pulp. Then he disappeared. I hoped he had traveled back to Earth and into one body, though I wasn't sure what happened to him. I watched the demons as they jumped and celebrated the pool of blood left by the life player. Their elation made my anger rage.

I continued the fight, helping to dismantle the demons' power. I breathed a sigh of relief each time one was catapulted into the abyss. I smashed their heads, drove my dagger into their bodies, and had my own screaming celebration with each success. My body throbbed immensely, but I didn't care. When the demons had disappeared, I traveled back to Adonis's home. Level four won? I hoped so.

Lying on the couch, curled up in a fetal position, I groaned.

"Well done," Adonis praised.

"I'm in serious agony." My body hurt more than I had realized.

"No pain, no gain," Adonis joked.

"Funny," I muttered. "I hope this means I've won four levels."

"That's exactly what that means."

I sat upright. "I saw a life player...he got the crap beaten out of him... he cried out for help, but I was attacked by too many demons and couldn't make it over to help him."

Adonis stood up and turned his ancient TV to a news channel. Seriously, the TV looked like it was one of the first ever made. The screen flashed "Breaking News." A female newscaster came on and was reporting that Hurricane Katrina hit the Louisiana shore.

I sat there in shock unable to speak. Adonis shut off the TV and shook his head. "That's what happens when Vorago gains power," he explained. "If Vorago's army takes one of us down and a life player loses a level, they gain immeasurable clout on Earth. With a hurricane like that, there must have been many life players that lost their level at the same time."

I found my voice. "Hurricane Katrina? That's impossible. That happened five years ago in 2005. How can that be on your TV now?"

"Bladen, the time in Arcis seems to go by more quickly than on Earth, right?" But in reality there's no time in Arcis. Our successes or failures there can change any time in history here on Earth. When I turn on any television, I can make the TV show the effects of any of our battles in Arcis."

"Amazing…but the life player I saw. Why him, not me?"

"It could've been you, but maybe they chose that life player because he had more strength than you. The stronger the life player they destroy, the more wickedness they can spew on Earth."

"The life player I saw…he's okay, right?"

Adonis gazed thoughtfully. "When a life player is attacked that way, sadly, he could be injured enough to be in a hospital, but they can't kill him, at least not in Arcis. They can steal his power, just like we can theirs."

"Yeah, but what happens to demons and life players when their power's taken away?"

"Demons never gain it back, and only the most powerful and useful life players gain theirs, others are no longer life players. The game is over for them. Their frustration now begins by having to sit back and watch these events unfold — powerless."

That blew me away. I never knew I could lose my power.

Adonis's face showed overwhelming grief. "You look upset, Bladen, but there's more I need to tell you."

"What?" I felt sick to my stomach.

"I found out who murdered the life player that lived in your room." Adonis was hesitant to tell me.

"Go on," I insisted.

"A male life player died there. His name was Mark…and the murderer…well…Julia's father committed the crime.

I lost my ability to speak. My heart cried out for Julia. She knew her father was a sick, vindictive man, but did she know he was *this* much of a monster?

"Does Lisa know this?" I asked, furious.

"Yes."

"What about Julia?"

"Of course not."

"Why? That's crazy. She needs to know." I stood up and met Adonis face-to-face. "Do you know that when I leave here, Julia wants me to explain to her what's going on in my life, because she can tell I'm keeping something from her."

Adonis's face shone with concern. "What are you going to tell her?"

"I haven't decided yet, but don't worry. I won't tell her anything that concerns you or her family, though I *can* tell her my story. If I tell Julia I'm a life player, she'll wonder about you too." I knew I sounded desperate.

"I need to talk to her mother first, but you're right. I think it's time she knew the real truths behind her father and sister…and me for that matter. But for now, like you said, just tell her what you need to."

I calmed down and asked Adonis about the dove and voice I'd heard in my head the last time I left his house.

He didn't answer right away. He stepped into his kitchen and came back with a cup of tea. He took a sip and then set it on the coffee table. "I have mechanical doves I send out that have hidden video cameras in them," Adonis explained. "I launch them on occasion…when I'm concerned about Julia, so I can make sure she's safe. As for the voice you heard in your head, it sounds like someone's telepathic and is watching out for her. I've never heard of this, which is quite unusual."

"Mechanical doves? The one I saw crapped on her head," I said, puzzled.

"That's impossible. They're not real. What happened to that bird?" Adonis asked, alarmed.

"I killed it by accident. It wouldn't leave us alone. I knocked it with my hand, and it fell down dead."

"Where's the bird now?"

"I picked it up and threw it in the woods in your backyard. Julia and I buried it."

Rushing to the door, Adonis commanded me to show him where I'd done that. We stepped outside. My eyes adjusted to the late afternoon sun that hung low in the almost autumn sky. The lengthy blades of grass, badly in need of mowing, swooshed against our legs as we made our way to the scanty woods in the back of the house.

I couldn't find where we had buried the dove. I kicked my foot around and looked under the leaves but couldn't find the hole. But Adonis could. He went back to his garage to get a shovel. He came back and dug it up. "Here it is, and it's definitely dead. No way it was one of my mechanical ones."

The dove lay on the ground, a mangled mess. I took a closer look and noticed something shiny in it that looked like a box. "Adonis, come and see this." He came over and inspected it. He pulled a handkerchief out of his pocket and wrapped it around the dove.

"Come back to my house with me," he said. Adonis took the bird into his messy garage and placed it on top of one of his paint-splattered workbenches. He pulled out his jackknife and cut into it. With tweezers, he plucked out the miniature, metal box, and in one swift movement, he smashed the box with his hammer.

"What did you do that for?"

"I believe it was a camera like the ones I use. But that's not possible." Adonis answered, deep in thought. "This isn't good, Bladen. I have a feeling this came from Shamus, and if he found us again—"

"Shamus? Do you think he's on to you?"

"I don't know, but there are too many strange things going on—the fact that a life player was killed in *your* dorm room. That's an uncanny coincidence don't you think? And now this? Who could have known the mechanical doves I sent out were to watch Julia—and then copy it with a real dove? A real dove with a camera? Ingenius."

"What should we do?"

"First, we must hold an emergency Assembly, so all life players know that more danger may be near. I don't want you driving here for training anymore, either. I'll come and get you. If you're with me too much, that'll draw attention to both of us." Adonis paced again and then stopped. "There's just one more thing, Bladen…I need you to protect Julia. You're the only one I trust. Don't worry about Lisa. I'll have her covered."

"How do you want me to do that?" I asked.

Adonis and I left the garage and walked back into the living room. He went into a closet in the hallway, came back with a rugged looking gold chain, and handed it to me. "Here, wear this."

"A necklace?" I asked, with uncertainty.

"Yes, put it on. When you rub it, it'll become lustrous. Your body will go through a transition and you'll become invisible and be teleported to wherever you need to go. If Julia's in immediate danger, you'll be teleported directly to her location. If there's impending danger, you'll be teleported into a gray room, where you'll be able to see clues as to what might occur in the future. In that way, you'll be able to protect her. It won't work, however, if you choose to misuse it."

"So you mean, no using it when she's changing clothes?" I retorted, lightheartedly.

Adonis chuckled with one eyebrow raised. "Remember I'm like a father to her, do anything out of line, and you'll have to answer to me."

I laughed and thought, guess he doesn't know I spent the night with her.

"Adonis, if life players are told about this situation at an Assembly, then your identity will no longer be anonymous," I said.

"No mate," Adonis corrected me, "Julia and Lisa's anonymity will be gone, not mine. That means regrettably, they might have to move again—soon." The thought of Julia moving sucked. I didn't want to think about it.

Adonis and I said our goodbyes. He told me Berard would find me once more for the Assembly, and he wanted me to tell Julia he'd visit her later on, to reveal their own family secrets.

I ran my fingers through my hair, as I drove the short distance to Julia's house in my car. I felt a knot in my stomach forming. I worried about how she might respond to me as a life player. Somehow, I had a premonition she wouldn't be happy about it.

I didn't need to knock on the door. Julia opened it, anxious. I followed her inside where she had set up a snack for us—raw carrots and celery. I wasn't excited about the food, until I saw a plate of chocolate chip cookies. Now *that* was cool.

"Thanks for the snack," I said, picking up a handful of cookies, "that was nice of you." I stuffed a couple of them into my mouth.

"You're welcome…I figured since you're going to tell me your cryptic secrets, like I told you mine, you might get hungry."

"Is it poisoned?" I asked, trying to keep things light.

"Of course not, silly. If I did that, I'd never get to hear your secrets."

I deliberately chewed on a cookie at a snail's pace. Julia stood with her arms crossed, tapping her foot.

"I know you're eager to hear what I have to say, but I'll be honest with you. You probably won't like it, so I guess, I'll cut to the chase."

"I'd appreciate that," she said.

I told Julia about Arcis, about Berard, and all about what I had experienced so far. I enjoyed watching her attempt to control her emotions, especially when her eyes grew as wide as quarters. Otherwise, she remained quiet and contemplative. I begged her to believe my story. I didn't want her to think I was crazy. When I finished, Julia wanted time to think about what I had said. Before I left, I told her Adonis wanted to talk to her, too.

"Adonis," Julia said, surprised. "Why?"

"He has his own family secrets to tell," I informed her.

"What is it, Bladen? You know don't you? You have to tell me." Julia looked scared.

"I can't. You'll have to talk to him yourself. But, if, after discussing things with him you need someone to talk to, then please call me." I hated leaving her that way, but I had to.

I went back to my room, wondering what would happen next. Would I hear from Julia, or would Berard come and get me for the Assembly? I had a hard time concentrating.

I took out my guitar and started to play a song by Boston. I didn't think to put on my headphones, so that only I could hear. Instead, I played "Hitch a Ride" with the volume turned so high, I bet the whole dorm could hear it. After I finished rocking out the tune, I heard applause and shouts. I gave an encore.

When I quit, I laid in my bed, arms folded above my head, until the phone rang. I glanced at the clock next to me—9:47 p.m. I answered the phone and heard Adonis on the other end, panicked. "I talked to Julia tonight, and she flipped out on me. I tried to call her later, but she didn't answer the phone, mate. I went back to the house. She's not there. Have you heard from her?"

I sat upright then bolted out of bed. "No I haven't, but she seemed like she took my news okay. What do you want me to do?"

"Help me find her. Do you mind?"

"Adonis, relax." I reassured him. "I'm sure she's fine. I'll swing by her house. If she's not there, I'll drive around and look for her."

Adonis took a deep breath. "I hope you're right."

I hung up the phone, reached for my keys, and ran to my car, feeling more uneasy than I had led on to Adonis. I sped toward Julia's house. It started to pour rain. I had just put my windshield wipers on high when I noticed a girl with long, soaked hair running in the dark. I rolled down my window to get a better look and thought it might be Julia.

"Julia?" I yelled, as loud as I could. The face in the darkness turned toward me. I knew it had to be her. "Get in the car, Julia." I stopped the car and reached over to open the passenger door. She ignored me and kept jogging. I shut the door and drove after her again. "Come on, it's late and dark," I pleaded through the open window. "Please get in the car."

This time Julia paused. When I hit the brakes and pulled over, she climbed in, shivering from the cold. She kept her face turned away from mine. Without saying a word, I drove to her house. I pulled in the driveway, and turned off the ignition.

"Do you want me to stay?" I asked. She didn't answer. She sprang out of the car and ran into the house, stalling only to unlock the front door. I ran after her and tried to get in, but she had already locked me out.

I stood there, getting pelted with torrents of rain, and continued to ring the doorbell. You know, the one that plays Beethoven's Fifth. I pushed it again and again, hoping it would drive her crazy. Before long, I was drenched like Julia. I pounded on the door and almost gave up, until the door finally sprung open and hit my arm.

"Sorry," she mumbled.

I stepped out of the rain into the foyer and shook the water out of my hair like a wet dog. Julia sat back down, crouched over with her elbows resting on her thighs, her face pressed against her hands.

I sat next to her as I listened to her sobbing, and put my arms around her. She dropped her hands and buried her head in my chest. I stroked her hair. My heart wrenched as I heard her weep in pain. We stayed like that for so long, her hair eventually dried. Her crying stopped and a hiccup like sound replaced it that made her body shudder against mine.

"Everything's going to be okay," I kept repeating.

After my muscles ached from being in the same position for so long, Julia drew her face back away from mine. "This is the worst day of my life," she cried, with fresh tears streaming down her face. I tried to wipe them away, but there were too many of them.

"First Josh and then you with your unbelievable story. You threw me. You did. But not like Adonis. Now I have a father and sister out there somewhere, who are not only murderers, they're death players that want Mom and me dead."

I hugged Julia again and tried to reassure her that things would be okay. She shook her head in disbelief. "Julia," I said in a quiet tone, "If I could take it all away, I would."

She stared at me with desperate eyes. "No…no…you can't. You're involved in all of this. You don't understand…I hate my life. I hate this, and you…you…I thought you'd be something happy in my life, but instead, you're a part of something I don't want to have anything to do with." Her cutting words stung. It wasn't my fault her father and sister had become sadistic death players.

Taking her face into my hands, I spoke to her from the depths of my heart. "I'd give all this up for you."

"And then what? Down the road, you'd probably despise me for taking you away from something you love."

"That would never happen," I insisted. I could tell by the look in her eye, she didn't believe me. I felt sorry for her, but at the same time, she had ripped my heart easier than a sword.

I looked at my watch—3:18 a.m. My eyes felt heavy. I went into the kitchen to get a drink for both of us. I found some Celestial Seasoning tea called Sleepy Time. It sounded good. I brewed two mugs in the microwave and brought them to Julia, but she had already fallen asleep. I set the tea on the coffee table and picked up a blanket to tuck around her. I took a few sips, before I fell asleep on the big chair for the second night in a row. I tossed and turned.

I woke much too early and was thankful for a dreamless night. The sun was still below the horizon. I checked Julia. She was still asleep. I couldn't help but notice the peaceful look on her face that would be stolen away once she woke up. My heart ached for her. My feelings tormented me.

In the kitchen, I made an omelet loaded with melted cheese. My stomach felt too sick to finish mine, but I wanted to make a plate for Julia, anyway. I halfheartedly left for my dorm to get my books for class. It was Tuesday, which meant Biology and Angelina.

MORE TEARS

"Hey, you're my partner for class and lab." I heard Angelina's cheery voice.

I turned to look. "Great," I said, with a weak smile.

The class got better, though. We were going to study snakes and lizards, their venomous bites, and how that related to medicine's ability to lower blood pressure and minimize blood clots in human beings. Sweet, I thought.

We found out that on Friday, in lab we were going to observe a rattlesnake attack a rat, and then our professor planned to monitor the venomous bite's effect on the rat's blood pressure and heart rate. Now that sounded fun.

My next class, Intro. to Psychology, was meant to be. We studied social psychology, in particular, why women had a tendency to marry a man like their father—strange that we'd be studying that particular topic–a little scary when I thought about Julia's father.

I spent the rest of the day doing boring stuff like my laundry to take my mind off things. I cleaned my room and eventually studied. I didn't have the heart to turn on the Arcis game. I never heard from Julia. I called Adonis to make sure she was all right. He told me she stayed home for the day to rest, and that she still felt quite upset. Lisa was traveling home as we spoke to stay with her.

That night I worked at the Bistro. It was hectic for a Tuesday, and to make my life even lousier, Angelina sauntered in. She nodded hello, when I hurried by to wait on another table, but she left me alone after that.

I caught my breath when Julia strolled in with Gloria. Even though her eyes were red and swollen, she looked beautiful in green jeans and a black turtleneck with her hair pulled up in a high ponytail. Silver hoop earrings dangled from her ears. After she told me she wanted nothing to do with the life I'd chosen, it bugged me how much it hurt to see her. I didn't talk to her either. Someone else waited on their table, and they both left once they ate their food. I was ripped she came in, knowing I'd be there.

As soon as possible after work, I drove back to my dorm. Once my head hit the pillow, I began to drift off, until I saw Berard … and it wasn't a dream. No, this can't be happening, I thought, groggily. But Berard had other plans. He shook me awake to take me to the uncomfortable, unpretentious school bus, which took us to the next Assembly.

I didn't think I needed to be there this time. I already knew the topic of the meeting, and yet I had to participate. I sat there grumpy with my arms crossed and my eyes half closed. A huge poster of Julia and an outdated photo of her family hung sprawled across the stage for everyone to see. Adonis went on and on, giving the life players a full update on the possible danger regarding Julia's dad and sister.

Just before the end of the Assembly, a spotlight beamed down on me. "This is the life player I've chosen to protect Julia," Adonis bellowed. I shot upright in my seat, unaware that he had planned to announce anything about me. "This is Bladen. If he needs any assistance, you'll need to help him, even if it means putting your lives in danger to the point of death." The few life players I had encountered turned to stare at me. I felt like I wanted to crawl under a rock. I breathed a sigh of relief, when Adonis called everyone up for the supper provided. I left feeling renewed, one of the promises for attending the Assemblies, and I didn't feel quite as exhausted mentally or physically; though, I was still upset about Julia.

The next day, Wednesday, I had chemistry again—the class I shared with Anthony. After class, he marched up to me. "You have no idea how lucky you are that Adonis chose you," he whispered, his voice dripped in envy. "What I wouldn't give."

Yeah right, I thought, if he only knew.

I didn't have to work again until Thursday. After classes, I studied, worked out, and then jammed on my guitar again, only this time not as loud. I didn't feel like an audience. I was strumming my favorite part to the Goo Goo Dolls song "Slide," when my phone vibrated in my pocket. I picked it up and saw the name Simms—Julia. I wondered why she was calling. My hands shook, my heart pounded, and my stomach felt sick from anxiety.

"Hey," I said, trying to sound calm and cool.

"Hey," Julia said.

"Julia?" I asked, pretending like I didn't recognize her.

"Yeah, don't you know my voice by now?"

"Sure, I guess," I said, still trying to act like I didn't care.

"I think we need to talk. I owe you that at least," she said sweetly, which I thought rather odd.

"What do you have in mind?"

"We can take a drive."

"When?" I asked.

"I thought now, if you're not too busy."

"I'm a little busy. I can be at your house in an hour. Does that work for you?"

"See you then," she said, and hung up the phone.

By the time I'd pick her up, it'd be about 3:00 p.m—still daylight. I had bad feelings about where this conversation would lead. I threw on a sweatshirt and didn't care about my messed up hair. I left right at three, knowing I'd be late.

When I pulled into Julia's driveway, she came out immediately as if she'd been waiting. She wouldn't tell me where we were going. She gave me directions and said she'd explain where we were once we got there. It felt like she was playing games with me, which I found annoying, but I didn't say anything.

"Do you feel okay? You're hair's a mess, and your face is scruffy." Julia had noticed.

"I feel great. Why? You don't like the scruffy look?" I asked, running my fingers through my hair to make it even more messed up. "Any reason why we have to go for a drive to talk? Couldn't we have talked at your house?"

"My mom's home."

"What difference does that make?"

"I didn't want her to listen."

"With the amount of time she spends at home, I doubt she'd try to overhear our conversation, anyway," I answered, dryly.

"Actually, now that I know the truth about things, and I was so upset, she said she'd try to work from Burlington more often and spend extra time at home with me."

"That's cool, but that still doesn't mean she'd listen in on us." I felt sympathetic for all Julia had been through, annoyed with myself for having that reaction, and annoyed with her for leading me on. Yeah, my affection for her ran too deep.

"Hey we're here. Take a right turn," Julia said. We pulled into Sandbar State Park, a recreational area that had been closed for the season. We parked outside of the locked, metal gate.

We walked down to the beach and sat at a wooden picnic table; neither one of us spoke. The late afternoon sun glistened on the water and made me think of the day Julia and I had biked to the beach downtown. I reminded Julia, not only about that afternoon, but also how I had observed her watching the father that had been there as he played and laughed with his daughter.

"You had a yearning expression on your face that day," I said.

Julia looked pensive for a moment before she responded. "I'm glad you brought that up. It makes it easier for me to talk to you."

I beat her to it, you know, to save my self-pride. "I know what kind of life you're looking for. You don't have to worry about it. We can just be friends." I acted casual about it. "Really, Julia, it's no big deal."

"How did you know what I was going to say?" She looked sincerely shocked.

"Does it matter? Besides, we didn't need to come this far to talk about it. I think we could've taken care of this over the phone."

Julia looked hurt. I'd heard about the "let's be friends talk" from buddies in high school, but this was my first experience. Even though I acted like I didn't care, the whole thing sucked.

"Bladen?" Julia said, her eyes welled up with tears that began to spill over.

"Yeah," I breathed, brushing her face with my fingertips to wipe away the tears.

"It's not that I don't care—because I do. I just don't want anything to do with the life you've chosen—the world that's made my existence so miserable. I want to marry a guy who comes home every day, who has a job that's not going to kill him, who will hold me and promise me the perfect family, in the perfect house. I even want the cute, white picket fence to go along with it."

I wished I could tell her I'd give her that, but I didn't know how my own life would end up. "I hope that all works out for you, Julia. I really do."

Julia nodded. We sat there for a while longer, watching the miniscule waves on Lake Champlain lap against the shore.

"Brr…it's kind of chilly," Julia said, as she hugged her knees.

I took off my gray hooded sweatshirt that said Freefall in green bold letters and handed it to her. "Here wear this."

"Thanks." She put it on. I couldn't help but be amused by how it draped off her small frame.

"I think it's a little big for you," I laughed.

"It's warm, though. How about you? You look cold. Are you sure you don't want it back?"

"No, I'm fine." I was wearing a plain white t-shirt that fit a little tight. I knew it showed off my muscles. I couldn't help but feel satisfied when Julia gawked at me but then shyly turned away. It felt good, like maybe I salvaged my ego.

We both wandered down near the water and strolled along the beach.

"Do you mind if I ask you a personal question?" Julia began.

"No, go ahead."

"You don't take steroids or anything like that, right?"

"No way, why?" I pretended to be shocked.

"Your muscles are kind of…large," she said.

Kind of? I thought. That was all she was going to give me? "I work out a lot. I'll race you to the end of the beach." Julia didn't answer, but ran ahead of me. Laughing, we both stopped where the sand turned into rocks. I grabbed her around the waist and pulled her to me. She caught her breath.

"I thought we were going to be friends," she said, as she relaxed in my arms.

"We are…and I need to get back. I have some studying to do. Before we go, can I give you one last kiss goodbye?"

Julia hesitated, but then nodded.

I barely brushed my lips against hers. Then I let go and sprinted to the car. By the time Julia caught up to me, I had already buckled my seatbelt. The car engine was idling.

"You're fast when you want to be," Julia gasped, in between breaths, as she climbed into the car and fastened her seatbelt. I put the car into drive and made the tires squeal as I pealed out.

"Too bad you'll never know how fast I *can* be," I snickered, good-naturedly.

Julia laughed, punched me in the arm, and told me to slow down. On the way back to Julia's house, we talked about our classes and work. She was enjoying her internship as a teacher's assistant at the elementary school. I told her I thought my job was cool, because it was a social place—lots of college students.

I pulled into Julia's driveway and left my car idling. Julia sat for a moment without getting out. "Thanks for being there for me this week. You're a good friend."

"Sure," I replied. I gave her a quick hug goodbye and pulled on the door handle next to her to open the door. Once out, she waved as I drove away. I felt heartbroken the relationship had ended before it had a chance to grow.

I trudged into my dorm and headed to my room. Robby was sitting there by himself with his iPod on, bouncing his head up and down to the beat of the music. His feet, crossed over at the ankles, were resting on top of the desk. At first, he didn't see me standing next to him.

Finally, he sprang to his feet. "Dude, how's it going? What are you doing here? Don't you have to work, study, see Julia? To what do I owe this honor of your presence?" Robby always sounded like a surfer dude.

I hit him hard on the arm. He punched me back. We scuffled a bit, until I had him in a headlock.

"Truce," he yelled. "You gotta show me how you do that. Seriously."

Once we stopped kidding around, I explained to him that Julia and I had a "sort of" relationship that had started, but then we decided to be "friends." I was thankful he didn't ask any questions and let it go.

Robby reminded me about the guys' weekend he had planned in the middle of October at his house. After dealing with Julia and Angelina's stuff, nothing could've sounded better. I spent some time on the phone, until I found someone to cover for me at work that particular weekend.

With everything going on, I doubted I'd make it home until Thanksgiving and would miss my usual autumn hike with my family. I called them to let them know. Christiana, the littlest, munchkin answered the phone, squealing in delight when she heard my voice. She handed the phone to Mom and Dad. They were disappointed I didn't have time to make a trip home, but they understood.

When I hung up the phone, I called Nicholas. We talked for an hour. He asked Stephanie to be his girlfriend and sounded totally crazy about her. He went on and on. I thought he'd never stop. It only made me think more about Julia.

Later, Robby and I went out for dinner. We played a few fun games of pool at Sunny's, a local eating-place and lounge. The restaurant wasn't a college hang out, so we didn't recognize anyone. I didn't have to worry about running into Julia. After eating a burger and fries, Robby beat me in another game of pool. I challenged him to a rematch on our guys' weekend at his house. I didn't think I'd win the rematch either, but I threatened to. Since I probably wouldn't be seeing Julia that much anymore, I was thankful for someone fun like Robby to hang out with.

Later that night, Jared came around. We talked a lot. He was cool, too. Like me, he played guitar, so we jammed a few songs together. Robby had an awesome voice and belted out the lyrics. We all joked around about putting our own band together. When I went to bed, even though my heart ached at the thought of Julia, I drifted off to sleep in no time.

As usual, my turbulent dreams erupted like a volcano, and I saw her. There *she* was in my dream, a luscious, long-legged, black and red spider—the black widow. My burning desire for her returned. She inched her way toward me. Feeling her breath on my face made every hair on my body stand up on end. I yearned desperately for her.

"Help me, Bladen," she whispered.

Startled, I woke up. "That insane spider again," I murmured in the dark. I felt tortured by the meaning of this dream and why my name had been called in it again. Unable to fall asleep, I took out my phone. When I began to watch the game Arcis, I saw the angry man wearing black, his back toward me. He stood inside the basilica, a medium-size knife in hand. He raised the shiny knife above his head, with both of his hands gripping it. He plunged it down into something. I couldn't see what it was, but I saw blood squirt out on both sides. It hit the window of the basilica.

The man turned. As soon as his fuming eyes met mine, I shut off my game. I knew he could see me. I just knew it. It made me feel unsettled. I hardly slept for the rest of the night.

The next day crawled by. I thought about Julia a lot. I even called work to see if they needed an extra hand for the night to get my mind off her. They didn't, and my boss told me to rest up, since I had to work for the next three days. I sat in my room, a Thursday night, with music blasting.

Adonis startled me when he tapped me on the shoulder. "Hey, what are you doing here?" I asked, looking toward the locked door. "And how did you get in?"

"I told you I'd come get you for your training. Let's go quickly, before someone knows I'm here. Put your hand on my shoulder."

I placed my hand on his shoulder, and we zipped along, landing in Adonis's living room. My body crashed down with a loud thump.

"Awesome, I didn't know you could teleport like that," I grimaced from the landing, although I was thoroughly impressed. "Berard has done that before but never with me."

"One of the perks of being a lord, mate. Now get up and let's train," he said, and extended me a helping hand.

Today we started with Kung Foo, then Judo. During Kung Foo, Adonis spun in the air and kicked me to the floor every time. When we practiced Judo, he also grabbed me and flung me to the floor each time. I made a lame attempt to defend myself. So pathetic, that Adonis stopped to ask me what was the matter.

"This isn't like you, mate. What's going on?" he asked.

"Nothing really…I guess I just have a lot on my mind lately."

"Does this have anything to do with Julia?"

"How would you know?" I asked, wryly. "Do you have some other super power that allows you to listen in on other people's conversations?"

Adonis sat next to me on the floor and placed his hand on my shoulder. He looked unswervingly into my eyes. "I do live right next door to her, and I've always been like her father."

It never occurred to me that maybe she told him about us. "What did she say to you?" I asked, brushing his hand off my shoulder.

"She said she cares a lot about you, but she wants nothing to do with the life we lead. She feels torn, but she thinks she's making the right decision for herself. Your friendship's important to her, though."

"Sounds like she told you basically the same thing she told me."

"I'm glad you brought it up because there's something you should know..." Adonis trailed off.

"What?" I asked, alarmed.

"Julia has a few dates coming up...you know...with other blokes."

"What do you mean...blokes? Guys? You mean guys? Like more than one?"

"Yeah...I just thought you might like to know, so you're not surprised if you see her out with any of them."

Fury dripped through my blood. "Why are you letting her do that? Did she tell you about her date with Josh?"

Adonis stood up, his back toward me and clenched his fists into balls. "I know all about that, and I know you took care of it... inappropriately..."

"Inappropriately?" I interrupted, disbelieving.

"You can't show your strength like that, mate. It's dangerous."

"Forget it," I spat. "Who cares. The fact is: you haven't prepared her to date or how to deal with guys."

"She dealt with you okay," Adonis said.

"Yeah, but I'm nice. And besides that, you can kill any human being with your bare hands. Have you taught her *any* of that? She's been sheltered, and now you're throwing her out there. That's like tossing a paralytic into a pond and expecting them to swim."

Adonis spun around, and stomped toward me, with anguish that gripped his face. "I tried, but she wanted nothing to do with violence after her father and sister committed their atrocities," he said, angrily. "She, in defiance, would learn nothing to defend herself. Why do you think I've asked you to protect her? You are nice. But come on…Lisa and I did the best we could raising her. There's nothing more we can do. We have to let her go."

I yanked the gold chain angrily from my neck snapping it and handed it back to Adonis. "Here…I don't want it. You can protect her. I don't want to see her. It might affect my ability to fight. I need to think of myself now."

Adonis took the chain. With a wave of his hand, he mended it and passed it back to me. "Please," he implored. "I need your help. I told you, I only trust *you* with her."

"Adonis," I pleaded. "You don't understand. I can't deny how I feel about her anymore. Seeing her will cause me too much pain. What good will I be for battle then?"

Adonis argued with me. "Unless she's in immediate peril, you won't even see her. The necklace can read your heart. If you believe she's in danger but she's not, then you'll be transported through a portal into a gray room. The room will be empty, and then you'll be bounced back to where you came from. That way you'll know she's safe. The portal is similar to the one I used to bring you here today."

"And what if she's in danger, and I *have* to see her?"

Adonis stared at me with beseeching eyes that reminded me of my little sister's puppy dog eyes she used on my parents when she begged for something. Typically, she got whatever she wanted.

Running my fingers through my hair, I answered, "Give me time to think about it."

"We don't have time, Bladen," Adonis said, closing his eyes and breathing deeply. "Julia's father and sister are closing in on us; they're nearer. I can sense them."

"If they're so close, why don't you move somewhere new, now? What are you waiting for?"

"We don't want to uproot Julia during her first year in college, if we don't have to."

"What if I can't fight, because Julia's on my mind too much?" I asked.

"Come on, Bladen. Do you think you're alone in this quest for love among the Simms' family? I loved Lisa way before you had your first crush, and yet I'm still able to accomplish the tasks at hand, and you will to. I'm sure of it."

"So you *do* love her," I said, but pushed it no further when I saw the anguish on his face. "I guess I know why you and I were meant to be friends…fine…I'll protect her."

Adonis looked relieved. "Thanks, mate. I knew you'd understand."

My training session ended, and Adonis teleported me back to my room. He said he'd return the next day to get me for training, before I went to work.

On Friday, I had my biology lab. Our professor brought us into the lab room where a giant glass aquarium sat on a table. Inside, some type of rattlesnake sat coiled around a branch. The branch was leaning against the glass wall and floor of the aquarium like it had been tossed in.

Probably someone terrified of snakes threw that stick in there, I thought.

Our professor gently tapped on the glass and motioned for all of us to come closer. While most of the students edged forward only a little, I shifted as close as possible. The snake seemed to turn and peer at us with its tail rattling like maracas.

Our professor, Mrs. Z, was breathing with witchlike intensity. Her glasses had fallen down across the bridge of her nose and revealed the excitement that shone in her eyes. Her lips curled up in wicked satisfaction, a side to her that I hadn't seen until now. I shivered as she spoke in her shrilling voice.

Man, I thought. That woman looks crazy.

"You seem to be an enthusiast," Mrs. Z said to me. "Why don't you come closer and have the honor of releasing the rat into the cage. You'll do that now, won't you? Come along." She handed me the rat and got ready to lift the lid to the aquarium. I stepped forward hesitantly and took the white rat by its tail. Its high-pitched squeal reminded me of Mrs. Z's voice. I tossed it into the cage like it was a hot coal. Mrs. Z quickly placed the cover back on the aquarium. As we observed our gory experiment, she explained that this type of rattlesnake, called a Mohave, was found in the Mojave Desert in California and happened to be one of the most venomous of its kind. It hadn't been fed in a while and was ravenous. Mrs. Z snickered and snorted, eagerly.

Standing up front, I had a clear view and could see the snake as it slowly became conscience of the rat. It pulled back and got ready to strike. In a blur, the reptile's fangs sunk deeply into its prey. I heard the poor rat screech and saw it tremble in pain. If rats shed tears, this one would have been in the middle of a downpour.

GIRLS

"I can't believe the school allows this kind of science experiment—sick," one student muttered, as Mrs. Z continued to enjoy herself.

Another student ran out. "I'm gonna throw up," she groaned.

Mrs. Z knew how to handle snakes. With great speed, she took this one out of the aquarium and put it into a second cage nearby. Then she put a monitor on the rat to show us how its blood pressure dropped. She planned to record it until the rat died. On Monday in class, she'd show us the rat's pattern of blood pressure as it fell and would explain the medical use of small amounts of venom to control high blood pressure, heart attacks, and strokes. We had to start our lab report with our partner but didn't have to finish it until next week. After explaining our homework, she dismissed us.

One student went up to Mrs. Z and asked her something I couldn't hear. Mrs. Z faced the departing students. "Hold up everyone…due to the upset of some students, I *will* give the rat an anti-venom shot in a moment, so the rat won't die." In a softer tone, she added. "Hopefully it won't die, anyway." Some students cheered, others jeered, a strange mix of responses.

"Cool huh?" Angelina sounded delighted. She came up behind me and linked her arm through mine. "Do you want to start the lab together today?"

"I can't. I have a chemistry lab today too, and I'm working later."

"How about tomorrow?"

"Sure, give me your phone number."

As the class left the room, Angelina and I exchanged phone numbers. Mrs. Z had already shut the light off, and we were the last ones about to exit. Angelina took the sleeve of my shirt and yanked my arm. I stumbled.

"Hey, what are you doing?" I asked.

"Shh," she whispered as she pulled me into a dark closet and shut the door.

"What are you doing?" I demanded a second time. I grasped the knob to open the door, wondering why I let her pull me in there in the first place.

"If you stay, I'll show you something cool," Angelina coaxed.

We waited a few moments in silence, until Angelina dared to open the door. As we stepped out into the now dimly-lit room, we verified no one else was around. Mrs. Z had pulled the curtains, hoping to trick the nocturnal snake into believing it was nighttime.

Angelina tiptoed toward the front of the classroom to the aquarium, where the rattlesnake rested, and the rat worked hard to breathe.

"I don't know what you're doing, Angelina, but we need to get out of here. Mrs. Z plans to come back and give the rat the anti-venom shot," I warned. I didn't trust Angelina. She gave me a bad feeling.

"I think she already gave it one before she left," Angelina said. She waved her hand in front of the lock and opened the lid. I was sure Mrs. Z had locked it, considering how dangerous this type of rattlesnake would be if it was let loose.

"Are you crazy," I argued.

In one swift movement, Angelina took the snake out of the cage and held it by the head with one hand and by the body with the other.

"Oh come here and look. Isn't he beautiful?" Angelina cooed.

"Where did you learn how to handle snakes like that?" I asked. "It's not exactly your average female talent."

Angelina slipped the snake back into the aquarium. She closed the lid and waved her hand in front of the lock one final time. She turned toward me and quickened her stride, then slid her hand into mine, and pulled me toward the door. We left the room, making sure nobody saw us.

Once we were far away from the lab, Angelina answered my question. "I have two older brothers. One of them used to be into unique reptiles. I played with a lot of strange pets when I was younger."

I released my hand from hers. "You're a…different girl…full of surprises, aren't you?"

"I hope that's a good thing," Angelina beamed.

"Uh–yeah," I said, not so sure.

When we left the building, I told Angelina she had some explaining to do about how she managed to magically open the aquarium. She gazed at me with mischievous eyes and annoyingly told me she'd tell me some other time.

That night at work, I ran around like I was on fire. The Bistro was insane. The usual people I knew came in—Robby, Jared, and the girls. Angelina strolled in with one of her girlfriends, and then Julia and Gloria waltzed in with two guys, or blokes as Adonis would say. Regardless, the girls obviously had dates.

Great, I thought as my heart sank. To make things worse, their table was in my section. I casually walked up to them and gave them their menus.

"Hi guys, can I start any of you off with a drink?" I asked.

They gave me their drink order. I turned to leave. "Look at the muscles on that guy," I heard Julia's date mutter. "He's probably a male bimbo." The two guys at the table snickered. I wanted to pound them, but I didn't want to lose my job.

I brought their sodas and set them on the table. "I asked for my soda with lime," Julia's date complained. Even though I knew he never asked for lime, I took his glass, apologized, and came back with a slice of lime on the side.

"I asked for lemon, idiot," he sneered, this time.

I was ripped and forgot to care about my job. I knocked his drink on his pants and laughed when the shade of his face turned into the color of a plum.

"Oh sorry," I said, not feeling sorry at all, "let me get you a towel to clean that up."

Julia looked embarrassed. Gloria shook her head in disbelief. I was angry Julia didn't have a backbone and stand up to this guy. Her date demanded we give him his dinner free, and although my boss was ripped at me, he gave me a pat on the back when I told him what had happened. In this type of situation, the usual punishment was for the wait staff to pay for the customer's dinner. However, my boss gladly offered to do that for me. I guess he *could* be cool sometimes.

They ate their meal after that and left me alone, until Julia stood up and headed straight for me.

"I'm sorry about that," she said, filled with remorse.

"Your not that hot at choosing dates are you?" I said, angrily and turned to walk away.

"Well, I chose you didn't I," she retaliated.

"Not really," I answered, angrily and left to go to the bar, leaving Julia behind.

Angelina sauntered up next to me when I got there. "Want me to make her jealous for you?" Angelina asked, with her lively grin.

"What are you talking about?"

"I'm talking about Blondie. I think you know that," Angelina answered, and kissed my cheek when Julia was still looking. Angelina continued to whisper in my ear. "I can see the guy she's with is a real jerk, and right now everyone at their table's watching us—gawking is more like it." Angelina kissed my cheek one more time, a little closer to my lips. I searched around for my boss. I knew he'd be mad at me this time, but he didn't see us.

"Thanks," I whispered, to Angelina.

"Hey," Angelina said. "How 'bout I call you tomorrow to work on our lab report. Maybe around ten in the morning?"

"Sure," I answered.

Later that night, I crawled into bed and fell asleep. I had that horrible nightmare once more, you know, the relentless, recurring spider dream.

A lonely black and red spider inched up next to me, her expression looked empty and sad—a tear rolled down from her right eye. The hairs on my body and legs stood on end from fear, curiosity, and desire. Out of my peripheral vision, I saw a reflection in the glass on the aquarium next to me. It contained two black widow spiders. I stopped breathing when I saw my mirror image between these two venomous killers. Then one of the female spiders laid down and closed her eyes.

"Help me," she breathed.

I woke up with a start, my breath harsh and irregular. In case you haven't noticed. I almost always wake up from these dreams out of breath. I fell back to sleep, until my head pulsated with pain. I woke up again.

I heard a familiar voice in my head say, "You'll choose the right one."

"What? Who are you?" I shouted like a fool, waking up Robby.

"Wh...wh...what, man, is someone breaking in?" Robby fell out of his bed to the floor. He picked up a chair and thrust it into the air ready to fight. When I couldn't stop laughing, Robby threatened to hit me in the head with the chair.

"Go to sleep, dude," I told him, and put my hands up in the air to protect myself. I knew I needed to ask Adonis about the voice in my head. He had to know why it continued to happen to me.

The next morning, the sound of my phone woke me up. I heard Angelina's voice on the other end. "Good morning," she sang bright and cheerful. "Are you ready to do our report?"

"Are you kidding me? What time is it?

"It's nine forty-five, and you said ten o'clock worked for you. Get out of bed you lazy head and meet me at the library in half an hour." Angelina hung up the phone.

I was almost on time and met her at just a little past ten. Angelina arrived before me. I searched around for her and couldn't believe when I found her at my usual study table hidden behind the bookshelves. I went up behind her and covered her eyes with my hands. She sprang to her feet, took hold of my arm, and tried to twist it behind me. I was obviously stronger and grabbed her by both her wrists.

"Ow," she grumbled, pulling hard to loosen my grip. When she looked at my face, she relaxed. "Oh, it's only you."

"Only me?" I mused, letting her wrists go. "Who did you think I was that made you react that way?"

Angelina seated herself stiffly on the chair. "Never mind, are you ready to start our report?" Angelina wore a plain black t-shirt. Her body looked poured into her torn blue jeans. Her thick, black hair cascaded around her nearly makeup-less face. Her striking dark features made her emerald eyes appear illuminated—like they were stolen from a tropical rainforest.

"In a minute," I answered, running my hand through my hair, a habit I had acquired, considering how often it stuck out.

Angelina giggled.

"What's so funny?" I asked.

"Your hair's a mess," she said.

"Sorry you don't like the messy look," I said, sarcastically.

"No, it's sort of cute." She giggled again.

I sat down across from Angelina and leaned toward her. "I'm not the best student, but I'm not stupid either. What kind of malefic magic can you conjure up that makes you able to open locked cages and manipulate people?" I whispered. "And now you jumped at me like I lit your back on fire. Any explanations?"

"Malefic Magic? I wouldn't have thought a guy like you would even know what that word meant," she said, opening her notebook ready to work.

"Such stinging words. Look, if you want to be my friend and partner in biology, you *will* talk—got it?"

Angelina gazed at me amused this time. "Are you threatening me? Besides…who said I want to be your friend."

"I'm not threatening you, but I don't trust you either."

"I won't share anything with you," Angelina snickered. "If I don't feel like it—got it?"

I opened my notebook and began to study, ignoring our conversation. It took about forty-five minutes to complete what we could, both of us angry the whole time. I gathered my belongings and heard Angelina greet someone. I looked up and saw Julia.

"Uh…hi…I guess this table's taken," she said, nervously. "I'll find another one."

"Hey Julia, we were just leaving. You can have this one," I said, and threw my black backpack over my shoulder. "See you two later."

I felt Julia's eyes stare me down as I walked away, and sure enough, when I glanced over my shoulder, she was watching me. Smug Angelina had her arms crossed. If she wasn't a girl… I shook my head and let the rest of that thought trail off.

I made my way back to my room, left to wonder whether Angelina had the nerve to stay and talk to Julia or not. I didn't care. I looked forward to the upcoming guys' weekend. I needed a break from girls.

Later that night at work, Julia brought in a second date. I couldn't believe it. Adonis gave her a little breathing room, and she took off with it like she was in a marathon. Of course, she sat at one of my tables. I actually think she did it on purpose. I acted like I didn't have a clue who she was, which seemed to frustrate the daylights out of her. I couldn't help but smile with satisfaction.

It was Saturday night, busy as usual, and it was no surprise when Angelina sauntered in, making sure Julia saw her. Angelina always seemed to hang around like a parasite, though the expression on Julia's face when she came in was worth its weight in gold.

"Hey," Angelina said, beaming.

"What do you look so happy about?" I asked. Angelina plopped down on a barstool next to me, as I was picking up a drink order.

"Not much," she said, still smirking.

"Yeah, that seems to be your way…all secrets." My eyes mocked hers. "Why are you always around anyway? Are you stalking me?"

"Meddling in your life is becoming one of my favorite pastimes."

"What have you done now?" Irritation dripped from my voice.

"Let's just say, I helped you out with Blondie. I can tell there's something between the two of you, and now she knows how amazing I think you are. She's jealous as anything—mission accomplished."

I stuck my face into Angelina's. "Look Angelina, I don't need your help. I'm not interested in you. I think you're too forward, and I'd appreciate it if you left me alone."

Angelina glared at me for a second. "Have it your way," she said, and took off without ordering. Later she left a message on my phone. "Sorry I got under your skin." Yeah. I felt bad. I'm a pushover.

Time spent studying and engrossed in a pile of books was how I spent my days the following weeks, until Adonis showed up for training. I didn't bother to discuss Julia with him anymore, and he never mentioned her. In that duration, we practiced with guns and archery. His dismal, soundproof basement allowed me to practice using an assault gun and a machine gun, feeling the power behind each one without disturbing the neighborhood. I preferred the machine gun's ability to blast bullets that sounded like fireworks over any of the other weapons.

Adonis had a target hung up on one wall of the basement. I had to shoot from the opposite side and get as many bullets as possible out, reload, and repeat. It felt like I had trained forever, but in reality, only a half an hour had passed. He explained this type of training was for fighting on Earth in case any death players tagged a life player and went for the kill. Adonis was impressed with my good aim.

Following, we shot arrows from a cross bow at the same targets, learning this skill for warfare in Arcis. I shot one after the other with precision, though I didn't find it to be as gripping as the force of the guns.

I pulled an arrow out of the quiver that hung from my shoulder, placed it into the bow, and brought it back with all my strength. I released the string. The arrow sped, leaving a trail of smoke suspended in the air similar to the gases that mark a jet's pathway. On impact, the arrow made a popping noise. I watched as the target shattered into pieces and tumbled to the ground.

Adonis clapped in the background. "Well done, mate. Only the best life players have the capability to accomplish such a task. You're abilities are increasing at a remarkable speed. You'll need to watch your back, because as soon as Vorago catches wind of your successes, he'll hunt you down relentlessly, and send quantities of his followers to torture and kill you. You must never show your strength in public or draw attention to yourself like you've done in the past unless it's necessary. Have I made myself clear?"

"Yes sir," I answered, startled by his stern tone.

Later I asked Adonis again about the voice I'd heard in my head, but he still had no idea who it could've been. So much for being a lord, I guess.

We repeated the same exercises and went upstairs when we finished. Lisa was waiting on the couch for us to invite us both to dinner, which I thought rather strange. Maybe she hadn't spoken with Julia about what had transpired between us. I doubted that Julia would want me to have dinner with her family. I began to protest when Adonis accepted on both our behalf's. He told me to go to the house ahead of Lisa and him. I noticed the somber expression on both their faces and wondered what they had to discuss.

❖ ❧ ❖

The familiar sound of Beethoven's Fifth rang out when I pushed the doorbell. I cringed when I heard it, while my heart pounded. I didn't want to see Julia.

"Uh…hi, what are you doing here?" Julia asked, after she answered the door with her hands on her hips in defiance.

"Your mom and Adonis invited me to dinner," I answered, arrogantly.

Julia stared at me blankly. Her perfume emanated from her. "I have a date here, right now," she leaned forward in a whisper. I breathed in the recognizable fragrance as I brushed past her while she opened the door wider to let me in. Its odor felt like a prick from a rosebush's thorn.

My eyes lit up. "I can't *wait* to meet him."

He stood up when I strolled in, some new guy, at least the fifth guy in her life, including me, in the last few weeks. I guess she is on a role. This one, to my complete irritation, was disgustingly good looking, and, believe me, I'm not into checking out other guys. He could have been a model, though, with a cut bone structure and thick, sandy-brown hair. His brown eyes shone as he flashed me a grin as white as a sheet of paper. I shook his hand as the introductions were made. Brom was his name. A name I would've *loved* to make fun of. But I guess it wasn't his fault. He still had yet to find out what Julia was really like.

I knew *I* wouldn't be staying for dinner, and when Julia excused herself and left the living room to go into the kitchen, I excused myself and followed her.

"Which bachelor is this?" I asked.

"Excuse me?" Julia asked, acting like I had just asked her the most, difficult calculus question.

I spoke to Julia as though I was speaking to my six-year-old sister. "I'm sorry, I suppose I've lost count. Which bachelor is this, meaning how many dates have you been on? You've been out with so many different guys in the last two weeks. I'm having a hard time keeping up."

Julia rolled her eyes. "Are you keeping track? I thought you were cool about this."

"I was until you decided to set a world record, and from what I can see, you're choosing losers to go out with. Are you being careful, or are you gonna end up with another Josh?"

Julia stood right in front of me. "It's none of your business!"

I felt my cheeks burn with scorn toward her. "Do you like their kisses as much as you liked mine?" I could've kicked myself for having asked that.

"You're such a jerk!" she spat and hit my arm.

"And now you're hitting me?" My anger and hurt escalated.

Brom walked into the kitchen and cleared his throat. "Is everything okay?" he asked, nervously. "Sounds like world war three in here."

I walked up to him. "Brilliant observation Brom, but you should know that Julia and I have known each other since we were kids, and we're kind of like brother and sister," I exaggerated. "I hope you're nice to her because one of the last guys she dated wasn't, and…well…lets just say I had to take care of him, if you know what I mean." I flexed my bicep in his face and gave it a kiss. I winked at Julia. She stared on in horror.

"You two have fun," I called out over my shoulder, hoping she'd notice the smirk on my face, when I went to leave. Before I slammed the door shut, I heard Brom ask Julia what guys she had dated. He sounded ripped.

"You're staying, right?" Lisa called, to me as she walked back from Adonis's house.

"No thanks," I answered, coolly, "maybe some other time."

Lisa showed her disappointment. "That's too bad, Julia likes having you around."

I stopped dead in my tracks and gave her an intent stare. "Look, Ms. Simms, let's not fool ourselves. Julia's in there with a date, and right now she could care less if I'm there or not." Lisa's mouth dropped open. I apologized and told her I didn't mean to offend her, but I was just trying to keep it real.

I had thought Julia and I were meant to be. I believed Adonis had thought the same thing. Now I knew that wasn't how things would play out, and I had to let it go. Her rotten attitude made it a whole lot easier.

❖ ❧ ❖

It also helped that my guys' weekend with Jared and Robby finally rolled around. I had my bag packed and was ready to kick back and relax.

When we left, the crisp, late-October air chilled me to the bone. I huddled deep inside my red parka and cranked up the heat, as I drove my car to Robby's. It was Friday after classes, and Jared sat in the back tapping his fingers to the music that blared on the radio. In the front, Robby checked out any and all females in sight as we drove along.

"Hey Robby, how's Kaitland doing?" I asked.

"Ooh, she's great," he answered not going into detail. He answered like he was lost in a fog. I snapped my fingers in front of his face. "What… what do you want?" he asked, breaking out of his thoughts. "I'm sorry, whadya say? I didn't hear you."

"Kaitland," I said. "I just asked you how she's doing. Have you seen her much?"

"Yeah, she's not my girlfriend, though. You know, we see other people. She's cool about that."

Somehow, I doubted she was cool about it, but I kept my mouth shut. For the rest of the ride, we joked and laughed. We had fun chilling, without discussing anything in particular.

We drove past the almost barren trees. Their branches reached out to us like arms on Halloween night, a feast I loved as a kid. November, my least favorite month, was creeping in just around the corner, though I had the holidays to look forward to and snowboarding, of course. Tearing down the mountain was always a blast.

When we arrived at Robby's house, his parents rushed out, their faces beamed with excitement. His mom waved her hand like it was on fire.

"Uh wow, nice greeting," I said. "I guess your parents have missed you."

"Yeah, they can be a little embarrassing, but they're awesome," Robby agreed. He sprang out of the car to give them both a big hug, jumping up and down like a little kid.

I glanced back at Jared. He was watching Robby's parents with sadness spread across his face. I couldn't help but wonder why.

"You okay?" I asked. He ignored me, grabbed his bag, and jumped out of the car. I soon followed.

Robby's parents lived in a massive, dark-tan colonial with white shutters. The three-car garage made it look even larger. As we entered the kitchen, a sweet aroma struck our noses—an enormous plate of chocolate chip cookies. My favorite.

"Mmm, you're the best," Jared told Robby's mom, Madison. She was a robust, homemaker who looked fifty-ish. Her short, brown hair, decked out with auburn highlights, was messed up a little. Her face looked cheerful like she was always in high spirits.

Robby's dad, Alexander, was directly opposite to his wife. His hippy-style hair had been pulled back into a tight ponytail. It was jet black and showed no signs of gray. His body was pencil thin, and his smile took on a more serious tone. Robby's dad is a heart surgeon.

Robby's boisterous sister, Alyssa, came bounding in with a friend.

"Oh look, the twerp is here," she said.

WAR TRAINING
LACERATIONS

"Awe man, what is *she* doing here? I thought we had the weekend to ourselves," Robby piped in. Alyssa flicked his ear with her finger. Robby swatted her back.

"Thanks a lot," Alyssa answered, and then whispered something in her friend's ear. They both giggled and smiled as they checked me out. Alyssa introduced her friend, Tina.

"He *is* cute," Tina whispered.

"Boys for the weekend you're above the garage, and girls you're in the basement," Madison insisted, pointing her finger toward us.

"Don't worry Mrs. Anderson. We'll behave," Tina said to Madison, "and try not to the bother the guys too much." She winked at me.

After that, we settled in. The room we were staying in was a game room, with a pool table, an iHome, and an old-fashioned pinball machine. A movie screen TV hung on the wall. Every video game console made was laid out on the shelf next to it with several DVD movies on the shelf below that. The room looked newly renovated, with cathedral ceilings and tan Berber carpeting. A huge picture window covered one wall.

"Your house is amazing!" Jared exclaimed.

"Thanks," Robby answered, and turned on the jukebox. A song by Yiruma blasted out. "My parents music," Robby said, "let me find some rock."

Yiruma? I thought. Julia. Thinking about her gave me an unsettled feeling. I excused myself and went into the bathroom. It freaked me out that I heard Yiruma again. I had never heard his music before Julia mentioned him.

As soon as I closed the bathroom door, I used my necklace for the first time. I curled my fingers around the gold and concentrated on Julia's safety. My body bounced back and forth into the gray room Adonis had told me about, except that it wasn't empty. There were blurry images on both sides of me. To my right, I saw Julia out with her new friend Brom in an Italian restaurant. Their conversation sounded garbled. The amusement on their faces made me feel a pang of envy I couldn't shake away. Unfortunately, Adonis was wrong. I *could* see Julia.

On my left, I saw a vague image of an unrecognizable man with blonde hair, talking on a cell phone. I moved closer to that particular wall and heard him say something about his daughter's twin and her mother. He also sounded like someone talking under water.

It hit me. Of course. Julia was a twin. The man's hair was the same color as hers, and he did resemble the photo I saw at the Assembly. Anxious, I exited the bathroom and told the other guys I needed to make a phone call. I stepped outside and called Adonis. He answered after only one ring.

"What is it, mate?"

"Adonis, it's me, Bladen."

"I know."

"How could you know?"

"Caller I.D.?"

"I'm calling from my cell phone, and I've never given you this number before," I protested.

"Bladen, never mind," Adonis said, "why are you calling?"

When I explained what happened, Adonis responded with silence.

"Hey—Adonis, you still there?"

"I need to go. We'll talk later. Don't worry for now, okay?" Adonis said, and hung up the phone.

I went back into the house and found Robby and Jared playing pool with the iHome blaring, no jukebox. We hung out until Madison called us for our dinner—loads of pizza. Pretty scary how much food three college guys could consume.

Later, after dark, the girls snuck into our room to hang out with us, and, without me noticing, Jared snuck out. Alyssa and Tina were both cool girls. Alyssa could have been Robby's twin. Her dark hair almost matched his. Her eyes were the same shade of brown. The one big difference between the two of them, she wasn't as flirtatious with the opposite sex as her brother. She didn't hit on Jared or me. Tina, on the other hand, was short with a bouncy personality. She laughed a lot. Her jet-black hair flowed to the bottom of her back and was almost too long for her height. Her sapphire eyes danced with delight or danced with a desire for Robby. She obviously had a thing for him, but to my surprise, he didn't act like he cared. Something's gotta be wrong with him, I thought. After a few games of pool, which we won thanks to Robby, the girls left, and Jared had still not come back.

"Where'd Jared take off to?" Robby asked me.

"Beats me," I answered, unconcerned.

"Well…since he's not here, I need to talk to you about him."

"What's up?"

"Remember the first weekend at school, when he came in our room, and his eyes were bloodshot?"

"Yeah."

"Well, he's been like that quite a few times. I tried to talk to him about it…you know…brother to brother. He denies anything's wrong, yet he jokes about being dead. He acts real down sometimes and has told me how crappy his parents are. I'm worried he might be suicidal. Crazy thing is…most of the time he's fun to hang out with and smart…man is he smart…your talking the next Einstein, seriously. He's so lucky. He just gets everything."

"I don't know–," I began to respond, but didn't have time to finish. Jared stormed into the room laughing hysterically. He fell to the floor. When he looked up at us, his eyes were bloodshot.

Robby was mad and lost his cool. He picked Jared up by his shirt and shook him. "What kind of drugs you on, man? I can't believe you're acting like this in my house! My parents are gonna be ripped if they find out." Jared laughed the entire time Robby dragged him to the bathroom, even after Robby slammed the door.

"This is what I'm talking about," Robby said. His eyes blazed with anger. "What are we gonna do with him, bro? I swear he's never coming to my house again."

"There's nothing we can do right now. Let's wait until he sleeps it off. Okay? We'll talk to him tomorrow,"

Later Robby and I talked about girls, naturally. Even though Robby thought Kaitland was cool about dating other people, he thought she'd fallen pretty hard for him. "I'm not sure if I should break it off with her," he told me. "I'm too young for anything that serious…but forget me. What about you? You said nothing's going on with you and Julia, but I've seen you with a brunette who's a knockout. Who is she? Come on, man, give me the dirt."

Robby always made me laugh. "She's my biology partner, and she's weird. No big deal."

"You lie, man. She's gotta be the hottest girl on campus, and from what I've seen, she looks like she's hot for you too."

She *was* beautiful. I couldn't deny it.

Alyssa and Tina came back in real late. We hung out until the sun came up, and finally slept…a little. Jared passed out. The girls never asked why he "fell asleep" so early.

The next day, Jared denied everything when we brought it up to him. Robby was more concerned than angry.

On Sunday, we drove back to school as silently as snow floating down on a winter's day. When we got to the dorm, I told Jared I wanted to talk to him about what had happened. He told me, "No way." So—I let it go.

Sunday night I fell into another subterraneous sleep, seeing nothing but raven-like darkness until I began to dream. What else?

A spark of light, like a camera flash, lit up in front of me. I was paddling in a tiny vessel in what appeared to be the Tiber River again. A huge monstrous form, the same toothless creep in my past dreams, emerged from the waters. His mouth parted, about to shout, until a giant, muscular figure adorned in armor with a mini Mohawk strapped to the top of his head came forth.

"I am Mars, here for blood." He peered at me and shrieked. His bloodstained lance spoke more than a thousand words. I watched him plunge it into the heart of not only the monstrous figure but also into the man sitting in front of me. Blood splattered all around.

He squinted at me, amused. "You're next."

I awoke startled, as usual, my breathing heavy. I felt something warm dripping down my arm—blood—the same blood that had been lavishly sprayed in my dream. My heart beat like a drum at an Indian ritual. I yanked a tissue out of the Kleenex box next to me and wiped it up.

At least it was Mars, I thought panicked, and not Ares, Mar's counterpart. Ares was the Greek god of war and had a more violent, ruthless reputation. Mars, on the other hand, was the Roman god of war. He was supposed to have been more civil. Maybe seeing Mars was a positive sign for me regarding whatever message, Vorago had tried to threaten me with. I felt sure my dream had been inspired by him.

I wanted to scream for a decent night sleep, but I felt my body balloon in and out, readying itself for Arcis. One part of me was lying comfortably in my bed, while the other prepared for a dangerous quest.

I landed in Arcis where barren trees were pushed up against a lonely landscape—the ugliest place I'd seen so far. Level five?

Benedict and Gianna floated down like feathers from the sky, their bodies illuminated like soft oil lamps in their long, ashen robes. Their compassionate smiles set me at ease. After a warm greeting, they explained my purpose for this exercise in Arcis. I was there not only to beat level five, squash impiety on Earth, but also for my own personal training, so that I would be fit for the battle in the bathing houses of Myndos, Turkey.

"Okay...what exactly do you want me to do?" I asked.

Benedict handed me a compass. "You need to travel from where we're standing now, until you reach the beach near Gianna's home. This compass will guide you on your journey north, until you reach your destination. Be careful using it. It's magical." The compass was the color of gray stones on the inside. The outside was the light-blue color of the sky. Depending on which way I held it, the two colors changed in the same way the animal world uses mimicry for protection, making it impossible for the enemy to see it.

"Sounds easy enough," I answered, without bothering to ask more questions. I already knew they'd probably tell me I had to figure it out on my own anyway.

Shaking her head, Gianna stopped me. "No, this training is only for those life players who will become the most dominant, Bladen. You must be vigilant because you can't cast any of the demons into the abyss. You must fight them, outsmart them, and continue to run north at lightening speed. They may continue to chase after you."

"You'll have to find a way to rest without being noticed," Benedict continued, "or you'll tire and never make it."

My heart sank—for a couple of seconds. "What are you saying? Is there a chance I won't be able to do this? What will happen to me then?"

"I feel strongly that you *can* achieve this," Benedict went on. "There's a fraction of a chance that you won't, and if that does indeed occur, the ramifications of what Earth will face—I wouldn't want to imagine—"

I stared blankly at the two of them, moving up and down on my tiptoes, hands in my armored pants. "No pressure, huh?"

Gianna spread her index finger and thumb about a half-inch apart and smiled wryly. "Maybe just a little."

"I almost forgot," Benedict said, reaching into a pocket in his robe. "You should eat this."

I took one look at what he handed me. "No way, I'm not eatin' that. You can't pay me enough to eat that junk. Don't you remember what happened the last time I ate it?" It was wormale! The potent food that blew my stomach up like helium.

"Yes, I do recall that. However, this will help sustain your strength," Benedict insisted, "and you need to eat only a little. You ate too much before."

I took one bite of the wormale and in an instant felt full. It *did* taste good.

Gianna took my hand in both of hers and warned me. "We won't be able to help you this time. You'll be mostly on your own, so be careful...okay?"

I loved that phrase, mostly on your own. I was curious to find out what she meant by that and to check out my new compass. I thanked Benedict and Gianna and said goodbye.

I was pumped for the upcoming challenge and set off running at a swift pace. I pulled out the compass and opened it. As expected, I was traveling north. When I shook the compass around, it began to talk. Cool, I thought, like my own personal G.P.S. in Arcis. I suppose Gianna and Benedict knew I'd need it.

The compass sounded like a computer. "Twenty-five feet north to your left and sitting high up on a boulder is a Terra...demon...Terra."

I slowed to a jog and pulled out my bow. I hid behind a tree and saw the demon. Its body was blown out in a massive block of fat, dark-green in color, with a white, scruffy wig-like bundle of hair that sprouted out from its head. Tattered clothing covered its pathetic body. The demon's back was facing me. Slowly, it turned around, smiling with its toothless grin.

"I've been waiting for you," it said, in a high, raspy voice just before it began its sinister cackle.

I had an arrow set and readied my hand to pull the string. Smoke filled the air when I let it go, blocking my view of the demon, though I still had the satisfaction of hearing it wince in pain when the arrow hit it. I sprinted away, past the obscure surroundings, only glancing back every few seconds to make sure the Terra wouldn't hunt me down.

My breath grew heavier as I ran. Again, the compass vibrated in my pocket like a cell phone. I answered it by lifting the latch on the front of it.

"Ninja ten feet to your right." It said without emotion.

Ninja, I thought. Now I felt like I was in the middle of a completely different video game. I turned to my right and saw him. He held a Frisbee-like disc called a ninja star. He cast it toward me at a startling rate. I ducked but not without it nicking the armor on the crown of my head. He threw a second one at me that soared at jet speed. This time it connected with my armor but bounced off. He dragged out his sword. Another ninja sprung up next to him.

The other ninja used kung fu and spun in the air toward me, wielding another ninja star. This one struck my cheek, where there was no armor to shield me.

"Crap!" I muttered in pain, clutching my face. My fingers smeared my bloody flesh.

They both charged toward me. A third joined them swinging nun chucks. I had no chance, but I did my best to ward them off with my sword. I plunged it into one of them and watched him drop. To my surprise, several other life players joined me. Their armor looked exactly like mine. Once I had backup, I pulled my nunchucks out as well. Somehow, I knew how to use them.

"Who are you?" one player asked, while his sword clashed together with one of the other ninjas.

"Bladen, and you?"

"I'm Joshua. You're a life player, right? I wasn't anticipating running into anyone out here." His voice sounded winded.

"Yeah, I'm a life player. I didn't expect to see anyone either." I noticed this life player's blazing blue eyes, fierce with determination.

I knew the ninja next to me wasn't a real ninja, just a demon in disguise, but still, it fought like a real ninja. In no time, we took all three ninjas down and bound them to a tree.

"Maybe I'll see you at the next Assembly," Joshua called, and sprinted away.

"What? How?" I asked, but it was too late. He had already dashed off, and there I was again left unaccompanied, racing northward toward my final destination.

I brawled with Terra after Terra—the land demons were ruthless. They used clone imaging to alter the shapes of their heads into everyone I cared about, from Julia and friends to my family. Even though they hoped it would make me powerless, it gave me dominance. I fought like my body was loaded with explosives. I stabbed my dagger into the stomach of one of them, slit the throat of another, and shot two others down with more arrows.

In due course, an Aer demon swooped down and lashed at my neck. I lost my breath and fell to the ground, only capable of going through the motions of breathing. I saw black and white spots and felt like I was going to faint. Finally, I caught my breath.

The Aer demon hovered nearby and snickered at me. Its large dragon wings spanned at least four feet and sagged from old age? I wasn't sure. I checked out its pea-size black eyes that seemed worn out against its prehistoric-looking body. It flew away, priding itself under its breath for a job well done.

Yeah right, I thought and stood up ready to fight again. My strength returned to its full capacity. Why don't you come back and play, little birdie?

At that juncture, the terrain around me began to alter swiftly from the dark, barren trees, to an unrelenting canyon like the Grand Canyon, to an ocean with raging waves, and then settling on a jagged, snowcapped mountain range as large as the Himalayas. I shivered from the freezing air.

"Screech, Screech." I heard Slaughter.

"Hey little buddy, good to see ya," I called out, happily surprised to see him.

"Who you callin' little?"

"Sorry, man. How are ya?"

"Here to help you is how I am," he answered with an attitude.

"How do you plan to help me?" I asked and gave him a respectful bow.

"You need to rest," he said, "or you won't make it. Hang on to me."

Slaughter enlarged his insignificant body, until it was at least six feet in width. A dignified crest sprouted from the top of his head that shone bright red in color, similar to a cardinal. It looked strange compared to his amethyst body. He smiled a human smile beneath the animal façade, pleased that I was impressed.

I grabbed hold of his talons. He breathlessly flew me to a cave deep within the mountains. I helped him start a fire, sat down, and warmed my body, leaning my head against the metamorphic rock behind me. Before long, I fell into a dreamless sleep.

When I awoke, there was a man resting beside me with lengthy blonde hair down to his shoulder. The gold in it shone from the light of the fire. Another Terra, I thought in disgust. I reached for my dagger and jumped to my feet. He glanced up in surprise, rose, and swiftly pulled the dagger from my hand. He took my arm and twisted it behind my back. I heard Slaughter's voice in the background. I yelled to him to help me.

"I am helping you, ya fool," he scolded me. When my arm was released, I turned and saw only the blonde fellow, no Slaughter.

"Who are you?" I asked, bewildered.

"It's me, Slaughter," he answered, grinning.

"Get out," I said in disbelief. The blonde guy with the angelic face was Slaughter? I thought he was only a bird—not just any bird, I'll give you. He was special. My eyes widened as I stared longer at him, until I recognized his dark-brown, intense eyes.

"You can shape shift into human form?" I asked.

He nodded.

"Cool." If I had a gift like that on Earth, I could only imagine what kind of trouble I'd get into. The idea made me smile. Soon after I had enough rest, I continued on, and Slaughter went his own way.

I had almost reached my destination, with the ocean just over the next slight hill. I couldn't understand why I needed the rest. I was almost to Gianna's, a winner. I started basking in glory. Within a few arms reach, I saw the transparent walls—Gianna's walls—my final resting spot, when I felt the hair stand up on the back of my neck. I turned around and wasn't prepared for what I saw.

"Crap," I mumbled under my breath. There were several demons from the land, sea, *and* air, all with similarities in their appearance: they looked like black skeletons with transparent flesh-like wings that spanned about three feet, and blood-red eyes that hung just below their horns. Wickedness emanated from every thread of them. I'll never win, but I'd rather be destroyed trying, I thought, worried about Earth and any catastrophes that could arise from my failings.

I pulled out my arrows, one of my best forms of attack, and let them soar one after the other. I shot demon after demon. They shrieked and fell down to the ground, until I drew my last arrow and released. That's when I turned to run and saw Gianna's heartrending face. She watched in horror from within her safe walls as the scene played out before her. The demons swarmed around me like bees. I must have looked like a dead carcass on the side of the road, clothed with ravenous flies. I felt unimaginable pain. A moan I didn't have control over came from deep within my throat. I saw only blackness, until I passed out and traveled through my phone back into one body.

When I regained consciousness, the three beating suns of Arcis were the last things I remembered. "Help me, please help me," I had cried out to Spero. A ray of light had flowed out from the suns and embraced me with its warmth. Now, I could taste the salt, feel the throbbing in my body, and see the pool of blood in front of me that came from my mouth and too many other places on my body.

"9…1…1," I croaked. As I repeated those three beautiful numbers, I imagined someone taking the excruciating pain away.

"What the…" cried Robby. "What happened?" He fell out of his bed, panicked. He fumbled with his phone, hair sticking up, eyes filled with sleep.

I heard him explain, "My…my roommate's on the floor, blood's everywhere. What do I do? Help."

BOTTOMLESS PIT

My body bounced against the stretcher beneath me, which caused agonizing pain, as I was wheeled toward the waiting ambulance. I pulsated in and out of consciousness and was barely aware of the firm straps that pinned me down to hard, cold metal. I did feel a needle of some sort pierce my right arm. By the time we reached the hospital, the pain lessened. They brought me to a room and I heard the click of the door's bolt as they locked it behind them. Fear gripped me for a second. I blinked, trying to see who exactly *they* were. I could make out one person's black hair as they moved me from the gurney to a bed. The other one wore a long, white coat and possibly glasses. It was too blurry for me to tell.

"Bladen, it's okay." The presumed doctor's voice comforted me. "I'm a life player too. We'll take good care of you."

"Are you sure he's going to be all right?" I heard one of them ask.

"Yes," the other answered. "He's healing extraordinarily fast, quite unusual."

I grunted in misery and felt another shot in my arm.

"This will help him sleep it off," said the one in the white coat.

It must have been much later when I gradually woke up. Most of my pain was gone, except for an ache on my skin near my throat and a few painful gashes on my face. I sat up woozy in a bed and rubbed my eyes.

"Brilliant," Adonis remarked. When my vision adjusted, I saw Adonis come into focus like the lens on a camera.

"Hey," I mumbled.

Adonis walked over and placed his hand on my arm. "You're almost entirely healed," he said. "You have no idea how amazing this is." He turned on the TV above my bed and showed me the news. Flight 8250 with 127 passengers aboard had gone down in Columbia. It was hit by lightening and crashed. The nose of the plane was torn away, yet there was only one fatality, a 73-year-old woman who died from a heart attack. They're calling it a miracle.

"That's you, right there. Because of your increased fighting capabilities and how rapidly your body is healing, a miracle has occurred. Congratulations, you're becoming a powerful life player. If all players fought with the same zeal and passion as you, evil would be conquered much sooner."

"When did this crash occur?" I asked, amazed.

"Last August."

The door opened, and a young doctor walked in just as I was throwing my shaky legs over the bed and onto the floor.

"Look at you! I don't think you'll need to be spending the night after all." He stood by my bedside and extended his hand for me to shake it. "I'm Dr. James. I'm a life player like you." He looked young and brawny, with curly red hair like Jared's.

With my jelly-like legs, I stood up and hobbled to the mirror. I gazed, wide-eyed at my reflection, as I watched the gouges on my cheeks quickly vanish before my eyes. I touched my face with the tips of my fingers, not believing what I had just seen.

"I do good work, don't I?" Dr. James chided.

I remembered Robby and asked Adonis about him. Adonis reassured me that he had already explained to Robby that my body might have experienced a seizure. Tests were being conducted, but I would be fine. After that, I stayed in the hospital for about an hour. Then they released me.

I briskly headed for the lobby door and nearly ran into Angelina.

"Hey, watch it! Why are *you* in such a hurry?" she muttered.

"Oh sorry. What are you doing here?" At first I thought she was there to see me.

"Haven't you heard?"

"Heard what?"

"Jared's in the hospital…suicide attempt," she whispered.

"No way," I answered strickened. "How do you know him?"

Angelina rolled her eyes. "Geek's group…you know…we're in a computer club together."

"You're smart?" I asked, not thinking. If looks could kill, I would've been dead. "I didn't mean it that way. Tell me what happened," I insisted and pulled Angelina aside, away from the door.

"He overdosed on sleeping pills. His roommate found him. He only had a faint heart rate by the time they got to him."

"Oh man, Robby's been worried about him. I knew Jared was depressed. I tried to talk to him about it, but he wouldn't talk to me."

"Who's Robby?" Angelina asked.

"My roommate. He hangs out a lot with Jared."

"Oh…I didn't know that…well, I need to go see him now, so I'll see you later," Angelina said.

"Wait," I stopped Angelina. "Do you want to go together?"

Angelina stared at me quizzically. "I thought you said I was stalking you and that you didn't want anything to do with me."

"I'm sorry. It's not like I wanted to offend you, but you *were* a little pushy."

"Yeah, I know." Angelina gazed up at me. "I'm sorry too, friends?" She offered her hand to me. I gave it a little shake.

"Sure," I answered. "Let's see if they'll let us visit Jared now, okay?"

We checked in at the nurse's station and was told that Jared was ready for visitors.

Angelina tapped on the door, and as there was no answer, she quietly walked in first. Jared, was lounging in bed. He glanced our way and then stared out the window at the pounding rain.

Angelina went right over and sat next to him on the bed. She handed him a sheet of paper. "I want you to read this…now, okay?" she said, and caressed his cheek. Jared held the paper in his hands. He took a few moments to study it and then put it down. Angelina gave him a huge hug. His eyes welled up with tears, but he blinked them back. Angelina whispered a few things in his ear that I couldn't hear, and Jared nodded his head. When she finished, she kissed his cheek and stood up. As she walked past me, she asked, "Meet me in the lobby before you leave the hospital, okay?

"Sure," I replied and went and stood next to Jared. He managed a feeble smile. "You don't need to tell me anything," he offered. "I'll be out of here tomorrow…I'll be seeing a counselor." His voice cracked as he spoke.

"You're one of Robby's best friends, you know?" I said, concerned.

"I know. He's a good friend."

"If you want someone to talk to, I'm always here. People care about you. I'm your friend, too."

Jared nodded. "I do want to talk to you and Robby…you know… to explain." I was about to protest and tell him he didn't have to tell us anything if he didn't want to, but he stopped me.

"I want you to know. It's important to me…I just don't want to talk about it right now."

"Sure…I understand…any time you're ready."

Jared nodded again.

I walked to the door and zipped up my jacket. "Want me to give you a lift outta here tomorrow?"

"Yeah thanks. They said I can leave around 11:30 in the morning."

I had my hand on the door handle ready to go, when Jared stopped me. "Hey, wait a second."

"Yeah?"

"Do you know what it feels like?" he asked, as he gazed somewhere on the wall behind me.

"What do you mean?"

"What it feels like…to want to take your own life," he went on stone-faced, as though he went back into his own dark, collected memories.

My heart thumped, and I answered honestly. "No, I don't."

Before going on, he disappeared into his thoughts for a few seconds longer before he described it. "It feels like the pain inside is so great, but nothing can be done about it–complete hopelessness. Then it's like this dark disease starts to cover every inch of your body, slowly, and can't be stopped…and the only desire is for all of it to go away."

Silence echoed in the room. Jared shook his head as though to clear it of any visions he had and gave me another weak smile. My heart was still pounding.

"I'm sure now everything will be okay," I said. At least I hoped it would.

"Yeah, I know it will," he answered, confidently.

We said our goodbyes, and I left.

I found Angelina in the lobby waiting for me. Exotic plants adorned the room, like the hospital staff had tried real hard to make the place cheerful.

"Hey," Angelina said, walking up to me.

I shook my head in disbelief. The whole situation felt surreal. Angelina and I hugged each other. It seemed like the right thing to do, at that moment. She looked upset, like her pretty face was trying to hold back a sprinkle of tears.

"It's probably none of my business, but what did you hand Jared on that sheet of paper?" I asked.

She let go of me and wiped her eyes. She reached into her purse and handed me another sheet of paper. "Here, you can read it. I don't mind."

I unfolded the white, lined paper and saw that it revealed Angelina's handwriting.

"Is this a song or a poem or something?" I asked.

"More like a poem for now, I guess. I need to add more words to turn it into a song, I think."

I read Angelina's words to myself.

Life is a poem,

A romantic song,

A dance on a moonlit beach,

A moment that won't last long.

Move forward,

Don't look back,

No one can replace you,

I hope you remember that.

Breathe in life,

Every breath has a number,

Live your dream,

Not a life in slumber.

Move forward,

Don't look back,

No one can replace you,

I hope you remember that.

Love is a starry sky,

A night's sweet kiss,

An everlasting hug,

A moment not to miss.

Move forward,

Don't look back,

No one can replace you,

I hope you remember that.

Yeah you need to remember that.

Yeah baby, remember that...

"Did you write this...by yourself...for Jared?" I asked, curiously.

Angelina took the paper out of my hands and placed it back into her purse. "Sort of," she answered. "Look...I have a lot of studying to do. I need to go." And like that she split.

"Yeah...I'll see ya." I called after her and watched as her hair bounced against the back of her tan, corduroy jacket. She paused at the door, glanced back and gave me a sweet smile, then walked out, pulling her jacket around her to fight against the torrential rain outside.

Angelina had diametrically opposing sides, I figured, ones I wouldn't have imagined existed. She had at first seemed as strange as a Venus Flytrap, but now she was as beautiful as a rose, a fascinating attraction. I didn't know her that well, but part of me couldn't wait to talk to her and find out more.

At 11:30 a.m. sharp the following day, I drove back to the hospital to pick up Jared. When I walked into his room, he looked ready to go, rocking back and forth, free as a pendulum, as he gazed out the window. He didn't hear me come in and was startled when he saw me.

"You scared me," he laughed, a little. His combed hair gave him a look I wasn't accustomed to. Typically, his untamed hair sprouted from the top of his head like weeds in a garden. Something else about his face seemed different too.

"Can you see all right?" I asked.

"Yeah, why?"

"You're not wearing your glasses."

"Contact lenses," he explained.

"I have to say, you look great, Jared," I said, glad to see him so put together.

"Thanks," he answered, as he shrugged his shoulders and looked away.

Neither one of us spoke on the drive back to our dorm. When we arrived, he grabbed his bag, thanked me for the ride, and headed inside.

Robby was in our room. His thumbs were hitting like pistons against his XBox 360 remote, as he battled some evil creature in a foreign land. I didn't really like regular video games all that much anymore, not after I had traveled to Arcis. The real thing was way more intense.

"Robby," I called, so he could hear me.

"Aw, you made me lose, and I was so close," he sputtered.

We both heard a knock on the door. Must be Jared, I thought.

He let himself in and stood ill-at-ease, his hands buried deep in his jean pockets. Robby did a double take when he saw him. "Dude, did ya get a makeover or what. Cool hair." Robby took the liberty of messing it up. Jared shoved him away, laughing.

Then a dim shadow crossed Jared's face. His smile faded away. He closed the door behind him. "If you don't mind, I want to get this over with."

Robby and I didn't say a word. We knew why he had come. I motioned to Jared to have a seat.

"Four score and seven years ago..." Jared began.

Robby grabbed a shoe and threw it at him. "Dude, you're not Abraham Lincoln and you sound like a nerd," he said.

Jared dodged the attack and threw the shoe back. "Sorry," he said, "but you should see the look of anticipation on both of your faces. I couldn't help myself. Are you guys that bored with your lives?"

"No way bro. I got the ladies," Robby said. "You know, if there weren't the ladies, then I'd be bored." He glanced at me and continued to ramble. "Nothing personal, man. As far as roommates go, you're cool...and I got the video games."

I hadn't been bored either, though I didn't say anything. I encouraged Jared to continue and glared at Robby to stop him from droning on and on like a moron.

Jared's nervousness showed. "Look...I'm going to give you guys the short version about my life...here goes...I don't live with my parents...um...they used to beat me up pretty bad, black and blue. Now they're both in prison. I know I look like a nerd. Believe me—my parents made sure to tell me that every day. When I came home with the highest grades, they laughed and called me all kinds of obscenities I won't repeat." Jared stopped and looked at Robby, who shook his head.

"I...I...was joking about the whole nerd thing," Robby said.

"I know," Jared answered, "don't worry about it. Just let me finish."

Robby nodded for Jared to go on.

"My parents also owned a business with my uncle, my dad's brother. They embezzled money. My uncle never thought in a thousand years they'd have it in their hearts to commit a crime like that against him. He never knew they abused me either. He thought of me as a shy child. I found out about my parents, when I overheard their conversation one night. After they downed a bottle of whiskey, they talked, more like slurred, about their exploits a little too loudly. Loud enough for me to hear anyway, and when the police came to question them at a later date, I told them everything I knew, including their abusive behavior toward me. I was eleven at the time.

When the police arrested them, they told me they wished I'd never been born, and that when they were released from jail, they'd find me and kill me. My uncle was horrified and shocked. He felt sorry for me, so he took me in and is now helping me pay for college.

I know taking too many sleeping pills was desperate, and when my uncle came to see me in the hospital—" Jared broke off, and put his head down. His voice choked up. "I'll never do it again…because my uncle was so sad. I didn't realize he loved me that much. He told me he understood after the way my parents had treated me."

Quiet filled the room as the warmth of friendship covered us. Of course, Robby's wild n' crazy personality broke the stillness like a rooster breaks the silence of dawn. He gave Jared a hug. "Look, bro, I'm sorry—I should've done something about this sooner. I saw it coming and should've told someone. You're a good friend. We're cool. I was thinkin' maybe you should hang with me more, man. I'll teach you to have fun with the babes. In return, you can help me with my grades. They need some work."

"What kind of fun do you mean exactly, Robby?" I mocked.

Robby winked at both of us. "Check this out," he said. He strolled over to the window, ripped it open, and whistled at some girls walking on the sidewalk below. Jared and I moved closer for a better look. "Hey baby, you look fine tonight. Why don't you come on up. We're in room 222, and we're waitin' for you."

The girls giggled.

Turning to us, Robby shrugged. "They may not come up, but I just made those girls laugh. Mmm…hmm, that's right. Hang with me, and we'll pick up chicks." Robby pointed to me. "Bladen…now he's always off doing his thang. I wish he'd chill with me more often." Jared and I laughed.

We told Jared his secret was safe with us, and we all went our separate ways. Case closed.

The next couple of weeks flew by. As the milder sunlit days ended, the long nights seemed lonelier. Thanksgiving grew near. I was excited to see my family, especially since my original promise to visit and go hiking in September had never been fulfilled.

My parents didn't miss me nearly as much as my littlest siblings, anyway. I knew what I'd find when I visited home. Christiana would probably beg me to stay and never leave again, complaining that everyone picked on her with imagined tales of sibling torture that had some grain of truth to them. Timmy would try to act like a dude, with all his eleven years of age, and I was sure Cynthia and April, both teenagers now, would be even more into boys, makeup, and their wardrobes. Nicholas planned to bring Stephanie home, which was a big ordeal. I missed them all.

Finally, Thanksgiving rolled around. I raced along curvy Vermont roads during the two and a half hour trip home. Fluffy, white snow sprinkled down like powdered sugar all around. The first real snow of the year always turned the bland, gray countryside into a shimmering snow globe.

When I drove into my parents' driveway, a car I recognized was parked there, taking up two spaces. Odd, I thought. It was the same make and color Lisa Simms drove—a dark, blue Volvo. Because of the angular way it was parked, I didn't have room and had to park further away from the house.

No one heard me as I let myself in, but I saw Lisa and Adonis standing in the kitchen, and my heart fell two feet when I saw Julia sitting at the table near them. I didn't have time to comment on our extra guests.

My dad was chopping vegetables at the counter, when he glanced up. "Bladen, hey!" He dropped his knife and gave me a hug. I greeted and hugged my mom, and then my siblings bombarded me. They all behaved just as I had expected. Little Christiana acted like a monkey and climbed all over me. I tickled her to the floor to make her stop.

Nicholas bounded up next with Stephanie, his face shining with adoration for his new girlfriend, their bronze skin, suntanned from the blazing, Costa Rican sun. They gazed at each other with affection, hands locked together, and, as expected, she was perfectly sweet. She was Costa Rican like my boss, a detail Nicholas had left out.

In contrast, Julia, who I spoke with next, had a sour expression on her face as though she had just polished off a bowl of lemons. I didn't want her around, and she looked like the feelings were mutual.

Lisa was bubbly as usual, and it was always great to see Adonis, even though I saw him several times a week already.

The first chance I had, I grabbed my mom and whispered in anger, so no one could hear me. "Why are the Simms here with Adonis?"

My mom looked surprised. "You know everything that's going on with Julia, finding out about their lives," she replied. "Lisa told me Julia's been upset, so I invited them for Thanksgiving. Your father and I wanted to give them support. Why are you so angry?"

"How do you know what's going on in her life?" I asked, stunned and confused. "You know about life players?"

"I thought Adonis told you," my mom answered, surprised.

"Told me what?" I asked.

"We need to talk," she said staring at me wide-eyed. She pulled me aside and led me down the hall. She told me she and my dad had both been life players when they were younger, and that Adonis had kept them up-to-date about me. I had nothing to explain. My parents knew it all! I couldn't believe they had all discussed *my* life with each other and thought I knew. Seriously, parents can be clueless.

Later that night after Julia and her mom went to bed, Adonis and I stayed up with my parents and worked it all out. Apparently, my parents stopped their role as life players when they got married. That was something new I didn't know. All life players had to be single and unmarried, so they wouldn't be distracted with family. I decided it was cool my parents had been life players. At least now, I wouldn't have to keep my life a secret from them. Julia had no idea my parents had been life players, and now my parents knew I didn't want anything to do with Julia. Of course, my mom insisted I be nice to her.

❖ ❂ ❖

On Thanksgiving Day, we chowed down way too much food: stuffing with celery, onions, and just the right amount of spices; mashed potatoes with melted butter, green bean casserole, and, of course, an enormous turkey cooked a perfect golden brown that looked good enough to be on a TV commercial. Everyone relaxed and had fun. After dessert, I noticed Julia had left and not returned.

My mom and Lisa had started to clean up and wash the mound of dishes. "I need more dish soap, Bladen. Could you be a dear and go downstairs to get more for me?" my mom asked.

"Sure Mom," I answered, and descended the stairs to our basement. Julia was standing by the sliding glass door that faced the east side of my house.

"I remember when your parents put on this addition," she reminisced, when she saw me come down. "There was a huge pile of dirt, right there." Julia pointed to the spot outside where it had been. "We had so much fun playing in it. Do you remember?"

Julia was talking about the right side of the house. Years ago, my parents built an addition with a basement and an upstairs that had two extra bedrooms and a living room. The basement was our rec room or the place where company stayed.

I walked up next to her. "Yeah, I remember you throwing mud balls at me," I teased, trying to be kind—my mother's advice. "I guess you always had it out for me."

Julia looked pleased at my kindness. Then she startled me. She threw her hands around my neck and pressed her mouth to mine. I tasted a hint of peppermint. Not thinking, I slipped my hands around her waist and returned the kiss. Our lips moved in harmony like music. Our breath quickened. Julia made a fist as she grasped a clump of hair at the nape of my neck. I pulled her closer, pressing her body against mine until, like waking up from a bad dream, her recent nastiness flickered through my mind—a PowerPoint picture show I didn't feel like watching.

I pulled back and released my grip around her waist only slightly. "Somehow I don't think Brom would appreciate this," I murmured.

"He's not my boyfriend," she whispered back.

I removed my arms brusquely from around Julia's waist. She stumbled back into the sliding glass door.

"Hey!" she grumbled.

"Really?" I responded hotly. "So, if he knew you were here kissing me, he'd be okay with that?"

Julia turned her head away.

"That's what I thought...let me recap the last few months for you. We were both attracted to each other. You can't deny that. One thing led to another, and it became more, but you dropped me when you found out I'm a life player. I trusted you. I could understand if I fought on the other side, one of the bad guys, but I'm one of the good guys. I don't get it."

Julia stared stone-faced at the snow outside. Her blonde hair revealed their faded summer highlights in the sunlit room. I resisted the desire to reach out and brush my hand against her face.

"So," I continued, "you started dating and just had to bring your dates into where I work—to smear it in my face, no doubt. Like that wasn't bad enough, you sat by and watched, while one of them tried to totally humiliate me...remember? You told me I was a jerk and hit me at your house. You're dating Brom, and now...you want to kiss me?" I moved closer to Julia and placed my hand around her shoulder. She caught her breath but didn't move. I nudged my mouth near her ear. "I don't think we're meant to be together," I whispered. "I thought we were, but I guess not."

We both stood still. The quiet felt endless as haunted memories of a love that would never happen filled our minds.

"We can still be friends, right?" she said, looking up at me with watery eyes.

"I don't know."

"Why?" she demanded.

"You haven't been a good friend so far."

"I'm sorry," she said, exasperated.

"It's only my opinion," I said, "but you have some growing up to do… maybe at some point we'll be friends again."

Julia glared at me.

Calmly, I went into the utility closet, grabbed the dish soap my mother wanted, and left. Feeling the heat of Julia's stare, I never turned back.

SIBLINGS

The next morning I woke up and ate a vegetable omelet with my family. Then I packed my bag to go. I didn't have to work until the next night, Saturday, but I thought I'd head back to school to get some extra studying done. Julia seemed stressed with me around. I was sure she'd be happy to see me go. My siblings were disappointed, but I assured them I'd be back soon for Christmas vacation.

Packed up and ready to go, I put the key in the ignition and revved the engine. I was just about to pull out, when Julia ran toward me. She left the front door wide open. I rolled down my window and felt an amused smirk creep on my face. Julia looked messed up with wild hair. She must have just jumped out of bed, I thought.

"I didn't know you were leaving today," she said, out of breath, while she placed her hands on the car door.

"I didn't think you cared," I mused, trying to hide my smile.

She placed a hand on her hip. "Funny," she responded, not looking pleased. "I wanted to make sure…um…about yesterday…that we keep that between us."

I enjoyed watching her squirm—more than I should have, perhaps. "You mean, you don't want me to tell Brom?"

"Exactly," she replied.

I revved my engine again, nonchalantly placed my sunglasses on the bridge of my nose, and unable to resist smiling any longer, I beamed, "Don't worry…I don't kiss and tell." With that, I stepped on the gas and took off, leaving Julia to spring back away from my car. I glanced in my rearview mirror and saw her glaring until I was out of sight. The ride back felt long, plenty of time to try to clear my head of hollow visions of Julia.

Back at my room, I studied for a while but had a difficult time concentrating. I left and worked out—hard, lifting weights like I never had before at the school gym, not caring about who saw my strength. The place was mostly empty, anyway, since it was a vacation week. Afterward I went for a long run, sweating bullets despite the cold.

That night, I wasn't scheduled to work at The Bistro. For the first time, I thought it would be fun to go there as a customer rather than an employee. When I walked in, I noticed the restaurant held different clientele than usual. There were fewer college students and more families with cute smiling kids.

My boss greeted me. I would've talked more with him, but out of the corner of my eye, I noticed someone I wouldn't have expected to see—Angelina.

I wandered over to her. She glanced up surprised to see me—pleasantly so. I was thankful for the warm welcome after dealing with Julia. She wore black jeans, and a silky, red blouse. She had her hair piled in a high ponytail and looked breathtaking as always. I sat down across from her.

"What are you doing here?" she asked. "I thought you'd be with your family for vacation."

"I *was* home yesterday," I answered, "but I have to work tomorrow. What about you? Why aren't you with your family?"

Angelina didn't answer right away. She stalled at the pool of ketchup on her plate. She rolled her french fry around in it, before she popped it into her mouth.

I tapped my fingers on the table. "I'm waiting."

Angelina gave me a half-smile. "My family's like a spider's web." She stared intently into my eyes, just long enough for me to feel a little uncomfortable before she went on. "We're full of intricate details."

That was it. A series of pictures soared through my mind. Angelina when she tried to attract me with her animal-like magnetism, I could hardly pull away. Angelina when she waved her hand over the snake's cage. She magically unlocked it and then relocked it later. And what about my dreams—the black widow ones, with the young woman that begged me to help her.

Before I could think of the consequences, I leaned closer to her and spoke in a soft tone. "Are you the black widow?"

Angelina's head snapped up. Rummaging through her purse, she found a twenty-dollar bill and threw it on the table. Before I had a chance to stop her, she stormed out of the restaurant. I waved goodbye to my boss and ran after her.

"Wait," I called.

Angelina glanced over her shoulder and broke into a run.

Wow, she's fast, I thought, but not nearly as fast as me. When I caught up with her, I grabbed her by the arm and swung her around.

"Why the abrupt exit?" I demanded.

"Let go of me," she pleaded.

We were both out of breath but something in her tone, and the fearful look on her face made me stop. I released her arm.

"What's going on?" I asked, more gently this time.

"You're not going to hurt me, are you?" Alarm still gripped her, which made me feel bad.

"No," I answered. "Why would you think that?"

The worry began to fade from her face. "I can't talk to you here. My address is 522 Lake Road. Find me there, and we'll talk."

With that, she strode off.

As I hurried to my car, I heard a *TAP, TAP, TAP,* behind me. I turned to look and saw the blind man with his walking stick.

"What are you doing out in the dark, old man?" I warned, startled by his presence. "It's not the safest time for you to be out."

That's not a concern for me.

I stopped scared stiff. "I hear you in my head, but your lips aren't moving. You're telepathic?"

I always knew you were a s-mart one.

He halted his step. As we faced one another, his mangled eyes became clear like the crested moon and as bright as the North Star, shining outward toward me. Its rays reflected off my jacket.

"You're the one I've been hearing in my head," I said, in awe. "Who are you?"

He vanished. Right before my eyes, he disappeared. Who was he? I thought he was a poor man on the street I felt sorry for. Now, I wanted to see him again—talk to him—hear his story.

I remembered Angelina. I ran to my car and typed her address into my G.P.S. before I forgot it. Then I sped away. My trusty G.P.S. took me right to her place. She lived in a condominium as a freshman... sweet, I thought. I went to the door and lifted my hand to knock, but Angelina opened it before I had the chance. She took my coat by its collar and wrenched me inside, locking the deadbolts behind her. Yeah that's right. She had four deadbolts on the door *and* an alarm. What's she afraid of?

I noticed the tiny kitchen on the left as I walked in and a quaint bathroom on the right. A dining room table sat situated near the kitchen next to a small, open serving window that was meant to hand food back and forth from the kitchen to the eating area.

Straight ahead, the living room had an adjoining deck that overlooked Lake Champlain. The bedroom was located on the right, directly across from the living room.

"Nice place," I commented, glancing around.

Angelina plopped down on a black, velvety couch and leaned over with her elbows on her knees, hands under her chin. "Normally, I'd offer you a glass of water or something, but not this time. Who are you, and why did you ask me if I was the Black Widow?"

I sat down on the glass coffee table across from her, and, unswervingly met her stare. "The question is who are you?"

Angelina gazed at me tumultuously though trying to hide it.

"You can trust me," I assured her and sat down right next to her.

"Come here and look behind my ear." Angelina pulled the loose strands of her hair back away from her face. She pushed her earlobe forward and pointed to a spot I was familiar with—the place where a life player's emblem was etched deep into the skin, similar to a tattoo, except that most people couldn't see it.

I brushed her smooth skin with the rough grain of my finger, pretending to examine closely, even though I already saw the mark there—a faded death player's emblem. I couldn't believe it.

"Why did you want me to do this?" I asked, not letting her know what I saw.

Closing her eyes, Angelina drew in her breath. "I guess you're not who I thought you were."

"Are you disappointed?" I probed.

"Never mind," she whispered.

"Who did you think I was?" I played dumb.

Angelina stood up. "Forget it. You need to go."

Smirking, I finally gave up my game. "You didn't want me to see your faded death player's emblem did you?"

She punched me. Honestly, I don't know why girls always punch me, but I was beginning to find it a little irritating.

"You're a jerk," Angelina said. Relief resounded in her voice. "I knew you were a life player. I had hoped even before you mentioned the whole black-widow thing."

"How did you know?"

Angelina put her hand on her hip. "Obviously, you have to be, or you wouldn't have been able to see my emblem."

A faded emblem, like Angelina's, meant that a life player had changed their mind and decided to leave Vorago in favor of Spero, but first they had to ask Spero for forgiveness for all wrongs committed. Then if they wanted, they could become a life player or enter regular civilian life. The fact that an emblem was faded meant that the change had not completely come to pass and the death player still had to prove herself during a probationary period. Funny, I had found out about my parents, and they had just explained all this to me. The timing was uncanny.

Because Angelina's emblem still appeared washed out, I couldn't completely trust her. I could as long as her emblem continued to fade and disappear. If her emblem grew darker again, then I'd be in trouble. That would mean she had chosen Vorago and her old life once more and would probably try to kill me. No big deal, right?

"Okay, I told you I could be trusted," I said, pointing to her ear. "I want to be able to trust you too. You need to explain."

She pulled the elastic from her dark hair, shaking her head as her hair tumbled down past her shoulders. She was stunning. I tried not to gape or look like an idiot.

"How about that glass of water now?" she asked.

"Are you stalling?"

"I'm a little nervous," she admitted. She sauntered into the kitchen and opened one of the oak cabinets.

She came back, handed my water to me, and, after I gulped down a few swigs, we heard a desperate banging at the door.

Angelina looked horrified. "Who could that be? Nobody knows where I live. I'm telling you, I *never* have visitors."

"Relax," I said. I felt apprehensive myself but tried not to show it. "Just look through the peephole, and see who it is."

"If anyone finds me, they'll blow the door off. I'm as good as dead," Angelina said, hysterically.

"Will you relax?" I said, once more.

Angelina pulled it together and looked through the hole. "I don't know who it is—some short kid."

"Let me see." I carefully pushed her aside, looked through the hole myself, and saw Berard.

"What are you doing?" Angelina gasped, as I began to unlock the series of deadbolts. She tried to pull my hands away from the door.

"Stop it Angelina. I know who it is," I said. My physical strength far exceeded hers. I gripped her arms to move her out of the way. She backed up, her face flaming with dread.

The instant the door flew open, Berard wrenched my arm. "You need to come with me…now!"

I glanced back at Angelina. "Stay here. I'll be back as soon as I can." She nodded her head and slammed the door as soon as I walked out.

The yellow bus was parked on the curb, with the door already opened waiting for us to enter. We both sprinted aboard and took a seat.

"Hey Berard what's going on? Why the hurry?" I asked, "and you look terrible, man." Strands of Berard's hair stood like electric poles on end. Dark circles were embedded beneath his eyes. He raced his fingers through his hair, messing it up even more.

"Seventeen life players were in Arcis in an arena…at different times," he choked, "and they were all tagged by death players. The death players were able to retrieve computer images of every one of them."

"Seventeen of them? Are you sure?"

"Yeah, I'm pretty sure, and now the death players will find them and assassinate them along with anyone else who gets in their way. We've never had so many tagged at one time."

"How did that happen?"

"I don't know. We're on our way to an Assembly. Hopefully, Adonis knows and will clue us in."

A young life player in front of us overheard our conversation. "I heard death players cheated and used illegal magic to force life players to gaze up into the stands," he said.

Berard turned to him. "Where did you hear that nonsense?"

"It's not nonsense," the life player replied. "I heard it from a reliable source."

"Who?" Berard demanded.

"Anthony," the life player revealed.

"Do you know who he's talking about? Berard asked me.

"I do know of an Anthony who's a life player. If *that's* the one he's talking about, he's one of the best."

The other life player nodded his head smugly. Berard harrumphed.

"What's illegal magic?" I asked.

The other life player snickered. "It's when Vorago and his crew go against natural law and use black magic to accomplish tasks they normally could never achieve. It's the ultimate way to cheat in the game."

"Oh," I answered. I didn't know what else to say, but I felt ripped with anger. When the bus stopped at the Assembly's meeting place, everyone scurried out.

Inside, the room reverberated with a bee-like buzz as everyone gossiped about the recent shocking news, but that didn't last long when Adonis entered the stage and held up his hands to subdue the crowd, hiding his identity behind his coffee-color cloak.

Even though I couldn't see all the life players this time, I could hear them.

"Quiet…everyone quiet," Adonis bellowed. A wavelike hush flowed through the room as Adonis went on to explain, "I'm sure that you've all been told that seventeen life players were tagged in the arenas in Arcis. That number is incorrect. I've learned…there were twenty-four."

The room swarmed with chaos. Adonis raised his arms again to hush the crowd.

"How do you know that for sure?" someone cried out.

"Spero and I have spoken with Vorago," Adonis said with sadness. His words dripped like water out of a faucet as he gazed out. "The news I'm giving you is accurate, and if we don't do something soon, all twenty-four life players will be murdered, so we've come to a compromise with Vorago and his savages. They've allowed us to fight with them on the Fields. For any of you who are not acquainted with this, the Fields are a middle ground—not on Earth or in Arcis. Rather, it's a realm where we fight with them to the death, until one side retreats. We've chosen this option, because I believe the outcome will be in our favor, and we'll lose fewer players. Not every life player will fight this battle, only the strongest, most powerful ones. Your patriarch will let you know whether you've been chosen. After the battle, we'll meet here again."

Once again, the racket in the room became deafening as fellow life players conversed about our recent dilemma. Adonis didn't bother to quiet the crowd. He tried to leave discretely, but as the curtain on the stage began to close, someone called out, "I heard the death players used black magic. Is that true, Adonis?"

Adonis spun around. "It doesn't matter if that's true or not. Our life players have to be protected. This is our only choice."

"How are we supposed to protect ourselves in the future?" another yelled. "How do we know this won't happen to any one of us?"

"We're working on that," Adonis replied. "I have another meeting with Vorago. If he's allowed his lot to cheat by using illegal magic, he *will* suffer consequences."

"What consequences?" another demanded.

Adonis put his hand up. "Quiet!" he growled. "I know this current report is mind blowing, but we *will* find out if Vorago is using black magic. I promise you, and if he is…a multitude of his power will be banished–forever."

The crowd applauded, then jeered. "Down fall Vorago, down fall Vorago."

"Let's go," Berard shouted in my ear, as he pulled me out of the crowd.

Back on the bus, above the bustling sound of the passengers, I turned to look at Berard. "Am I one of the life players going to the Fields?"

Berard studied my face. "I don't have the list of life players, yet. As soon as Adonis gives it to me, I'll let you know."

I rarely saw Berard anymore, other than trips to the Assemblies. When I asked him why, he told me that I was privileged to have Adonis train me rather than him.

The bus driver almost dropped me off at my dorm, but I asked him to drive me to Angelina's instead.

When I stepped off the bus and said goodbye to Berard, he never questioned me about Angelina. I was glad. I didn't feel like offering any details.

Pushing the light button on my watch, I saw it was almost midnight. Rather than tired, I felt wired for sound from the Assembly. Angelina had left an outside light on near the front door for me. I knocked, not waiting long as she opened her door to let me in.

"What was that all about?" she asked, right after she shut the door.

"As soon as I trust you…*if* I trust you, I'll let you know," I answered. "Right now I think *you* have some explaining to do."

Angelina squirmed uncomfortably. At that point, I didn't care. We both sat on bar stools at the granite countertop near the serving window. She looked tired, lonely, and afraid like a lost kitten, but without knowing much about her, I stared at her hard and offered no comfort.

Angelina began after a few nervous gulps and a feeble smile. "I have two older brothers. Adam's the oldest. He's twenty-four. I haven't seen him in two years. Accursio's nineteen. He's my Irish twin. He's only ten months older than me. When I was a kid, I thought we had the perfect family until my parents began to fight—*a lot*. My parents were both death players. When my mother realized what that would mean for us, she wanted out…but my dad was like, no way. Then my parents divorced, and I never had contact with my father again. I was fifteen at the time.

"Soon after, my mom was murdered. I don't know who did it, but it was probably another death player or maybe my father. I bet Accursio knows. He worshipped my father. Adam took my mother's side. You should be able to guess what happened after that.

"Accursio became a death player, and I left with him. Adam took off into hiding. I don't know where he is.

"Later things turned sour. Accursio became enraged with life and hungered more and more for the kill. He's one of the fiercest, most powerful death players out there. I was appalled at how much he prized killing. So I left, met with Spero, and now here I am…living alone, until I've proven myself as a true life player."

"H…how do you live? I mean…how do you pay for things?" I asked, and pointed to the expensive condominium we were sitting in.

"I don't know if my father's dead or alive, but once my parents' divorce became final, my father started to wire each of us a large sum of money every month. I'm not sure how long we'll receive his money. I've been trying to save some and not spend it all."

"What about Accursio? Doesn't he want you dead?"

Angelina's eyes welled up with tears. She brushed them away. "He probably does. That's why I'm in college, so I can get a good enough job and not rely on my father's money. I'm worried Accursio will track me down by tracing my father's money to me. I can't change which bank the money's deposited into. I keep changing my address, though, and I've moved around. I've also changed my look. Hold on a second."

Angelina went to a drawer in her oak hutch, came back, and handed me a picture in a gold frame. It held a photo of a gorgeous, blonde teenager with dark-brown eyes. The girl wasn't smiling.

"Is this you?" I guessed.

"Yeah," she laughed. "Big difference, huh?"

"You look...like a different person," I answered, staring at her and then back to the picture. "You did an amazing job transforming your looks, but you look beautiful either way."

Her cheeks flushed at the compliment. "Anything else you want to know?"

"Your parents...they were married with children and still death players?" I asked, thinking that when my parents were married they stopped playing the real game of Arcis.

"Once a death player, always a death player. That's the motto, unless you're like me. Then you live a life of hiding or are murdered like my mom, but Spero knows. He told me he'd send someone to help me. When I met you, I knew right away that you could be that someone. I felt so desperate to find out. That's why I used some magic in front of you—to see how you would respond."

"Can you use magic now?"

"No, my gifts, or rather curses from Vorago have been taken away. I could use them weakly before, but I don't have any power right now. I feel like a lamb waiting to be slaughtered." Angelina attempted to laugh.

"Can I look behind your ear again?"

"Why?"

I took her hands into mine. "You trusted me with a lot...and...I just have a feeling." I gazed deeply into her eyes, wishing I could open a window into her heart. "Can I look?"

She nodded.

I moved her hair back and carefully pulled her earlobe back toward her face. "Just as I thought."

She pulled back. "What...what do you see?"

I rubbed the area behind her ear. "It's lighter than it was before. I think...you revealed yourself to me...and somehow that must be a part of proving yourself. Keep it up, and this emblem will be gone in no time."

I stood up. My watch showed almost 1:00 a.m. "I need to go...it's late. I'll come back and check on you. If you need anything, make sure you call me okay?"

"Bladen?"

"Yeah."

"Thanks," she said, and gave me a hug.

I put my face into her hair and caressed it with my hand. "Everything's going to be all right."

"I hope so," she said.

We both said goodnight.

Back at my room, I made a lousy attempt to sleep. It had only been one day since Thanksgiving, but the night was so long, it felt like a week had passed. I knew being friends with Angelina would be risky for me. I couldn't stop thinking about it.

I allowed my imagination to take hold of my brain. I had horrifying images of masked death players that tortured me, tied me up, and bound me with ropes covered in spikes. Then I imagined they lit me on fire. I could visualize the snickers of delight on their faces, as they chanted with joy while murdering life players.

I shook my head and hit it on the side a few times. Stop it Bladen, I thought to myself. What was wrong with me? Part of me *really* wanted to be Angelina's friend, but the other part of me thought, What am I crazy? How can I be friends with her? I could be killed. I'm too young for this. I thought this was a glory job, not a death wish. I beat myself up like this for a good portion of the night. It was one of the worst nights I ever had. Dread covered me like lava until I felt like I was gonna puke.

At last…sleep won out, but the petrifying images joined me in my dreams like an addiction heat-seeking missle, and, I saw Vorago. He stood dressed in a gray cloak, with a hood that covered his head. Wisps of his hair curled out around the sides of his hood; shadows crossed his face and revealed black, wrinkled pits under his eyes. His blood-red lips curled up in malevolent satisfaction. They moved, spewing bits of saliva at me, and with almost inaudible sound, he mouthed, "You'll die on the Fields."

ANGELINA'S SECRET, CONTINUED

B ring it, Vorago, I thought heatedly to myself when I woke up. I swung out of bed and fumbled for my phone. I wanted to call Adonis to see if I was a chosen life player to fight on the Fields. Rubbing my eyes to clear them of useless sleep, I saw the time—5:12 a.m. It wasn't that early, birds were up.

I dialed the number, *Ring, Ring, Ring.* It rang at least twenty times. Uh, maybe it was too early—

"This better be good," Adonis snapped as gruffly as a bear hoarding his honey.

"It's not that early."

Adonis let out a crotchety sigh on the other end.

"I want to know if I'm fighting on the Fields."

"No!" Adonis emphasized.

"Why not?" I demanded.

"You're not ready."

"What do you mean I'm not ready? I just fought brutally in Arcis. You saw the way my wounds healed in the hospital."

"That was Arcis. This is gun warfare, and you haven't been trained enough," Adonis said, firmly.

"Train me now, then," I insisted.

"You're still a novice. Give me one good reason why this is so important to you, and maybe I'll think about it."

I racked my brain. What story could I use to convince him? I settled on the truth and told him about my rotten night's sleep that ended with the swirling venom from Vorago. Adonis was silent and hopefully thoughtful on the other end. I couldn't take it any longer. "Well?" I sat on the edge of my bed in the dark and listened to Robby's blissful breathing as he slept.

"No, baby," Robby laughed.

Unbelievable, I thought. He even dreams about girls in his sleep. I jumped when I heard a deep voice clear his throat and grab me by the sleeve of my cotton T-shirt. He placed a hand over my mouth to muffle my scream.

In the amount of time it takes a lightening bolt to strike, I landed in Adonis's house. "It's only you," I said, and taking the opportunity to catch Adonis off-guard, I shoved his shoulder with the palm of my hand and swiped my foot behind his and made him crash to the floor.

"Who said I'm not ready?" I scoffed. "Pretty funny when the student defeats the teacher, huh?"

He put his head down and then flung it up, got to his feet, and slammed his body into mine. We hit with a few martial art moves, some kicks to the head, and after a while, we ended in a truce.

"Fair enough," Adonis said, "but just because you've proven yourself in most areas of warfare, doesn't mean you've trained enough with guns."

"Why can't you help me out with that? You know…blow on me or something, and have those little shiny things come at me."

"Nice choice of words," Adonis laughed. "That magic is mostly used for warfare that's allowed in Arcis. On the Fields, you rely mainly on your own strength and wit."

"When are we fighting on the Fields? How much time would I have to train?"

"I'm not sure," Adonis answered, giving me his full attention. "Right now, we're trying to find out if Vorago let his death players use dark magic to tag our life players in the arena. We're giving it two weeks. If we're still unsure, we'll go to the Fields. We won't be able to hold them off any longer. They'll want to start killing our players."

"I don't get it. Spero should know whether illegal magic was used or not. Why wouldn't he do anything about it?"

"He gives all living things the right to make their own choices. So in a way, we become the product of ourselves."

"I get that. I do, but what if someone on our side helped the death players cheat. You know, gave them our secrets. It's possible don't you think?"

"You're saying maybe it wasn't black magic, but rather a life player who spilled knowledge about Spero's plan of attack?"

"Or maybe it was both."

"It's possible. What makes you think that?"

"I think it's best to consider all possibilities. What else would explain that angry man who wore black and who would beckon to me from the basilica while I played the game? And who, I have a feeling, could see me too."

Adonis didn't have an immediate answer, "I'll look into this," he reassured.

"Do you think I'll be ready in two weeks?" I asked.

"Yes, but only with my instruction. You'll have to work hard, Bladen. You could die. I don't understand why you feel the need to do this now, when there'll be other battles on the Fields."

Since I had spoken with Angelina, I felt more zealous about my choice to be a life player, but I didn't know how to explain that to Adonis. And I definitely didn't want to tell him about Angelina. I was afraid he wouldn't approve, since her washed out emblem still adorned her neck.

Besides, the thought of killing human beings on the Fields didn't exactly thrill me. I felt scared stiff and didn't want to be slaughtered myself, though I wanted to crush Vorago and his following, ending his reign of power.

"It's difficult to explain," was all I told Adonis, since I had a hard time finding the right words.

He didn't push the matter any further but insisted that we begin immediately. We walked down to his cold, musty, soundproof basement where we spent a couple of hours loading and shooting assault rifles, machine guns, shot guns, and pistols.

Even though my aim was fairly accurate, Adonis still breathed his magical dust on me to improve my shot. Of course, he did that after I almost blew his brains into smithereens.

I was shooting a machine gun and thought he was behind me. When I heard a noise at the door to my side, I turned while the gun was still pelting bullets and almost took him down. Luckily, he fell to the floor faster than a short fin mako shark can swim, but oh man, did I make a mess out of his cement walls. Adonis was ripped. He screamed at me, arms flailing, "What are ya CRAZY!" I never saw his face look so wild, and I'm not so sure I care to see *that* again.

For the next two weeks, Adonis had me on a strict schedule. I went to class, studied hard, worked at the Bistro, and trained for battle.

In between all that, I checked in on Angelina every day. I felt bad she lived all alone, and somehow during those visits my feelings for her began to change—to grow. My heart throbbed whenever I neared her door, and when she began to open it, before I had the chance to knock, I wondered how she felt about me. As far as my feelings for Julia were concerned, she was lost in the dust—a faded memory.

As the two weeks came to a close, I decided to tell Angelina that I'd be fighting in the Fields. If I had a fatal outcome, I wanted her to know. The next time I visited her, she swung open the door with a smile that lit up her face.

"What are you so happy about?" I asked, as I glided into the entryway.

"Happy birthday," she sang.

Inside on the table, I saw a double-layered chocolate cake—my favorite, and a huge birthday bag with red, blue, and green frilly string that hung down on the sides.

I never told anyone about my birthday, not even Robby. I was too busy to think about it myself, with my only reminder being the two cards and new, striped sweater I had received from my parents.

Angelina could be so sweet—first her letter to Jared and now this. I thought her kindness made her look even hotter. Her hair was pulled up on the sides and clipped in the back with a beaded barrette. Wisps of her long bangs cradled her face. She wore black tights covered by a jean miniskirt and a matching black top.

"How did you know it was my birthday?"

Angelina put her hand on her hip and answered in a sassy voice. "I have my ways."

I was surprised. "Thanks…but why did you do this for me?"

She thought for a moment. "You've been here every day to make sure I'm okay. I wanted to repay you."

I had the urge to give her a hug, brush my hand against her cheek, and feel the softness of her lips on mine. What was I thinking? At first she creeped me out.

"Come on, open your gifts," she said, interrupting my thoughts. "You're going to love them." I opened the gift bag and took out a small rectangular package. It was wrapped in paper decorated with swords.

"Nice paper," I commented.

"I thought it matched you perfectly," she gushed.

I opened the gift and found a digital camcorder. I stared at Angelina, stunned that she had purchased something so pricey.

"Don't worry about the cost," she said, as though she could read my thoughts. "My father wires me a lot of money…open your next gift."

I had two other presents to open. One package contained a cool, long-sleeve t-shirt that was illustrated with a dagger jammed inside a viper, blood oozed out of the sides of it. The other gift was a pair of faded Levi jeans.

The camcorder and clothes were awesome. "My presents are great…wow…I can't tell you how much I appreciate this," I told Angelina. "But why did you think you needed to repay me? I came because I wanted to."

"Really?" she asked, as though she didn't believe me.

I strolled over to her and caressed her face with the back of my fingers, like I had wanted to earlier.

She stared into my eyes, searching. "It wasn't too long ago, you acted like you hated me."

"I didn't know you then," I justified.

"I suppose I acted like the predator and you were my prey." Angelina slowly let her fingertip meander its way diagonally across my chest. She glanced at me, as though she needed my approval. She had no idea what she was doing to me. I could feel my blood pumping through my veins.

"And now I suppose for the last two weeks," I whispered, "I've been the predator preying on you."

She flashed a relieved grin. "I think I like that much better."

Cradling her face with the palm of my hands, I placed my lips on hers and kissed her softly, once, twice, until the third time when my tongue parted her lips and passion caved in.

We kissed with fervor, our hunger unleashed. She took my hands and walked me to the couch. When I sat down, she sat on my lap and pressed her warm body against mine.

Angelina's lips felt rich and moist. She moved her body rhythmically against mine. We craved each other out of need. I began to feel like a drunken fool with desire, a way I had never felt before. I kissed the left side of her neck, starting from the top and slowly going down.

Even though I didn't want to stop, I knew I had to. I drew my head back and buried it in her neck, as I listened to our heated breath.

Angelina stopped and placed her hands on the sides of my head. She kissed my hair. "Is something wrong? Why did you stop?"

"How did you get it?"

USERNAME: BLADEN

"Get what?" she asked, as she tenderly scattered more kisses along my forehead.

"Your nickname, the black widow." Angelina got up from my lap and sat next to me with mixed emotions displayed on her face. I continued. "You told me how you became a death player, but you never explained the rest... I want to know what your life was like then."

Angelina gazed her eyes down away from mine. "Death players don't live like life players— alone," Angelina disdained. "They live in packs like animals. They even call the place where they live their den. Five death players lived in our pack, two guys, and three girls. One of the guys was my brother, Accursio.

If a death player tagged a male life player who lived in our district, it was my job to find him and lure him in. That's why I had the magnetizing gift and was nicknamed the black widow, so the life player couldn't get away." Angelina laughed with disgust. "Then... there was a special place where I took them that we referred to as the "post." At the "post," Dylan from my pack took care of them, if you know what I mean."

Tears began to spill down Angelina's face. "I don't know how I ended up there—how I could've done it."

I put my arm around her to console her and handed her a Kleenex from a box on the coffee table. "How many life players did you assist in killing?"

"That sounds horrible when you say it that way. I became a death player when I turned sixteen. I helped with two, one each year when I lived with the pack. You have to understand, Bladen. If I didn't do it, they'd kill me." Angelina's face filled with shame.

I stroked her hair gently. "I understand. You must have been scared. How did you finally get out?"

She took my hand into hers and traced the lines on my palm. "Everyone in my den became angry at me, because I couldn't do it the first time, couldn't make the kill. I wasn't sure how the magnetic thing worked, and I could barely keep the life player at the post. I almost lost him. Dylan snatched him away from me, angry and tortured him before he killed him, while I went into the woods and threw up. The second time went more smoothly...I still couldn't make the kill, but at least I didn't have to touch him. I could hold him at the "post," but after both times, I sobbed for days. Accursio and Dylan were enraged at my behavior."

"What do you mean you didn't have to touch the second life player?" I asked, confused.

Angelina's face pinched up with remorse. "I had to kiss the first one until Dylan got there." She paused and her breathing became erratic before she continued. "Accursio and Dylan beat me up after that...that's when I knew I had to get out, because I knew I could never actually kill someone."

Angelina gazed at me again with fear in her eyes. I encouraged her. "Don't be afraid to tell me. Spero forgave you. Now you're becoming a life player. I won't hold your past against you either. It's obvious you've beaten yourself up enough. And you were in forced situations...you didn't even want to be in."

Angelina's next words tumbled out. "I want you to know that Dylan was my boyfriend but not by choice. He chose me, and I couldn't do anything about it. He didn't love me or like me for that matter. He wanted to be with me, because he was filled with lust. I figured if I looked ugly, he'd leave me alone. I gained weight, didn't wash my hair, and made sure I looked as awful as possible. The next time a life player was tagged, I refused to do my job. Accursio and Dylan beat me up again, worse that time. They broke a couple of ribs, swore at me, called me horrendous names...Then Dylan began to lust after one of the other girls, anyway.

"So, they kicked me out into the street. I had nowhere to go. I walked to a hotel and was pulled into the game through my phone there. That's when Spero enveloped me with his warm embrace and invited me to join him, and gave me the opportunity to become a life player. And like I told you before, he promised he'd send someone to help me, that would be you. I'm worried, though, because...it's dangerous for you to be with me. If Accursio ever found me and you were with me...he'd kill us both."

"Don't worry about it," I answered, undisturbed. "You know, I saw you symbolically in my dreams…I had some…where a black widow asked me to help her."

Angelina looked shocked. "You did? Is that why you asked me about it?"

"Yeah, after I listened to you and put two and two together, I thought you were the girl in my dreams. The dreams must have come from Spero."

Angelina hugged me.

Listening to her story was like opening that window to her heart, and I felt shaken by the strong feelings I had for her in such a short period of time. Julia now seemed like an unimportant crush.

Julia—

The thought of her gripped me with some sixth sense, and I at once felt the need to check in on her. I ran my fingers through my hair and told Angelina I'd be right back. I excused myself and went to the bathroom. As soon as I shut the door, I clutched onto the supernatural gold chain that hung from my neck and was teleported back into the gray room.

To my side, I saw the same blonde, middle-aged man I had seen before. "It's okay, baby, we'll get to them soon." His snakelike voice hissed. "We're getting closer every day." I had a difficult time seeing the young woman whom he was speaking with, but gradually she came into focus. Julia. The young woman the man spoke with looked just like Julia. I stared, amazed.

Before I had time to reflect, I bounced back into Angelina's bathroom, with Angelina standing in front of me.

"Do you always make it a habit to join someone when they're taking a whiz?" I asked.

Angelina placed her hands on her hips and scoffed. "Only when I continue to call someone's name, and they don't answer me. When I opened the door you were gone, and now you magically reappeared. Any explanations?"

What should I tell Angelina? Part of me thought about Adonis and what he'd say in my shoes. Part of me was dying to tear open my soul and let her in, yet at the same time, her death player's emblem hadn't completely disappeared. I decided to inform her that I was Julia's protector, and my gold chain was an enchanted gift from Arcis.

Angelina didn't act too happy about it. "Julia? You mean Blondie? What does she have to do with any of this?" Angelina asked, with wringing envy. I explained that Julia had players in her ancestry. I didn't want to specify if they were life or death players, and I was relieved when she didn't ask.

"You sound jealous," I mused.

She turned away and pouted. "I knew there was something between the two of you."

"Julia doesn't know I'm protecting her," I added.

I pulled her around to face me. She wrapped her arms around my neck and clasped her hands. She pressed her body into mine. "I told you about Dylan. Tell me about Julia." She sounded desperate to know.

I encircled my arms around her waist, our faces only inches apart. "There's nothing to tell. Our moms have been friends since high school, and Julia and I have been friends since we were kids."

Angelina still didn't believe me. "I know there's more. I can see it in the way she looks at you while at the Bistro."

I lightly kissed Angelina on the mouth, and in between the array of kisses, I told her everything about Julia, even the part about how she dumped me, when she found out I was a life player.

"You mean right now, if she didn't break it off with you, you'd be with her instead of me?" Angelina looked dejected and pushed me away.

I put my arms back around her waist and expressed myself with fiery emotion, something I wasn't used to doing. "Angelina," I whispered, "It's *you* I want. I don't know what it is between us. Can't you feel it?"

She nodded. "Yeah, it feels…electrical, hard to control. I can't stop thinking about you."

I kissed her soft, satiny lips again until I realized I forgot to let her know my upcoming plans on the Fields. I picked her up and walked back to the couch to sit down. I must have looked serious.

What is it? What's wrong?" she asked.

"You should know. I'm going to be fighting on the Fields soon."

Her emerald eyes widened in alarm. "The Fields? Why? What's going on? You could die there."

I placed a finger over her lips to shush her. "What do you know about the Fields?"

"When death players believe they can murder more life players there than on Earth, they choose the Fields. Something must have happened to cause this. What is it?"

I told Angelina twenty-four life players had been unfairly tagged, through black magic or some other means, so we chose the Fields in hopes of losing fewer of our players.

Angelina's face looked like her brain was thinking a million miles an hour. "I don't know how that could've happened, but you should know death players always have a strategy. Usually, while some death players distract life players, others scatter around and get ready to attack. In the past, they've gathered in a circle and sang beautiful chants that hypnotized the life players. The hidden death players then began to shoot. The sight…of devastation…"Angelina turned away from me, visibly upset.

"Were you there?"

Angelina shook her head. "No, but one death player recorded it. They forced us to watch it during training." Angelina studied my face. "You must be powerful. Only the strongest from both sides are chosen to fight there."

I glanced at my watch. "I guess…I wanted to let you know, though, in case I don't make it back…right now I need to go."

"You can't leave until you have some of your cake," Angelina insisted. I stayed for a little longer and ate way too much of her mouth-watering, chocolate cake. When I went to the door, Angelina looked concerned.

"Be careful and come back," she said somberly.

I kissed the tip of her noseand vowed, "I will."

Back at the dorm, Robby and Jared were chilling with Kaitland. She stood snuggled against Robby's side, her face radiant, as she played with a claddagh ring on her finger.

"Hey guys, what's up?" I asked.

"And girls too?" Jared smiled, looking like an over-filled water balloon about to burst. "Robby has some news." He sounded like a radio announcer.

Robby glared at him.

"Go ahead and tell him," Kaitland said, and whispered something in his ear that I couldn't hear.

Robby stuttered. "Well...Kk...Kaitland and I...are...um...a thing... you know...a couple."

"Cool...congratulations," I said, sincerely. I couldn't tell if Robby was happy or in shock. The news blew me away. Crazy-for-girls Robby committed to a relationship? I wanted so badly to rag on him, but I held my tongue.

We all joked around for a while, but I never had the chance to talk to Robby alone. I had to hurry before Berard came, which was a bummer. I was dying to find out how Robby and Kaitland had hooked up into something serious.

As soon as I went to take a shower, Berard arrived to pick me up for the final Assembly before the battle that was for chosen life players only. I really needed that shower, but I guess it would have to wait.

When I entered the Assembly room, I found Adonis. I let him know that I teleported to the gray room again and saw the same middle-aged man, presumably Julia's father and what must have been Julia's sister. He blew me off and let me know we'd discuss it after the Fields.

Yeah right, after the Fields, I thought. That's if I make it and don't die or get mutilated. I couldn't believe he wanted to wait to talk to me about it.

Next, I clued him in to the death players' battle tactics that Angelina had warned me about. He was furious and informed me the chant probably was one that contained black magic, but at least the information gave him a few extra moments to prepare more for our own strategy. He also told me sternly that when this battle was over, he wanted to talk to me about Angelina. I was annoyed with his overbearing attitude but wondered what he had to say.

When all life players had arrived, a few of them handed out bulletproof vests for protection, black masks that covered our entire heads except for our eyes, and earplugs.

Glancing around, I recognized some familiar faces—Anthony and Gregory. Then I saw Joshua, who I had met in Arcis during my last training session. He saw me also and nodded his head in recognition. Since we were about to ascend to the Fields, I had the ability to see every life player present, whether I had met them before or not. All our faces shone serious and taut. Beads of sweat formed on some life players' foreheads.

As soon as a few of the needed items had been passed around, Adonis strolled tensely to the middle of the stage, where he began to give instructions in his booming voice. He wore a gray cloak that covered his head and revealed only his mouth.

"I have learned that in the past, on the Fields, death players have used black magic," he said.

Adonis was interrupted by the squabbling noise from the life players, who were fuming when they heard death players had deceived them again. Adonis subdued the crowd. "Everyone settle down...you need to stay focused on the tasks at hand." He then described what I had told him and how black magic was used on the Fields in the past. That it was planted in a chant the death players sang that hypnotized life players and gave death players the advantage in battle. Adonis explained that we needed our earplugs in battle, so if the death players used a chant this time, we wouldn't hear it.

"Furthermore, we'll have our own strategy. I've decided to let your patriarchs join you on the Fields." The life players rambled on again in excitement but stopped when Adonis raised his hands. "If death players become too powerful, your patriarch will appear next to you to assist you.

When and if that occurs, death players will not be able to see them." Loud applause went out in the crowd. Adonis shouted, articulating each word carefully at this point. "We will use our own methods to win this battle. We…will…NOT…BE…OVERCOME." Deafening cheers, louder than those you hear at football game, filled the room.

Adonis still kept his hands raised high, continuing to hush the crowd before he went on. "There's more you need to know. The time in the Fields is similar to the time in Arcis. If you fight for half a day on the Fields, then less than a quarter of a day will have passed on Earth. The time on the Fields goes by faster than it does on Earth. That's because the Fields are much closer to Arcis. Any questions?"

Adonis continued. "We want to win this war, and we…will be… VICTORIOUS! And it will be done as rapidly and skillfully as possible." More shouts and clapping came from the crowd.

Adonis pointed to the back of the Assembly room. "The weapons you'll need are there in piles. You are to take one weapon from each pile, then take the belt and attach your weapons to it. Does anyone have any questions?"

"How long will we be on the Fields?" A voice rang out.

"You'll be there until one side retreats. If we have too many men fall, then Joshua will give you the signal to retreat. He'll put up the life player's flag that holds a picture of Spero on it." Adonis then searched around for Joshua and told him to stand up for all of us to see. He was the same life player I had just nodded to, the one I'd seen in Arcis. Adonis bellowed again. "If death players retreat first, they'll hold up Vorago's flag."

Another life player's question reverberated in the room. "Adonis, with these masks the death players can still see our eyes. Does that mean they can mark us on the Fields?"

"No, life players can only be tagged in the arenas of Arcis," Adonis explained.

When all questions had been asked, Adonis encouraged us more. "Don't fear life players. You're among the best players, and your courage will…not…wane. Go now, and do what must be done." As the group cheered again, we went with our patriarchs and picked up our machine guns, pistols, bullets, daggers, and hand grenades. You name it, we had it. After every life player attached their weapons to their belts, we teleported without delay. As fast as lightening that whips through the spring sky, we landed on the Fields.

BLOOD SPLATTERS ON THE FIELDS

I saw a picturesque sight before me as beautiful as a Monet, with lengthy blades of lush green and crisp, tan grass that stretched as far as two feet high. A summer like sun was setting low on the horizon, with a deep, blue sky and a few feathery, white clouds that adorned the foreground. A warm breeze stroked my face.

Slowly one by one, the powerful life players that teleported to the Fields appeared. Every one of them looked pumped with anticipation. Within seconds, all one hundred landed ready for battle, guns in hand, tip toeing around to seek out the filthy death players.

As soon as the sun melted away, an eerie, icy darkness prevailed. The landscape became a shadow land. Faintly in the background, I heard the low bass-tone chant commence. I felt lethargic and remembered that I needed to put in my earplugs. Once they were inserted, I became alert, as though I had gulped down one too many cappuccinos.

The death players emerged disguised with clear masks that looked like the nylons bank robbers wore in old movies. Normally, I would've thought that was funny, but since I was standing at death's door, I felt gripped with fear.

The life players clustered together and charged at the droning death players. Shots rang out, and death players fell. The remaining ones staggered and scrambled in awe to get away. Awesome start, I speculated. We fooled them. When the chanting had ceased, I removed the earplugs.

I felt a tap on my shoulder and nearly crapped my pants, as a death player grabbed my mask and a handful of hair underneath while he etched his blade teasingly down my throat. I felt the warmth of my blood, as it trickled down my neck.

"If they were all like this one," the evil one snickered, "we'd be out of here in no time."

I tried to see how many had circled around me. How could I have been so stupid? I paid so much attention to the other life players' escapade that I let what was happening around me slip by. Now I had to pay the price. I was going to die. I wished they'd hurry it up.

The knife they held penetrated further into my neck. I let out a muffled groan as more shots echoed. To my surprise, I heard a few thumps in the grass as the blade at my throat fell. The three death players that had surrounded me lay lifeless on the ground.

"Be more careful next time!" A life player thundered at me.

I tried to see who it was. His voice sounded familiar. His eyes illuminated in the dark like two spotlights but then became glazed over and distorted in shape. My first thought—the blind man?

I had no time to think about it. A death player jumped in the air, his foot ready to kick me in the face. I grabbed it, and flipped him to the ground. At least five others were near him. I took hold of my machine gun and let it fire. I didn't stop until about one hundred bullets had raced out. It was a cool gun. It vibrated against my body, violently. When I was finished, I was the only one left standing.

My breath quickened and sweat poured. Approximately fifty feet in front of me, death players had outnumbered another life player. I reloaded my gun and began to shoot again. I felt charged with fury, but I was careful not to strike the life player. When the other death players fell from my shots, the life player saluted me and went off in another direction.

The air became still and held the pungent smell of stale gunfire. I lay on the ground, veiled with the long hay-like grass that covered the Fields. I needed to catch my breath.

Then I heard a group of death players begin to whisper. I tried not to make a sound. I pulled the pin on one of the hand grenades that had been attached to my belt. Silently, I tossed it toward them. The moment it hit, I saw the display of fireworks. It lit up the moonless sky—more death players down.

I couldn't celebrate or put a number on the death players that ate the ground. There was a reason for that. Ahead of me, I witnessed a life player clutching his face and screaming in agonizing terror and pain. His glazed eyes that shone between his fingers sung the song of defeat. His voice became silent as he bounced to the ground.

I sprinted, recharged with the power of fuel that sends a shuttle into space, and ripped off the mask on the player. I couldn't think straight, as the sound of multiple weapons resonated around me like a symphony, and the realization of death entered my heart. I heard a voice crying in anguish. The voice belonged to me. And I was holding the dead body of my new friend—Gregory. War sucks, I thought, repeatedly in my head until someone hollered, "Cease fire!"

I glanced around, wondering if the death players had retreated. I waited for their flag to rise in defeat, but it never did. Rather, a massive door-like structure opened. My mouth dropped open when I realized it was a giant portal, and at least one hundred more death players charged out. The vile expressions they wore seethed through their masks. One of them, obviously the leader, bounded out with a snarling, chained anaconda.

Chaos resulted as life players turned away and sprinted to escape.

"Wait," Joshua's voice shrilled out in the dark, smoky air. He looked stricken with tension so tight, it could be cut with a knife. His white stallion trotted into the middle of our group. He sat high up on it with a tiny whistle in his hand. When he blew it, an ear piercing sound came out.

The death players clutched their heads and fell to the ground. Our patriarchs then joined the battle, maiming them and slicing their anaconda into deli meat. If the death players were going to use illegal magic, then we had our own tricks up our sleeves, ones that were legal.

Definitely, the death players raised their flag that held Vorago's smug face, and, in an instant, we were all teleported back to the Assembly room.

I wasn't sure how many of our own had been killed, but the room swarmed with life players discussing the battle, many of them groaned from their wounds as doctors and nurses hurried in to aid them. I felt dizzy with the amount of blood I was losing from the slash on my neck. A young nurse with pinned up golden hair, kindly took me by the arm and walked me to a seat. In no time, she bandaged me, and after I had the sandwich and mineral water that healthy life players were handing out, I felt some strength return.

A little later, Adonis strode onto the stage. A hush fell over the crowd. "Victory has been ours today," he roared. "Congratulations are at hand for all of your courage and bravery. Vorago lost twenty-eight death players today." A handful of cheers went out from the audience, but Adonis stopped them. "Loss of life due to war is not to be glorified…we've also lost men today—three of them."

He listed their names, but I only recognized Gregory's. Then reality hit me hard. I should've dropped. I placed my fingers on the dressing on my neck and thought, if the death players hadn't been messing around, wasting time, I would've been dead. Even if that mysterious life player showed up, he would've been too late.

"The bodies will be on this stage in a few moments," Adonis continued, "encased in glass coffins. Each of you will be able to gather around them to pay them homage."

"Remember all, we still don't know how our life players became tagged. Finding out how *will be* one of our most important missions in the immediate future."

"On a final note, I've already heard from Spero, and he's told me that Vorago is enraged. There's no need for concern, though. Vorago chose the Fields, and now his death players have lost the ability to find the tagged life players...my friends...the death players are at an all time low. Very soon, we'll travel to the area in Arcis that looks like the bathing houses of Myndos, Turkey. Some of you may remember this, as we've already discussed it at an Assembly in Arcis. If we unleash our power there, Vorago will lose much more of his. We WILL cripple his army, FOREVER!" The crowd roared so loudly, Adonis couldn't help but grin.

We had a break before the exposition of the deceased life players. I crept amongst the group, grieving over our losses. Some faces still looked in shock. Others anxiously discussed the next battle.

I thought about one person who could help to relieve the aches of my spirit, and when I gazed around, I saw her—Angelina. What is she doing here? I thought. My heart skipped a beat.

Our eyes locked. A relieved smile emerged on her tearstained face. She ran over to me and threw her arms around my neck. We embraced in a tight hug.

"Ow," I cried out, as her hand pushed against my wound.

"I'm sorry, I didn't see that," she said, inspecting my bandages. "How badly are you hurt?"

"Never mind. I'm fine. What are you doing here?"

"Look," she said proudly, pulling her hair back and her earlobe forward. I moved a wisp of hair that fell back and saw that the death player's emblem had been replaced with the life player's.

"Congratulations," I whispered, as I brushed my lips over the emblem and down the side of her neck.

"You shouldn't do that here," she warned breathlessly.

Apparently not, I thought to myself with sarcasm, as I glanced up to see Adonis on stage, pointing to me and motioning me to go to him.

I gave Angelina another hug. "I'll be right back."

When I went into the room behind the stage, a place I had never been before, I was surprised to see Julia. "What are you doing here?" I asked. "Are you joining our troops?"

Julia barely glanced up. "Fat chance," she snapped, as Adonis and Lisa both strode toward me.

"Bladen, I'm so thankful you're okay," Lisa gushed, embracing me with motherly affection.

Adonis shook my hand. "Come with me."

I followed Adonis into another room in the back, where he left the door slightly ajar.

I stared at him. "So, what do you want?"

"First things first, mate. You did a super job fighting, but you were almost killed. I told you I didn't think you were quite ready."

My eyes grew wide. "How did you know I was almost killed, and who was the guy that saved me, anyway?"

"He's the blind man you've seen downtown. He's one of the only old life players allowed to help on Earth. He's like a special angel chosen just for you."

I stood speechless. Why would he be chosen for me? I wondered.

Adonis went on. "For now, you need more training. Make sure you fit it into your schedule."

I nodded.

"Also mate, we believe the angry man you told me about from the game, the one who seems to be watching you from inside the basilica, is leaking secrets from our side and betraying Spero. We're not letting others know about this until we have more information, but since the man seems to want to make contact with you, we may need your help in the future. Understood?"

I nodded again.

"The next thing we need to discuss…with your chain…you've seen Julia's father and now sister…they're closer. We found that out last week. I need to move Julia and Lisa. It's almost the end of the semester. Julia will take her exams, and then I'll be taking her and Lisa away. It *is* earlier than we had originally wanted, but I don't think we have a choice at this point in time."

"Where?"

"Back to Alaska. That's why Julia's mood was so sour when you greeted her."

"I don't get it."

"Get what?"

"Why don't you stay, meet Julia's father face-to-face, and take him down?"

"I don't think you understand how powerful his evil is. If there's ever a confrontation with him, many people *will* die, which brings me to the third thing I needed to discuss with you— Angelina."

"What about her?" I retorted. "She's good, not evil."

Adonis patted my shoulder. "I know. That's not the problem—it's her brother, Accursio. He's as violent as Julia's father. That means…if he ever finds out that Angelina has decided to join us, he'll kill her and whoever else gets in his path. He'll murder you too, Bladen."

"I'll take my chances."

"Have it your way, but at least let me help you."

"How?"

Adonis blew the sparkling dust toward me in the same way he had in the past. "There…now you can protect Angelina with your chain, the same way you protect Julia."

The door flew open and crashed against the wall, as Julia stormed into the room.

"Protect me? What are you talking about?" Her anger weighed so heavy, it would have tipped a scale.

Adonis said to me. "Go, I'll take care of this."

I left the room and found my way back to Angelina. She was waiting for me on the stage, where three other men were wheeling out the coffins that contained the dead life players.

Joshua stood among the bodies, ready to say a few words of praise and consolation for their bravery and the sadness inflicted by their loss. When he finished, we had a moment of silence, until the remaining life players passed by each coffin, saying their final goodbyes. One young life player fell to his knees and cried out. "It's not fair." A nurse went to his side and helped him up as she soothed him. I felt choked up myself.

"It's time to go," Berard spoke, quietly behind me. I hadn't known he was there. Angelina and I followed him to the exit where we needed to wait for our bus. By the door, there stood a tall, strawberry-blonde, middle-aged woman.

"Hello, Angelina," the woman said, and stretched out her hand to shake Angelina's. "I'm your matriarch. My name is Anneliese."

She had to have been six feet tall. I looked at Berard's mere height. "Angelina, why is your mentor so much larger than mine?"

Anneliese raised an insulted eyebrow at me. Berard suddenly grew three times his size, as he snarled at me.

"Hey!" I jumped back. "Okay okay, I get your point." We all laughed.

Once we stepped on the bus, silent reflection filled the air, as life players gazed out at the sun-filled sky. It was still daytime on Earth.

"Goodbye," a few life players quietly called out, when the bus reached Angelina's condo.

I put my hand on a few shoulders. "Good job," I said to them, as I went to get off the bus with her.

"It's snowing...how can that be?" Angelina screamed with delight. "There's barely a cloud in the sky, and the sun's shining." She ran around her front lawn, tongue stuck way out to catch the falling flakes. I couldn't help but laugh at how silly she looked. She grabbed me by the hand. "Come on, catch the snow with me."

We both ran around like little kids, catching and eating the snow on our tongues. One of Angelina's neighbors peeked out her window from behind golden curtains. The old woman shook her head. We laughed.

When we went inside, Angelina fixed hot cocoa with extra marshmallows. It tasted good. Then she came up behind me and slipped her hands around my waist. She insisted I tell her how I received the wound on my neck. I told her the gory details of the battle. She was more than upset by how close I had tasted death.

I turned to face her. She was filled with blazing emotion as she put her lips close to my ear. "I'm falling in love with you," she whispered. "If anything happens to you, I'll die."

Angelina and I were of one spirit, both destined life players. Falling for her felt like jumping out of an airplane. There was no turning back. Before our wanting lips met, I caressed her face with my fingertips and replied, "Ditto."